www.MinotaurBooks.com

DATE DUE		
JAN 0 6 20		
		PRINTED IN U.S.A.

www.MomentsInCrime.com

GetCozy: The ultimate cozy connection. Find your favorite cozy mystery, grab a reading group guide, sign up for monthly giveaways, and more.

www.GetCozyOnline.com

MINOTAUR
BOOKS

www.minotaurbooks.com

"Suspenseful...Mayor's New England eye mercilessly details what he sees without the 'calendar nostalgia' that usually clings to such villages and backwaters...The clever plot expands like a dark whirlpool and reveals the underbelly of Vermont and Maine."

—*Providence Journal-Bulletin*

"As with all Mayor's novels, the plot remains fresh and timely. Through his in-depth knowledge of police work, forensics and the medical field, combined with his ability to evoke the Vermont landscape, Mayor deftly brings the reader deep inside the story, taking us along the trail of meticulous detective work needed to bring out the truth."

—*Brattleboro Reformer*

...and for Archer Mayor and his other Joe Gunther novels

"Mayor is a devil of a plotter."

—Marilyn Stasio, *The New York Times Book Review*

"Superb...Mayor spins out parallel story lines and weaves the strands together with deft precision."

—*Publishers Weekly* (starred review) on *The Second Mouse*

"An intricate, first-rate thriller...a riveting plot and exceptional writing."

—*Publishers Weekly* (starred review) on *The Sniper's Wife*

"The writing is strong, with sharp social observations throughout...Gunther grows on you from novel to novel."

—*The Washington Post Book World*

OTHER BOOKS BY ARCHER MAYOR

THE PRICE OF MALICE

MALICE

A JOE GUNTHER NOVEL

ARCHER MAYOR

St. Martin's Paperbacks

This is a work of fiction. All of the characters, organizations, and events portrayed in this novel are either products of the author's imagination or are used fictitiously.

THE PRICE OF MALICE

Copyright © 2009 by Archer Mayor.
Excerpt from *Red Herring* copyright © 2010 by Archer Mayor.

Cover photos of road © Craig Aurness / Corbis; leaves on ground © Joe Sohm / Getty Images; trees © Stockbyte / Getty Images.

For information address St. Martin's Press, 175 Fifth Avenue, New York, NY 10010.

EAN: 978-0-312-53246-8

Printed in the United States of America

Minotaur Books edition / October 2009
St. Martin's Paperbacks edition / October 2010

St. Martin's Paperbacks are published by St. Martin's Press, 175 Fifth Avenue, New York, NY 10010.

10 9 8 7 6 5 4 3 2 1

To Paco, my longtime friend and sounding board

ACKNOWLEDGMENTS

As always, I owe a great deal of thanks to many people for the creation of this book. I start each new foray into Joe Gunther's continuing adventures pretty much as a blank slate, dependent on those who know far more than I for the interesting details for which this series has become known. It is those experts and advisors who deserve whatever praise you might have for any interesting and arcane tidbits you'll encounter. It is left to me to accept the blame for any inevitable mistakes and omissions left over.

My gratitude, therefore, to my readers and to the following:

John Martin
Anne Emerson
Rick Bates
Dick and Jean Hoyt
Paco Aumand
Eric Buel
Nancy Aichele
Castle Freeman, Jr.
Peter van Wagenigen

Nancy Polseno
Dan Davis
Sally Mattson
Lauren Petrie
Will Hoyt
Elaine Sopchak
Ray Walker
Julie Lavorgna
Lisa Keller

Also:

The Brattleboro Police Department
The Vermont State Police
Immigration and Customs Enforcement
The Vermont Forensic Lab
The Department of Children and Families

THE PRICE OF MALICE

CHAPTER 1

Willy Kunkle gently removed his one functional hand from the bare back of the woman stretched out beside him and reached for the softly buzzing cell phone on the night table. Unlike Sammie Martens—the woman in question—Willy had been termed a "vigilant sleeper," which sounded like psychobabble to him. He didn't need a shrink to tell him that he slept like shit.

"What?" he asked in a muted growl, noticing the first pale hint of dawn against the window shade.

"That you, Willy?"

It was Ron Klesczewski, chief of detectives of Brattleboro, Vermont, an old colleague of Willy's before he and Sam had left the PD to join the Vermont Bureau of Investigation, a new, statewide major crimes unit. As far as Willy was concerned, Ron was a perfect example of the Peter Principle. Way too touchy-feely for Willy's taste, he'd never have landed the top job if the rest of them hadn't jumped ship.

"Jesus, Ron. Who do you think it is? You called me."

Ron laughed, unfazed. "I'm just used to you yelling into the phone. You sound downright demure."

Willy rolled his eyes, as much at the word choice as at Sam's stirring from all the noise.

"What the hell do you want?"

"You're the VBI on call, according to your dispatch," Ron explained brightly, "and I got something for you."

"You lock your keys in the car again?"

Kleszczewski ignored him, slowly enunciating, "Ho-mi-cide."

Willy smiled abruptly, his mood improved as if by the flick of a switch. "Say that again for what's-her-name."

Ron repeated himself as Willy dangled the phone just above Sammie's exposed ear. He was rewarded as her eyes opened wide and she sat up in one fluid motion.

"Who is that?" she mouthed silently.

"Your buddy Ron," Willy said, bringing the phone back to his mouth. "Throwing us a local, at last. What is it, in under a thousand words?" Willy asked Kleszczewski.

"Single white male, done in with a knife; unknown assailant," Ron responded, his smile almost audible. He then gave the exact address on Manor Court, off of Canal, between Clark Street and Homestead—a hard-luck neighborhood a stone's throw from downtown. He hung up without further ceremony, having given Willy only precisely what he'd requested.

Willy laughed and closed the phone. "That boy's growing balls."

Sam was already across the room, getting dressed. "A minor miracle, given how much you bust 'em."

The name Manor Court sounded like a mass-produced, 1970s, northeastern development, in the way that Flamingo Estates brought to mind a Florida flophouse of fifty squirrel-sized apartments. In fact, it was neither a development nor a court, and hadn't been touched by a builder's level in 150 years. It was a residual holdover of

Brattleboro's nineteenth-century industrial past, when the town cranked out everything from parlor organs to baby carriages and had neighborhoods so clearly class-divided, it felt like some residents required passports for travel.

Manor Court had once been an open-ended street, which—as with some rivers—implied a sense of cleansing circulation. But subsequent traffic engineering had turned it into a J-shaped dead end, a tidal pool of sorts, located in a section of town relatively downtrodden to this day. The dominant architecture was both the famed working-class "triple decker" so much in evidence in a hundred other soot-stained, reinvented, ancient New England towns, and a less definable, two-and-a-half-story structure—often clad in scalloped, gray, pressed-board siding—whose sole distinguishable attribute was that it didn't look like anything more than a roof over four walls of marginal integrity.

The address Ron Klesczewski had offered was one of the former—and therefore of modest historical merit—minus any grace notes of subsequent care or maintenance. In fact, as Willy swung out of the car he and Sammie shared to get there, he wondered if the electrical and phone lines looping in from the nearby utility pole weren't the only modern amenities added over the prior seventy-five years.

Including the paint on the walls.

"You ever been here?" he asked his partner.

Sam was reaching into the back seat to grab a canvas shoulder bag she favored for crime-scene investigations. "Seems like our kind of place, but I don't know for sure."

Willy was standing by the car, studying the structure in the slowly growing dawn. It was peeling, sagging, and gaping where stair and balcony railings had vanished over time. His left hand, as always, was stuffed into his pants pocket—the useless tail end of an arm crippled years ago by a rifle round received in the line of duty. His powerful right hand remained empty. No extra equipment for him, not at this early stage.

"A hanging—about eight years ago."

Sammie pulled her head out of the car. "What?"

"A hanging," he repeated. "That's it. About eight years ago. That's how I know this dump."

She smiled, if just barely. Trust him to remember that—and almost everything else, in fact, except the everyday rules of social conduct. In that way, he reminded her of an idiot savant who could play the concert piano but not read a comic book. The man was a dinosaur—an old-fashioned, old-school cop—a black-and-white man in a colorful world. She loved him for that, among other quirks.

She adjusted her bag and motioned across the street. "Shall we?"

There were already two PD cruisers parked by the curb, along with an unmarked Impala that should have had "cop" stamped on both doors. A couple of patrolmen were stringing crime-scene tape around the building, and a third was loitering by the entrance at the top of the rickety porch steps, clipboard in hand.

A broad smile creased his weather-beaten face as he caught sight of them approaching.

"Oh, oh—watch out. It's the cavalry."

The two of them spoke simultaneously, Sam saying, "Hey, Zippo. How you been?" while Willy responded, "It's the brain trust, asshole, come to save your butt again."

Zippo just laughed, knowing them both well. "Beauty and the Beast. God help us." He jerked his thumb over his shoulder and applied pen to clipboard as he spoke. "Second floor, apartment three."

They filed by, into the fetid embrace of the dark first-floor lobby, stifling even at this early hour. Summer had kicked in at last, following a winter of more snowfall than the region had seen in years. Typically, it had taken barely a week for everyone to switch from enjoying the warmth to complaining about the heat. New Englanders tend to be hardier in the cold than they are in its absence, making Florida as the terminus for so many of them conceptually rational only because of its universal air-conditioning.

"Jesus," Willy groaned. As Sam well knew, the man—despite his marginal manners—was a neat freak at heart, and while he spent most of his time working in these environments, his soul quailed at the squalor.

At the second-floor landing, they were met by a poster boy for the average American male Caucasian.

Sammie walked up to him and gave him a hug. "Ron, it's great to see you. How's the family?"

Ron nodded to Willy over her shoulder. "Hi, guys. Everybody's great. How're you doin', Willy?"

Willy frowned and glanced at the open door of the nearby apartment. "I'm doin'. This the place?"

Ron broke from Sam and bowed slightly at the waist in mock homage. "It is. We've staged down the hall, there. You can get a Tyvek suit and booties and the rest from Phil. I also called the crime lab. Their ETA is maybe another two hours."

Willy's frown deepened. "I'll believe that when I see it. You're making this sound like a whodunit."

Ron nodded. "So far, it is. The dead guy is Wayne Castine, thirty-two. He was stabbed a bunch of times, and maybe shot and beaten, too. It's hard to tell with the blood. It's all over him, and all over the apartment."

"He live here alone?" Sam asked as Willy headed for where Phil was waiting with the crime-scene equipment.

"He didn't live here at all, and the woman who does swears she doesn't know who he is." Ron paused before rephrasing. "Correction—she says she doesn't know Wayne Castine. Making a visual ID on this guy is a little tough right now. She might know him but not his name."

"Do we know *her*?" Sam asked, in the age-old shorthand for, is she in the computer for any past misbehavior?

"Some speeding tickets," he answered. "Two DUIs over the past two years; a couple of domestics as the victim; a few public disturbances involving alcohol. She's been a person-of-interest in a dozen or more cases, hanging with a tough crowd." He held his hands out to both sides, palms up, in a hapless gesture. "Name's Elisabeth Babbitt—British-style spelling. Calls herself Liz. She's pretty down and out, like everybody else on the block. Only moved here a couple of months ago. Lived in West Bratt before that; Bellows Falls before that; north of Putney in a trailer before that. And that's just the past four years."

Willy returned, awkwardly zipping up his white suit while holding the hat, gloves, and booties, all with one hand. Everyone knew better than to offer to help. Sam took advantage of his approach to get outfitted herself.

"Not to sound obvious," Willy said, having overheard the conversation. "But if the guy's too messed up to recognize, how do you know who he is?"

"Wallet," Ron explained shortly. "It was poking out of his front pants pocket. I could snag it without disturbing anything else. I had dispatch run his license through CAD, and there were enough common traits to make it look pretty likely he's the guy, including a tattoo on his forearm."

Willy pursed his lips but withheld comment, pointing toward the apartment with his chin instead. "She find the body?" he asked.

"Yeah, after a night of barhopping."

"She share the place with anyone?"

Klesczewski shook his head. "Not that you can tell. I didn't get into the nitty-gritty with her—didn't want to trample too much ground ahead of you guys. But I got the feeling she wasn't beyond getting help with the rent the old-fashioned way."

"She's a hooker," Willy restated bluntly, leaning against the rickety railing and pulling on the booties as Sam returned, typically all ready to go.

"Amateur, I'd guess," Ron suggested. "Officially, she works at the grocery store."

Willy nodded.

Sam asked, "What do we have on Castine?"

"He's a kid diddler," Willy said without looking up.

They both stared at him, taken off guard.

"You know this guy?" Sam asked.

"I know about him," Willy answered her, intent on his task. "We never busted him when we were with the PD, but he was a person-of-interest a dozen times or more—buying booze for kids, crawling around the edge of underage parties, offering rides after school. One of those scumbags you know is dirty, but you can't catch him."

Sam glanced at Ron, who shrugged and said, "He's right. I don't have much to add. He lives in a one-room efficiency on Main Street—or lived, I should say. I have someone sitting on that. He worked as a part-time stacker and loader at one of the lumber companies. I got someone else getting a list of coworkers and buddies there, along with anything that might be interesting." He added carefully, seeing Willy's expression darken, "Nothing too intense. We're not conducting interviews—just collecting data."

Willy laid one latex glove on the railing, wriggled inside of it with four fingers, and finished pulling it on with his teeth. "How screwed up is this scene, with all the pickpocketing and whatever?" he then asked.

Ron was ready for that one. "Babbitt found the body, used the phone to call 911, and then waited right here. The responding officer—Rich Matthews, who deserves a high five as far as I'm concerned—grilled her first for a couple of minutes, and then literally tiptoed in to determine that Castine was really dead and alone. He didn't touch anything; came out the same way he went in; and then sealed the place up. He even took his boots off before he went in."

Willy scowled. "That's weird. He nuts? What if somebody had been hiding in the closet?"

Ron tilted his head to one side. "I know, I know. A little over the top. But he's fresh out of the academy and a little paranoid about scene preservation. I already talked to him. Anyhow, the scene's pretty good."

"Except for you," Willy commented.

"True," Ron admitted. "I suited up to confirm what Rich had seen, mostly because he is new. And along with the wallet, I took some baseline shots. But that's it."

"You call the ME?"

"Him and the state's attorney, but I also told them to hold tight until the crime lab arrived."

Sam reached out and patted her old colleague on the arm. "You did good, Ron. Like always. Thanks."

Willy didn't say anything, but moved to the apartment's door and glanced over his shoulder at his partner. "You ready?"

It wasn't much, Wayne Castine's last resting place. A hallway with a bathroom on one side and the kitchen opposite, leading to a small living room and a bedroom beyond. There were a couple of closets, with nobody in them, and a smattering of mismatched furniture. It wasn't terribly dirty, smelled mostly of cheap soap and makeup, and bragged of an awkward Middle Eastern motif, or maybe South American, consisting of gauzy scarves and odd pieces of fabric draped across the windows and over lamp shades.

Sammie studied Willy as he preceded her slowly down the hall, keeping his feet on the strip of brown butcher paper that Ron had laid out on the floor. She could sense through his body language—as he paused here and there, his latex-clad fingers sometimes extending as in a failed effort to reach out—a desire to absorb what might have happened in this now dull, quiet, otherwise mundane little home.

It was an understandable ambition, since what they could see, in the absence still of any dead body, spoke of grim and relentless violence. On the hallway's floor, smearing the walls and doorjambs, splattered and dripped and swiped as in a child's finger painting, was more blood than either one of them had witnessed in a long while.

Whatever else was left behind from the events of the night just past, certainly the lingering ghost of pure rage loomed large.

And that was before they reached the main attraction.

He was in the small living room, spread-eagled on his back, covered with enough blood to make him look more like a slaughtered carcass than a dead human being.

Even Willy, with his hard-hearted reputation, murmured, "Whoa," at the sight.

"Somebody was pissed," Sammie said quietly.

Willy reached into the pocket of his Tyvek suit and extracted a cell phone.

Sam glanced at him, surprised. He was usually ill-inclined to consult others on a case. "Who're you calling?" she asked.

She was struck by his tone of voice when he answered her. This was a man used to violence, after all. She knew that much from sleeping beside his nightmares.

But his words were somber and reflective as he flipped

open the phone. He spoke as a man who'd recognized something beyond the simple impulse of most killings. There was a presence crowding around them here—primal, angry, penned up, and very hot.

It wasn't the kind of thing for even Willy to confront cavalierly.

"I think," he told her, "it's time to wake up the Old Man."

CHAPTER 2

Joe Gunther was not asleep when Willy called from Manor Court. Nor had he been for hours. He was fully dressed, sitting by the window, and in trouble. At least, emotionally. Lyn Silva, the woman he loved, had gone into an introverted tailspin, cutting him out of her life.

And he had brought it about. Not directly—not by anything he'd done—but he had been the bearer of bad news from a recent trip to Maine, concerning her family, and was now paying the price.

"What?" he answered the phone by his side.

Willy was uncharacteristically brought up short. "Boss?"

Joe answered in a more neutral tone. "Hey, Willy. What's up?"

"You okay?"

It was an unusual question from this particular man, and Joe immediately sensed Willy's regret at having asked it. He knew him like a son, and had more than once protected him against those who'd wanted to fire him over trying to figure him out.

Joe therefore let him off the hook. "Yeah, fine. Just spilled some coffee. Bad timing."

Willy bought it, or played along. "Losing your grip. Bad sign. Incontinence'll probably be next."

Joe suppressed a sigh. "Glad you're concerned. I take it this isn't a social call. You are not a morning person."

"Klesczewski called us for a homicide on Manor Court," Willy explained casually, keeping to form.

"Here? In town?"

"Yeah. Number forty-two, second floor. It's a blood-bath."

Joe was struck by the description, given the jaded source. "We know who did it?"

"Not a clue. Wanna come out and play?"

Joe cast his eyes onto the scene he'd been watching emerge from the shadows of night—his own small, pleasant backyard, stuffed with bushes and flowers.

"Yeah," he said, in fact happy to apply his mind to almost anything by now. "Be right there."

Manor Court had come alive by the time Joe pulled off of Canal Street and into the dead end. People were standing on the sidewalk, along the balconies, and lounging in windows. Not a throng, and exhibiting no particular energy—this slice of society was used to seeing cops stringing crime tape. But whatever had happened at number forty-two was certainly more interesting than the first morning talk shows.

He parked behind Sam's car and got out, nodding to Zippo, still stationed on the porch.

"How're tricks, Joe?" the latter asked as he approached.

"I guess you'll have to tell me," Joe answered. "What're you hearing coming off the sidewalk?"

Zippo glanced at the few people standing outside the yellow tape and dropped his voice slightly. "I don't know how they do it, but word's already out who we got up there.

You can tell me later if I'm right: Ron hasn't said word one, but scuttlebutt is it's Wayne Castine."

Joe shrugged. "Willy didn't give me a name, but assuming it is, what're they saying?"

"That we're wasting our time; that we should dig a hole, throw him in, and call it a day. Another one said if we catch who did it, we should make him chief of police."

"You know who's saying all this?"

Zippo patted his breast pocket, where most cops keep their notepads. "I wrote 'em down. Couple of local losers; known them for years."

"Why the hostility? You know Castine, too? I never heard of him."

The old beat cop raised his eyebrows. "Me? Nope, which kind of surprised me. But according to these guys, he was a child molester."

Joe patted him on the shoulder. "Well, I guess we'll find out. Thanks, Zippo. I'll let you know if you get the Kewpie doll. I wouldn't doubt it, though. I mean, how many apartments are there on the second floor, right?"

Zippo gave him a knowing look. "Ah-ha, but that's the catch, see? It's not Castine's apartment. That I do know—it belongs to a woman who has no idea who the body is."

Joe pulled a face. "No kidding? Curiouser and curiouser."

"Still, I bet I get that doll," Zippo said, bending over his clipboard to enter Joe's name. "These people know the drumbeats."

Joe entered the building, paused in the lobby to get his bearings and absorb the place's familiar atmosphere, and then slowly climbed up the creaky, dusty stairway to the second floor.

Looming above, a wide smile on his face, Ron Klesczewski watched him come, waiting until he'd almost arrived to stick out a hand in greeting. "Hey, boss. Good to see you. I can't believe we work in the same building and never meet up."

Joe shook his hand, laughing at how Ron still addressed him. In the old days, Joe had indeed been his boss, as chief of detectives. "I know," he agreed. "Pretty dumb."

The PD and the VBI shared a roof in the town's municipal building, with the latter renting a one-room office on the second floor. But Ron's comment was well put—they were more likely to bump into each other at a place like this than around the water cooler.

"I'm running a survey," Joe said before Ron could begin his briefing. "Zippo told me that folks on the street have already ID'd the dead man as Wayne Castine. They right?"

Ron scowled and shook his head. "Unbelievable. Yeah, they are. I don't know how they found out, though."

Joe tilted his head and smiled. "Well, somebody killed him. Maybe the fact that word's already out will make this a lot easier than we think."

"I knew you believed in fairy tales," said a familiar voice.

Joe glanced at the apartment's front door and saw Willy standing in the entrance, clad in Tyvek.

"Looking at you, I believe in the Easter Bunny—minus the ears."

Ron burst out laughing, making Willy scowl. "Well, you're next," he said. "Assuming you actually want to help with this mess." He turned on his heel to reenter the apartment.

"Oh, oh," Ron whispered, his eyes theatrically wide. "Now he's all upset."

Joe picked up a white suit he found draped across the

railing and began putting it on. "What about the neighbors, Ron? You done any canvassing yet?"

"Mostly collecting names for you to chase down later. Not," he added quickly, "that I won't assign whoever you want to help out. You're doing me the favor here."

"Appreciate it," Joe grunted, bending over to slip on the booties.

"Anyhow," Ron resumed, "so far, we haven't got much. Nobody saw anything, nobody heard anything. The usual." He pointed upstairs. "There are two apartments per floor, six in all. The two above us are rented, the largest one, across the way, is empty, and the two below are full. But there are a lot of people involved, just so you know, and they're complicated to sort out. Everybody's living with everybody else; all the kids have different last names; people married and not, or married to people who aren't who they're sleeping with. Same ol', same ol', if you ask me. I've got names, birth dates, and phone numbers for a bunch of them, but there're several who aren't here who might have something to say later. Speaking of which, everyone here's agreed to stay in their apartments to preserve the overall crime scene, or ask for an escort if they want out."

Joe nodded as he pulled on his latex gloves. "Who lives with the woman who rents this place?"

"Nobody," Ron told him. "She's alone. It's the smallest apartment in the building."

"Zippo said she had no idea who the body was."

"Correct, at least not by name. They took her to the hospital to calm her down, so I haven't been able to show her his photo ID."

"Did you run that by any of the other renters?"

"No, nor his name, although I guess that's a moot point by now. At the time, I didn't want to foul your game, 'case you were looking for reactions."

"Good thought. Anyone living here with obvious red flags, like a mass murderer?"

Ron shook his head. "Nope, at least not yet. Cumulatively, though, you might be looking at a few dozen pages of rap sheets, and they run the gamut. Which isn't to say the guy wasn't done in by a newbie ten-year-old."

Joe had moved to the apartment's entrance and now looked back at his old colleague and raised his eyebrows. "Ron, you've turned into a cynic."

Ron smiled, but sadly. "Say it ain't so, boss."

Joe didn't say anything.

He proceeded as Willy had earlier—slowly, methodically, not touching anything, trying to read whatever story might be available. He saw blood spatter on the floor, with directionality heading the same way he was, implying a wounded person retreating from the front door. Bloody handprints indicated the same thing.

He paused, considering the possibility that Castine had answered the door of an apartment not his own, and been struck, stabbed, or shot by whoever had been on the other side.

But the blood didn't begin precisely at the door; its first appearance was about five feet inside. That could mean a hand covering the wound, delaying the blood flow, or an attacker hiding in the kitchen or hallway closet. If that was true, maybe Castine had been the one on the landing, letting himself in only to be assaulted once the door was closed.

Joe left it there, open to all theories, married to none.

He resumed his survey until he'd reached the cramped living room. Sam and Willy were both there, chatting softly. Beside them lay the remains of Wayne Castine.

Neither of his colleagues interrupted his silence, not even Willy, who could have repaid any cracks about resembling an earless rabbit.

Joe stayed on the butcher paper a moment, before carefully and slowly putting one white-clad foot down on the bare floor beside the body, so that he could crouch beside it, immediately above the head.

Castine was open-eyed and -mouthed, halfway between looking startled and dreamy. He needed a shave and a haircut; his clothes were old and worn—a T-shirt, jeans, and a cheap pair of running shoes. His hands were calloused and scarred by a life of manual labor, and perhaps a few fistfights. He had several tattoos.

He was also so covered in blood that the sole standout was a single patch of pale, bare skin along his left cheekbone—as artificial-looking as if it had been painted in place.

Joe gazed along the body's length, noting multiple "defects," as they called them forensically, on the front of the shirt and pants, put there by knife or gun. Most noticeable were three wounds to the groin—rare enough in a homicide, and usually never found without, as Willy might have put it, "a good story."

But Joe didn't ask him—not yet—instead returning to the victim's face. That had received several hard blows. One eye was deformed, its supporting orbit presumably crushed; the nose was bent awkwardly; the upper lip split; three teeth were broken, their jagged profile adding a grotesque element to Castine's peculiarly passive expression.

There are multiple theories about how homicide victims retain telling details of their fate, including the old saw that the last image to strike the retina remains forever, ripe for discovery. Some, even now, claim a body's facial expression can tell if the killer was friend or foe. In court, Joe had heard it said that a corpse's look of "peacefulness," or lack thereof, reveals if pain was a factor.

To Joe's eye—which had studied hundreds of bodies over the decades—none of this had merit. In Wayne

Castine's case, for example, everything *but* his passive expression told of an agonizing death, delivered by one or more people hell-bent on making it so.

Joe finally rose, stepped back, and commented, "Not that much blood around the body; he must've bled out by the time he dropped."

"From one of the groin wounds, alone," Sammie rejoined, taking up the Socratic invitation. "You can see where the left pants leg is soaked all the way to filling the shoe."

"Could even be the primary cause of death," Willy added. "The shoe print matching that sneaker begins about halfway down the hall. Probably the femoral artery."

They all paused a moment, configuring the scene as it might have happened.

Joe then said, "Ron told me the renter didn't know him, even though everyone else seems to. You want to fill me in?"

They did so, taking turns. In short order, Joe learned about Liz Babbitt, her possible alternate source of income, her peripatetic lifestyle, Willy's anecdotal knowledge of Wayne's carnal interest in children, and the fact that he had an apartment on Main Street, now under guard.

After they finished, Joe checked his watch.

"Got a date?" Willy asked. "Better be for lunch."

In fact, the sun had begun to assert itself with confidence, and was beginning to drive a bright shaft into the room across the body, further darkening the congealing blood. It would be another hot and humid day, and Wayne wasn't going to improve with time.

"No—I'm just wondering how to manage decomposition and keep the place intact for the crime lab," Joe admitted. "They may still be an hour or more out."

Actually, while the point was cogent, it wasn't why he'd checked the time. He'd wondered what Lyn was doing just

then—whether she was still fast asleep, or having break-
fast in the kitchen he'd grown accustomed to sharing with
her, at least from time to time.

"We can't get an air conditioner in here without screwing everything up," Sam said, bringing him back. "But
why not drop a blanket or something across the window
at least?"

Joe nodded. "Get Ron's people to do that. Why don't
you two start interviewing neighbors? I'll get Lester to
come in early and have him check out Castine's past—see
who he might have ticked off enough to deserve this. I'll
go chat with Liz Babbitt."

"What's that gonna produce?" Willy asked with his
usual lack of decorum.

"Maybe nothing, but she still hasn't been shown the
guy without the bloody makeup," Joe said. "Could be she
knew him by a different name."

Willy wiped his forehead with his sleeve, revealing the
source of some of his irritation. "Whatever. I just want to
get out of this damn sweat suit. I hate this weather."

"It's going to be a long day, Willy," Sam advised him
gently as she headed toward the hallway.

He fell in behind her. "You're telling me. I say we arrest everybody on the block and interview them in some
air-conditioned cellar. They'd probably thank us."

Joe stayed behind, letting the silence settle back, as he
imagined it had after Castine's last breath. Somebody—or
maybe several people—had no doubt stood as he was
now, considering their handiwork. But had the feeling
been triumphant? Guilty? Stunned that some plan had
gone wrong? One possible motivation had already surfaced, linked with Castine's sexual appetites. Would it end
up being the right one?

He let out a sigh. Only serious digging would reveal
that, but while therein lay one of the job's rewards, he

found his enthusiasm flagging. Lyn's struggles with what he'd inadvertently brought her were proving surprisingly distracting, which in turn reinforced how fond he'd become of her.

That was largely good news, of course. For a couple of decades, Joe had kept company with a woman named Gail Zigman, whom he'd loved dearly—and still did platonically. But she'd broken it off, partly because of her own political ambitions, and partly because of the occasional perils of his job. Lyn's appearance had greatly eased the resulting loneliness. That he'd now done something through his work to throw her for a loop was no subtle reminder of what had befallen him and Gail.

For several years, Lyn, the daughter of a Gloucester lobsterman, had believed that her father and older brother had been consumed by a storm at sea like so many fishermen before them—lock, stock, and fishing boat. It had been a complete and utter heartbreak, uprooting and transforming the remnants of the family, but it had at least shared with so many other similar losses a touchstone of commonality. The survivors of dead fishermen, like those of slain soldiers, had the knowledge that they were not alone in carrying their burden. It wasn't exactly a comfort for Lyn, but it eased her isolation, if only fractionally.

That, however, was before Joe, chasing a drug case in faraway Maine—some two hundred miles from Gloucester—discovered the Silvas' boat, the *Maria*, covered with algae but fully intact—its name carefully painted over—tucked away in a very bad man's boathouse.

Gone was the time-honored legend of decent men lost at sea, replaced by the haunting, corrosive possibility that everything about father and brother—including their disappearance—might have been a corruption of lies.

To Joe, her brooding withdrawal had seemed extreme. The two men were just as missing, and their reputations—

so far—just as inviolate as before. All he had found was the *Maria*. Even the bad guy had claimed to have found it afloat and empty long ago, and to have applied the salvage-of-the-sea convention to his own selfish and illegal advantage by hiding it. There was nothing to say that the two men still hadn't perished at sea, in poor weather.

But the fragile shell of tradition had been smashed for Lyn, leaving only questions, doubts, and a nagging disillusionment. Joe might have been only the proverbial messenger in the affair, but he was taking the full brunt of an untold quantity of baggage that she was choosing to keep to herself.

As a result, although they were now both living and working in Brattleboro—she as a bar owner, and he as the field force commander of the VBI—they hadn't spoken or seen each other for over two weeks.

Joe hated it. His age alone put him at the top of his profession's food chain. Most of his police academy classmates had long ago retired and a couple had died. He had witnessed much of what life had to deliver—the bloody chaos of combat, a young wife taken by cancer, a career of dealing with the destructive impulsiveness of a violent and selfish species. He had resisted becoming a hard man, but he had certainly become an experienced one.

All of which helped him resent the hell out of now feeling like a jilted teenager.

He blinked and refocused on the remains of Wayne Castine, struck by the absurdity of even thinking about such things, here and now.

Time to get a grip.

CHAPTER 3

Joe paused at the emergency-room reception window at Brattleboro's Memorial Hospital and waved to the white-haired nurse on the other side of the glass.

He leaned over so that his mouth was near the slot. "Hey, Elizabeth. Haven't you retired yet?"

Elizabeth Pace looked up and smiled broadly. "You old goat. You should talk. At least I tried it once—did you know that? Lasted about three weeks."

She hit the electronic button opening the sliding-glass door into the ER, and swiveled her chair to face him as he stopped at her counter.

"That's a little friendlier," she said, reaching up for an awkward hug.

He patted her shoulder and kissed her cheek. "You must have maxed out your retirement years ago," he said.

She laughed. "Six, to be exact. I think I'm working for thirty cents an hour by now. You, too?"

He shrugged. "Something like that. I don't bother counting."

She shook her head. "Warhorses. What a breed. I'll take a wild guess and say you're here to interview Ms. Babbitt."

"I am. How's she doing?"

"Better now. She was pretty worked up when they brought her in. Is the scene as bad as she's saying?"

Joe grimaced. "Maybe worse."

Elizabeth's face saddened. "What a shame. The things we do. Take a left at the corner, Joe, second room on the right. We thought we'd give her a little privacy."

Joe pushed himself away from the counter. "Thanks. She been medicated with anything?"

"Amounts to a sugar pill, really. Nothing that'll get in your way."

Joe thanked her again and walked down the short hallway, following her directions. He had ambivalent emotions about this hospital—what the locals called BMH—despite the fact that the town's small population and his own familiarity with it virtually guaranteed that he could have found ten other friends on this floor alone.

But his wife, Ellen, had died here of cancer, decades ago, when his career as a cop had barely begun. His youthful sense of invincibility had undergone daily batterings entering a building that had come to embody a shrine for the dying. He respected the people working here, knew that Ellen got the best care possible, and had been coming here himself ever since, for any number of reasons. But like a well-trained Pavlovian dog, he'd never forgotten the place's initial role in his life, and it always made him uneasy.

He reached the door in question, knocked quietly, and pushed it open slowly, allowing whoever was behind it time to adjust for a visitor.

At first sight, Liz Babbitt struck him as more caricature than human being, especially in the ER's sterile, starkly mechanical setting.

Her eyes were red-rimmed and heavily made-up, a steel stud gleamed against one nostril, her hair was teased, carefully chaotic, and dusted with something sparkly, and her emaciated, nervous body was clad in a garish mismatch of tight-fitting, exotic, borderline punk evening wear. She was bright and angular and a little bit wild, and—in this monochromatic environment—struck him as a hapless, endangered life-form, en route to some awaiting nature preserve.

"Ms. Babbitt?" he asked, his voice soft.

She nodded once, quickly, the gesture matching the furtive look.

She was sitting on a chair against the wall, her thin legs stuck out at contrasting angles, her arms crossed tightly across her narrow chest.

He perched on the gurney in the tiny room's center. Behind them, beyond the closed door, the phone was ringing on Elizabeth Pace's desk.

"My name's Joe Gunther," he told her. "I'm one of the police officers investigating what you found last night."

She nodded again, her eyes still glued to his.

"Before we get into that, though," he continued, "I wanted to know if you're okay. It must've been a huge shock."

"Fucking nightmare," she said shortly and without emphasis.

His turn to nod. "I bet. I hear they gave you something that should help a little."

"Yeah—like totally useless. Like, I mean: nothing. You know?"

"Still, you seem a little better."

"No thanks to them."

She was in her mid-forties, which he knew from his research, but while her language said she was far younger, her face was ten years older. He imagined that when it came to drugs, she knew her way around.

"I was told you haven't lived in that apartment long."

"A few weeks."

"And you've never heard of the dead man?"

"No way."

"Are you from around here originally, Liz?"

"Who cares?"

He smiled slightly. "I do. I like to know who I'm talking with."

"Syracuse."

"What's your birth date?"

She told him, with the bored ease of someone who'd been asked that question by a lot of cops. Sadly, Gunther had met nine-year-old kids with the same facility. Willy and Sam had mentioned her recent past; Joe had subsequently read up on a misspent youth in New York State. Liz was no heavy hitter, but she'd been paying her dues on the fringes for a long time.

"What brought you to this area?"

She smiled without humor. "What else? Some guy."

"Guess that didn't work out," Joe suggested sympathetically.

"Shit. When does it ever?"

"That's gotta be tough, knocking around, looking for the right fit."

She dropped her stare for the first time and looked at the floor for a moment. "I don't give a shit anymore. I take it as it comes."

Willy had commented earlier, embellishing Ron's less florid report, that this woman had "more handprints on her than a doorknob." It was becoming evident to Joe that Liz might have accepted the description, which, to him, amounted to the most poignant aspect about her.

"I know you already talked to the other officer, Liz, but could you tell me what happened last night?"

She hitched her shoulders in her quick, birdlike fashion,

eyes back on him. "Nothing to tell. I got home, walked in, and found . . . it."

"Did you see anyone on your way into the house or going up the stairs?"

"No."

"About what time was this?"

"I don't know—three or four."

"And you called 911 right away?"

"I think so. I ran outside first."

This matched what he'd heard, and what he'd listened to on the 911 tape.

"What had you been doing before that?"

Her face hardened. "Getting drunk and laid. Is that any of your business?"

Joe gave her a pleasant smile and shrugged. "I don't know yet. Maybe not, but I have to ask."

"Why?"

"What if someone wanted to get you in trouble? Distract you while this was happening at your apartment, and then saddle you with the fallout?"

Her eyes grew round. "You're shitting me. Is that what happened?"

Joe shook his head. "Not that I know of. But weirder things do all the time. That's all I'm saying."

She looked thoughtful for a moment before conceding, "Okay."

"So," he repeated, "how did you spend your evening?"

She took one long, black-painted fingernail and daintily scratched her forehead. "I don't remember everything. I know I was at Kelly's for a while, then The Purple Mountain, or maybe it was the other way around. I went to some guy's apartment with a bunch of other people."

"You remember the address, or any names?"

She looked exasperated. "Right. Names. Bob, Bill,

Frank, whatever. Like I know or care. I think the apartment was on Canal, not real far from the Sportsmen's."

"You drink a lot?"

"I always drink a lot," she said aggressively, hard again.

He returned it in kind. "You said you had sex."

"Yeah, in some guy's car. Forty bucks for a fast fuck." She stuck her wrists out. "You gonna arrest me?"

"Never crossed my mind," Joe said, suddenly gentle. "You're the victim here."

He leaned forward and asked quietly. "Liz, during all this, did you ever get suspicious of anyone, or get a feeling that something wasn't completely right? Any weird comments or questions or some act that struck you as out of place?"

She slowly lowered her arms, convinced by his tone, and a little frightened by it as well.

"That's kinda creepy, you know?"

"It may not mean anything," he reassured her. "You just never know."

She studied the floor a moment, before answering, "No."

He shifted his weight slightly. "Okay, so you finally head home. Was that alone?"

"Yeah. I was tired. My head hurt, and I wasn't feeling too good."

"When you reached your door, what do you remember doing?"

"I told you. I walked inside and I found the guy."

"Did you use your key?"

She looked disgusted. "Well, of course I . . ." She then paused before adding reluctantly, "But I didn't need it."

"Your door was unlocked?"

She nodded, looking fearful again.

"And you're sure you locked it when you left?"

"You seen where I live?"

He leaned forward once more. "I'm not doubting you, Liz. I'm only asking you to be absolutely positive. Are you sure you locked that door?"

Finally, she nodded deeply and with conviction. "Yes, I did. I'm really big on that. I got broke into once, back in Syracuse, and I lost a brooch my gram gave me. The only thing I ever loved from the only person I ever loved."

"And you're also sure you didn't get broken into this time? The lock was good and the door a tight fit?"

"Yup."

Joe nodded encouragingly. "Okay. Almost done, at least this time around. I may be coming back for more questions later, though."

"I know," she said, but without hostility.

He pulled out a blow-up of Wayne Castine's driver's license photo and handed it to her. "Have you ever seen this man before?"

She studied the picture. "Is this him?"

"Yes."

She handed it back. "God, it was hard to tell. I mean, he doesn't look at all like that guy, all bloody and stuff."

Joe didn't answer, his question still hanging in the air.

She finally shook her head. "He doesn't look familiar. I mean, you know how I am, and kind of what I do. I don't remember a lot. People come and go. But I don't think I ever knew him."

Joe replaced the photo in his pocket, not surprised, but a little disappointed. "Did you touch anything when you entered your apartment?"

"No," she said emphatically. "It was way too gross."

"How 'bout the lights?" he continued. "On or off?"

She stared at him in silence, suddenly brought up short. "Oh, my God," she said. "You did it again—made it creepy."

"How so?"

"The lights. That's another thing, like with the key. I always leave the hall light on when I go."

"But not this time?"

"No. I did. It's just that it was off when I got back. And it wasn't busted, 'cause it worked when I flipped it on."

"So it was dark when you opened the door—dark enough that you couldn't see?"

"Right. I pay the utilities, so I leave everything else off."

It was Joe's turn to pause, thinking back to an earlier consideration. Had Castine been waiting inside and been surprised by his visitor? Or had he been the one knocking on the door? And more pertinent to what Liz had just said, regardless of who was seeking entry, could that person see who was standing before him, or what might have been clutched in the other person's hand?

Joe slid off the gurney and stood up. "Liz, you've been great. I'm sorry this happened to you, and I wish I could make the memory of it disappear. There are people I can recommend you talk to. Won't cost you anything."

But she was already shaking her head. "I don't like those people," she said, awkwardly putting a thin, limp, bony hand into his proffered one. "I just want to go back home."

He looked down at her regretfully. "You know that can't happen for a while, right? The whole apartment's a crime scene. Do you have friends you can stay with, until you get resettled?"

Again, the short, sharp, humorless laugh. "I got places I could stay, but I wouldn't call them friends." She hesitated, then conceded. "Okay, maybe I will . . ."

She left it hanging, but Joe understood, and handed her two business cards from his wallet. "One of these is me, with all my pager and phone numbers. Call me night or day if you think of anything else, or even if you have a

question. The other card is from a shelter that'll be happy
to put you up for as long as you need it. I'll make sure
they know about you, if that's the way you want to go.
They're really good people—probably better than others
you've dealt with."

She fingered the two cards without looking at them.
"That mean I'll never get back into that apartment?"

"Not for a while," he told her honestly. "Plus, it's a
pretty big mess, and who knows what the landlord's going
to want to do."

"Ugh," she said unhappily. "That asshole."

Joe was standing by the door by now, ready to leave.
"That strikes me, Liz; I do have one last question. When
you rented the place, did you have a new lock put on the
door?"

She looked at him blankly. "He gave me a key."

"New or old?"

She scowled. "That cheap bastard."

That was answer enough.

CHAPTER 4

Brattleboro is a standard hub town on one hand, and a quirky cultural oasis on the other. Housing some twelve thousand people by night, it swells considerably during the day, inflated by commuters from surrounding villages, including nearby New Hampshire and Massachusetts. But, in part because its three interstate exits are the first in a state famous for independent thinking, social activism is valued as one of the town's dearest assets. In the sixties, when both I-91 was being laid down and the counterculture was escaping the cities for visions of a sylvan paradise, the combination of Vermont's Bing Crosby beauty, its Ethan Allen outspokenness, and its sudden, easy access made it almost irresistible to a legion of urban dropouts.

However, other things were happening now—so many decades later—less amusingly anthropological, and more in common with a host of other erstwhile New England industrial beehives. Brattleboro had lately become as buffeted by tough times as many of its less lively and opinionated ilk. The middle class was struggling to hang on, while the poor—once cared for and comforted by Brattleboro's socially conscious soldiers—were growing to stretch the limits of the town's hospitality. It had gotten to where the have-nots were threatening to outnumber the haves, causing the old-time altruists to groan under the weight.

There was an interesting by-product to this—a blurring of rich and poor neighborhoods. In modern times, Brattleboro had always bragged of some societal blending—it had been a source of pride that such disparates could live cheek-by-jowl. But now the crowding was involuntary and more noticeable, the crime rate more pointed, and the tolerance becoming frayed.

Manor Court was an example of this: an entire street given over to the marginally solvent. The apartment that Wayne Castine had once called home was another. Perched high above Main Street—with its traffic, commerce, and upbeat pedestrian bustle—his one-room efficiency was an unqualified dump.

Joe found it after climbing several floors, engulfed by the day's escalating heat. He also found it under guard, at the end of a long, empty, evil-smelling hallway, by a single perspiring Brattleboro beat cop, who was clearly wondering why he'd spent half a year at the police academy preparing for the likes of this.

"You the VBI?" he asked as Joe approached.

Joe opened his jacket to reveal the badge clipped to his belt. "One of them. Joe Gunther." He stuck out his hand for a damp shake.

"Officer Nelson," the cop said, as if still trying out the name.

Joe raised his eyebrows. "No shit. Your parents named you Officer?"

Nelson stared at him for a short take, unsure of how to react. "Oh, right," he finally managed. "It's Gary. Sorry. That's a good one. I heard about you."

"But not for my sense of humor."

Again, the pause, punctuated by a blink. "You used to work for us."

"For about seventy-five years. Good ones, too." Joe pointed at the door over Nelson's shoulder. "That Castine's home-sweet-home?"

Nelson stepped aside as if the floor had suddenly softened beneath him. "Not what I would've called it."

"You been inside?" Joe asked, surprised.

"No, no. I meant the whole building. Kind of a shit hole."

Joe laughed. "Now I know why your folks didn't name you Realtor."

He fished out the key he'd secured from the landlord, and stepped up to the door.

"The crime lab ever get to the scene?" Nelson asked.

Joe paused, impressed that the man even knew the lab had been called. "About fifteen minutes ago, from what I heard. Bet you wish you were there."

Nelson looked embarrassed. "I'm okay doing what I'm told."

"It's all right," Joe reassured him, unlocking the door. "You're entitled to a little ambition. The PD should treat you well—it's that kind of department."

He paused a moment before leaving the cop to the hallway's pressing silence. "You hear or see anything or anyone since you got here?" he asked.

Nelson shook his head. "It's been quiet. Just the usual sounds through the walls."

"Why don't you knock on the other doors up and down the hall, collect people's names and DOBs, and ask them if they knew this guy, or anything about him?"

Nelson's face brightened. "Sure. Thanks."

Joe stepped inside the apartment and closed the door behind him. He had considered inviting Nelson, to show him the ropes, share the case a little, and feed the kid's enthusiasm for the job. But at the last minute, he'd demurred, assigning him the mini-canvass instead, less because of

Nelson than for his own reasons. On a straightforward murder case, he would have been more inclusive and tutorial, but a gut feeling about this one was already warning him to pay closer attention. Something offbeat was afoot here, and he wasn't sure what.

He stood with the closed door to his back, motionless, surveying the single room.

It was an awful place—small, dark, foul, looking like the aftermath of a Kansas twister, minus the missing roof that would have only improved things. Instead, it felt like the den of some creature, custom-made from a child's nightmares.

Slipping on a pair of latex gloves, Joe reached out and switched on the overhead light. A bare bulb hanging at the end of a wire illuminated the room's center, casting an angular glare into all four corners. The single window was closed and covered with cardboard, duct-taped in place. The heat and stench made Joe's nose tingle. He carefully removed his jacket and hung it on the doorknob, already feeling the sweat trickling between his shoulder blades and down the backs of his legs.

He mopped his forehead with his forearm and pulled out a small flashlight. Distracted as he was by the clutter and his own wandering thoughts, he would need the bright halo of light to focus his concentration. He had to survey the room methodically, like an archaeologist, scrutinizing one square of an imaginary grid after another.

It was onerous work, time-consuming and mentally taxing. As he pawed through discarded, soiled clothing, rotting food, child pornography of all kinds, and unsettling discoveries like a stack of children's underwear, still in its original packaging, he became aware of a man whose entire life had been given over to the exploitation of the very young in any number of perverse ways.

Joe Gunther by now was at least aware of most human depravities. But this stuff got under his skin.

There was a computer, of course. Nowadays, that was a given, like oxygen. He wondered, as he often did, if the people who'd first conjured up a fully computerized world had ever imagined that their machines would be so routinely used for such pursuits.

It was a laptop, which he didn't bother turning on. He knew what it contained, and only hoped that it might also provide insight on Castine's recent movements and interactions. There, computers provided some redemption for the abuse they were put to: They remembered their instructions, and could often be used to thrust their erstwhile masters into the limelight, like unseen and unappreciated servants of old.

But there were less exotic methods of tracking people, too. Everyone had to eat, for example, and few people of Castine's habits bothered to cook. They bought fast food and junk; they were given receipts that ended up crumpled in plastic bags or stuck to damp bottles found thrown in the odd corner. And that's where Joe located them and placed them into a careful pile, arranged by date and time stamp, including two from the day before.

He found a phone—and noted to get a warrant for its records—two pistols and a hunting knife, a few bills addressed to a post-office box, and a pay stub from the lumber mill Ron had mentioned. He uncovered the quasi-obligatory stash of bagged marijuana, alongside a Band-Aid box full of Ecstasy pills. In the bathroom—moldy, stinking, and humid—he discovered tubes of K-Y Jelly that made him shudder, and a scattering of prescription pills without a bottle.

Significantly, he hoped, he also discovered a receipt from an area psychologist named Eberhard Dziobek. He would certainly merit a conversation. Not only did folks of his calling generally keep records in some detail, but with a patient like Castine, he probably also had a list of people—family and others—who knew and interacted with him.

Because that was the primary goal right now. In a vague imitation of the old TV show *This Is Your Life,* the strategy was to dredge up as many players who knew Wayne Castine as possible, and to grill them about every detail they could recall—not just about the star of the hour, but about each other, as well.

He made one last find, mundane in itself but unusual in this context: he came across a large box of rubber bands balanced on top of the TV set, which—not surprisingly in his experience, especially in such surroundings— was a high-end plasma unit.

He picked up the box and examined it carefully, wondering if it camouflaged some more telling contents. But it simply contained the rubber bands pictured on the lid. Nowhere else did he find any stationery supplies, apart from a few scraps of paper and a couple of pens. He made a mental note of the discovery and moved on. The garbage he left for someone else down the line. This was a preliminary search—not the end-all, be-all. Ron's people would be following up.

Over an hour later, soaked through with sweat, Joe retrieved his jacket from the doorknob and reemerged into the hallway. As before, Gary Nelson was standing alone, looking forlorn.

He gave Joe an appraising glance as the latter locked the door. "Wow. You got trashed."

Joe stood holding his jacket away from him, sparing it from getting wet.

"That's one word for it."

"Find anything?"

"I got a start on a few things. How 'bout you?"

Nelson's eyebrows shot up. "Oh, right." He quickly extracted a notebook from his rear pocket and consulted it as he spoke. "I found two people on this floor. There was no answer at the third apartment. You want their names?"

"Just give me the *Reader's Digest* version. I gotta get back to the scene."

"Right—neither one of them knew him personally, but they met him once or twice, in the corridor or on the stairs. They both said he made their skin crawl, and one of them added that she wouldn't have wanted to be 'that guy's niece.' When I asked her what that meant, she said she'd bumped into Castine in the stairwell about a month ago with a young girl—maybe twelve or so—who he introduced as his niece."

"Coming up or going down?" Joe asked.

"Up," Nelson answered, looking grim.

"Any names?"

"No. I mean, there was a name, but the woman couldn't remember it."

Joe let out a sigh. "I guess I better talk to her."

Nelson shook his head. "I told her you'd want to, but she said she had to go grocery shopping before she went to work—that you could talk to her later."

He ripped out the page he'd been consulting and handed it over. Joe was impressed by the man's careful handwriting.

"That's a copy of what I got on both of them," he explained, adding, "The second witness didn't have much to say."

"What was the body language of the twelve-year-old?" Joe asked.

The young cop's face was animated, apparently grateful

to have an answer. "I asked," he said. "The lady said the kid just stood there. The two of them were holding hands— or Castine was holding the girl's, I guess—but there was no emotion, not a word, nothing. She stood there— period."

Joe waved the notepad sheet in the air. "Either one of them ever hear anything from the apartment? Crying, screaming, loud music to cover up noises?"

Nelson shook his head again. "Nope. And Castine kept to himself. That's what they meant by his making their skin crawl: he never said anything when he was greeted, never made eye contact, always seemed bummed out when anyone caught him in the open—like a rat in the sun."

Joe stared at him. "One of them said that?"

Nelson flushed slightly. "Not exactly. That part's mine. Sorry."

Joe kept after him. "He never said anything, and yet he introduced his so-called niece?"

There, Nelson was prepared. "That was the point—he wasn't asked. He just volunteered, like he was feeling guilty."

"He have any regular habits?"

The other man finally had to admit defeat. "I didn't ask. It sounded like he was a night owl." He pointed at one of the names on the page. "That one said that he came and went at all hours of the day and night."

Joe wiped his forehead again with his sleeve. "I better head out. The lab guys'll probably be wrapping things up. You got relief coming soon?"

Nelson checked his watch. "Another hour or so."

Joe patted him on the shoulder. "I appreciate your help, Gary. I'll make sure Klesczewski and your supervisor get told."

Nelson smiled. "Thanks."

Nelson waited until Joe was about halfway down the hall, heading for the top of the stairwell, before he asked, "Mr. Gunther, do we know who did it?"

Joe stopped and looked back at him. "Not right now." He then added, more hopefully, "Not yet."

CHAPTER 5

Unbeknownst to Joe Gunther, Lester Spinney nosed his car down Brattleboro's Main Street a few minutes before his boss left Castine's apartment building, headed for the same destination.

Spinney was a startlingly tall and lanky man, doomed to be nicknamed Stork by almost any group he joined. He was the odd man in Joe Gunther's four-member squad—married and with children, and the only one to have come from the state police instead of the local cops. In that last way, paradoxically, he represented the VBI's overall norm, since most Bureau cops had begun as troopers. It wasn't high-level math. With some three hundred people in uniform—in a state numbering only a thousand full-time cops, total—it stood to reason that the state police would be the biggest talent pool available. The irony was, of course, that when the governor signed the VBI into existence, he'd slapped the face of the VSP in the process. Their own Bureau of Criminal Investigation had once been assigned Vermont's major crimes, and now were restricted to pursuing whatever was deemed too time-costly for road troopers. A bitter pill only partially offset by making applications to the new VBI exclusive to the best investigators in the state—a clear advantage to old BCI members.

It had been an arcane political childbirth, made murkier by strong opinions and hurt feelings. The likes of Lester Spinney, however, had only benefited. Once struggling inside a tradition-bound—he would have said hidebound—organization with a promotion bottleneck, Les was now free to run his own cases with a minimum of interference, under the guidance of an almost legendary mentor—all for the same pay, benefits, and retirement as before.

This was not a man unhappy with how life could sometimes turn out. And the fact that he had to commute from Springfield to Brattleboro to do so, and work with the likes of Willy Kunkle, didn't faze him at all. He and everyone else knew Kunkle was on board solely because of Gunther's influence. In truth, that was exactly the point: Willy may have been a public-relations disaster. But he was an inspired cop, instinctive and canny and utterly committed. Given Lester's own quirky sense of humor, and how he'd often felt bound and gagged as a trooper, he was delighted to work with an outfit that would have Willy Kunkle as a member.

He reached the bottom of Main Street, and the double-sided chute of tall, weathered, traditional, red brick buildings, and veered slightly right through the complex intersection—Brattleboro's own "malfunction junction"—to engage onto Canal Street, on his way to Manor Court.

Springfield, his home forty miles north, looked a little like this, as did so many others. There was always a source of flowing water somewhere, for the energy and transport of yore; always the imposing, gargantuan architecture, speaking of nineteenth-century industrial might; and usually a fountain, gazebo, or commons with a war memorial, where patriots could gather annually in early November.

It was largely a throwback to a long-lost era, with its share of built-in irony, given how the world had since passed it by.

But to Lester, it was the culture that had shaped him, been the cradle of his thinking and his general world outlook. He was the result of New Englanders—hardy, inventive, independent; used to living in an environment where winter threatened to kill you for over half of every year, and where three of the region's most plentiful attributes—ice, lumber, and granite—had been creatively turned into three of its earliest commercial assets.

Such thoughts of cold and ice struck him as ironic now, as he drove through one of the hottest days of the year, knowing he'd soon have to abandon the car's air-conditioning.

Lester was less familiar with Manor Court than his colleagues, given his more recent exposure to Brattleboro, but just as with downtown, he wasn't out of place. All New England cops knew these blocks, along with the stories of those calling them home.

He traveled most of the dead end's length, and pulled up to the curb amid an array of cruisers, unmarked cars, a converted ambulance—now a mobile command post—countless people in uniform, and a large truck labeled "Vermont Forensic Lab." Sammie Martens was standing on the sidewalk, twenty feet away, staring up at one of the triple-deckers.

"Lost?" he asked, emerging into the blast furnace heat. "Ask a cop for directions."

She turned to him, shoving her dark glasses up on her forehead for better eye contact. "I know better," she said. "They have no clue, but they tell you anyway."

He slammed his door and approached her. "Looks like a doughnut truck accident out here. Getting anywhere?"

"Who knows?" she answered. "Right now, it's just a

bunch of hen scratching. We may have what we need and not even know it yet. What did you find out?"

Lester's job had been to dig deeper into Castine's background. "Not much more than what you already got. I have a family history, and a long list of contacts off the computer. We'll have enough interviews to last us till next year, unless we get lucky."

Sam made a face. She wasn't fond of working indoors. High-strung and energetic, she was restless by nature.

"What's the game plan right now?" Spinney asked, already beginning to sweat. By contrast, his colleague looked dry and comfortable, which only made him feel hotter.

Sam pointed at the crime-lab truck with her chin. "They're close to wrapping up. The boss'll be here soon. Willy and I have been canvassing the neighbors. So, I guess, that's the assignment for the time being, until we get together and compare notes. You want to help me work this one?" She gestured to the building beside them, two doors down from the crime scene.

Spinney cast an eye along the street. There was now a fair crowd, being controlled by police tape and uniformed officers. He noticed several news crews, with and without TV cameras. Fortunately, in a state this size, even a crime this gory couldn't generate much of a zoo—there was only one major TV station—from far-off Burlington—and a mere sprinkling of newspapers and radio stations.

"Sure," he said, turning to the tired three-story building at hand. "What's your pleasure?"

She shrugged. "There're two apartments per floor, usually. If you want to take the top, I'll take the second."

"Deal," he said, heading for the porch steps.

Lester hadn't visited where Castine had been discovered, but he knew there wasn't much difference between structures. Even 130 years ago, architects and builders—

especially of workers' quarters—had a fondness for the economies of duplication. The fact that today's residents had evolved from factory drones to either working sporadically or not at all hadn't altered how their housing had ended up smelling, looking, and falling apart.

Les climbed the steps slowly, hoping to control his sweating. Behind the closed doors he passed, he heard children crying, TVs blaring, and inanimate objects being shifted, dropped, or thrown around. Arguments delivered with more or less effort formed a muted chorus overall, making him feel he was swimming within the circulatory system of a large, unhealthy, living entity.

At the top landing, he was faced with two apartment doors, one muffling more of the same audible chaos, the other obstructing what appeared to be total silence.

Hoping for a peaceful start to an onerous process, he pounded on the silent door.

The effect was startling, immediate, and painful. With his hand still in the air, Lester saw the door fly back on its hinges and a small, round-shaped man barrel out at him like a two-legged cannonball, catching him in the solar plexus and sending him staggering back against the far wall, where he smacked the back of his head and collapsed.

"*Runner*," he shouted weakly as his attacker took the steps two at a time.

On the second floor, Sammie heard the crash of the door, followed by Lester being sent flying. She had just had her own door opened before her, revealing an oversized woman with a baby bottle in her hand.

She quickly said, "Please close the door, ma'am," and braced herself for whatever was coming.

Lester's nemesis appeared at a dead run, bouncing off the wall at the bottom of the stairs so that he could better sprint the length of the landing.

In the two seconds allowed her, Sam took in her surroundings tactically, assessed her opponent's size and speed, and chose how to stop him.

Shouting, "*Stop. Police,*" she went at him like a linebacker, at an angle to shove him up against the landing's railing, and maybe even over its top. Being a small woman—and ex-military at that—had trained her to fight dirty when necessary.

The idea half worked. She did clip the man, and he did go careening against the railing, but she was the one who went over, ending up like a damsel in distress, hanging by her hands over the void, while the man with a plan kept charging like a miniaturized rhino on speed.

"*Runner,*" Sam screamed in turn, swinging her feet over to the banister below and letting go to make a clumsy landing on the uneven steps. "*Stop that man.*"

Outside, Joe Gunther had just exited his car and was about to call to Zippo, still positioned at the crime-scene building, when Sam's voice came echoing into the street two doors down.

Both men stared in astonishment as the runner in question blew out of the entrance, leaped off the front porch in one jump, landed on the sidewalk in a crouch, and took off like a sprinter for the far distant junction of Manor Court and Canal Street.

He didn't make it. Cops were all over that sidewalk. And within several paces, one of them stuck his foot out and tripped the fleeing man, just as four others landed on him like bears on a seal.

They were still sorting out who was who when Sam appeared and dove into the pile, pulling away cop after cop to reveal the man who had run her over.

She grabbed him by the shirtfront and yanked him to his feet. "You little peckerhead," she yelled into his face. "What the *fuck* do you think you're doing? You are under arrest. Do you understand that?" She shook him until his head was a blur, adding, "And count yourself lucky I don't shoot you right now."

She felt a hand calmly settle onto her right shoulder and twisted around angrily to stare into Joe Gunther's eyes.

"It's okay, Sam," he told her quietly. "We got him."

She opened her grip and let the little man fall into the arms of the cops around him.

"Right," she said, regaining composure. "Sorry about that. He surprised me."

Joe smiled. "I got that part."

She suddenly asked, "Where's Les?"

"Why?"

"He was with me in there. This guy hit him first."

They both turned toward the building and saw Lester Spinney standing on the porch, holding the back of his head. He was dirty and covered with sweat, but he waved them off as they approached.

"I'm okay, I'm okay," he said. "I whacked my head is all. Who the hell is that little bastard?"

"Eddie Novack," said a familiar voice.

They all three looked over at Ron Klesczewski, who was standing nearby, watching his men buckling up Sam's prisoner.

"He stuck a gun in the face of a teller at the Exit One gas station last month—got away with a couple of hundred bucks. We've been wondering when he'd show up."

"Meaning he probably had nothing to do with our body?" Spinney ventured.

Ron lifted one shoulder equivocally. "I'd guess not, but this is one of those neighborhoods. You never know."

"All right," Joe stated, his eye back on the first building. "Why don't you ask him about that later, Ron? Lester, go to the ER and get a clean bill of health for that head.

Sam can drive you. It looks like the lab folks are wrapping up; I want to head 'em off before they leave."

Spinney opened his mouth to protest, but then stopped, knowing both the predictable response, and that Gunther really had no choice. Plus, were he to be perfectly honest, he'd taken a harder shot than he was admitting, and was curious about what damage he might have incurred.

Ron, Joe, and Willy therefore left the other two and walked over to a small group of people gathered near the back of the large lab truck, who were slowly and gratefully peeling off their suffocating Tyvek suits.

Ron pointed out his own department's mobile command post, parked a few feet farther along, and suggested, "You want to talk, feel free to use that—it's air-conditioned."

Joe approached a man with graying hair who was already stuffing his suit into a garbage bag. His polo shirt and pants looked as if he'd been caught in a drenching summer shower.

"David?" Joe began.

The other man turned and smiled. "Joe. It's been a while. Pardon the damp hand."

Joe shook it enthusiastically. David Hawke was one of the true old-timers, dating back to when the state police replaced their troopers with scientifically schooled and accredited lab techs. Hawke was among the key people throughout the state that Joe had made an effort to make a personal friend, rather than just a colleague.

Joe nodded toward the PD's smaller truck. "Care to retire where it's cooler?"

Hawke smiled broadly. "Jesus. Might put me into shock. There enough room in there for my whole crew?"

The other techs looked at him hopefully.

Ron gestured with his arm. "Complete with cold drinks."

The small crowd ambled next door to Ron's command post and gingerly squeezed inside, carefully maneuvering until everyone had a place to perch and something cold to drink.

David passed his can of iced tea across his forehead before popping the tab and taking a long swallow.

"God," he finally said. "That is truly what the doctor ordered. This is not the worst scene we've ever processed, but it's close."

"Speak for yourself, Doc," said one of his junior colleagues, whom Joe recognized as the new photo tech.

The rest of them laughed sympathetically.

"Anything you can tell us right off?" Joe asked after a suitably polite pause.

"With the usual caveats, sure," David told him, continuing after another pull on his drink. "The ME will have her say about cause of death, but since transport was delayed until we got here, we did take a look, and I feel safe saying he was done in by a sharp instrument, versus something like a gun. But he was also badly beaten, so who knows? Is that convincingly enough stated for you?"

It was humorously said, but Joe noticed Willy shaking his head at the caution. Still, he kept quiet, which was good enough for the moment.

"Nice work, by the way," Hawke went on, "shading the windows from the sun. It did keep the heat down a little, and may have helped the blood from degrading too much for DNA analysis."

Ron nodded his appreciation. "Thanks. It was all we could think of."

"Next time, though," Hawke added gently, "call us and let us know of the situation. We can live with the body being moved and refrigerated, assuming you photograph and video the bejeezus out of it first. Better that than lose degradable evidence."

"My screwup," Joe said quickly. "I should've thought of that."

Hawke waved it away. "Not to worry. God knows, we all have too much on our plates, and from the looks of it, I'm guessing it all came from the victim anyway."

"You figure out how it went down?" Willy asked.

David pointed to one of his colleagues. "Robin's the one with the most schooling in reconstruction. I'll leave that to her."

Robin Lerner, the sole female of the team, was another forensics tech Joe knew from years past—one of several, in fact—which spoke well of Hawke's ability to retain good people, despite Vermont's inability to pay them appropriately.

"The story is mostly in the blood spatter analysis," she said, cautioning, "but that can be a tricky way of looking at something like this. You can end up seeing what you want, instead of what really happened."

"Whatever," Willy muttered.

It was offensive, but thankfully, Kunkle was well known, including up in Waterbury, where the lab was housed.

Lerner chose to laugh, although Joe noticed the momentary narrowing of her eyes. "Okay, okay," she said. "Point taken. Here's my educated guess, since for the moment, it doesn't really matter: I think Mr. Castine was inside the apartment, most likely answering the door, when he was attacked. It looks like it was fast, brutal, and may have involved at least a knife and possibly a blunt object, like a small bat or club."

"Did he put up a fight?" Willy asked.

"Hard to tell," she answered. "I'll leave that to the ME. She'll be able to wash the blood off and better examine the body's surface areas. I didn't see any broken fingers or obviously skinned knuckles, but the hands were a mess and difficult to visualize."

"I found some weapons at his apartment," Joe contributed. "That doesn't mean he didn't bring another one here, but he also may not have been expecting trouble."

"And there were just the two of them?" Ron asked.

Hawke answered that. "We discussed that when we were up there. There are two sets of bloody footprints—the primaries, belonging to Castine, and one set of secondaries, which were much harder to isolate and clearly document. It struck us that either the killer had been lucky that way, or very careful to avoid the blood."

"Doesn't that run at odds to the rest of it?" Joe asked.

"You mean the general savagery?" Hawke countered. "I suppose it could. It's also possible that the attacker's fury was very focused, very planned."

Willy again. "Fingerprints?"

"A lot of those, although only Castine's in blood."

Joe leaned forward on the bench seat he'd chosen. "David—or anybody, for that matter—this may be way outside what anyone can answer, but I was wondering: Could you tell if Castine had only been there last night, or if he was using this place as a home away from home? I mean, for example, did you find his prints generally throughout the apartment, or mostly in his own blood?"

Lerner answered him. "I'd say the latter, but as you all know, fingerprints in general are a Hollywood obsession, where they're the end-all, be-all. In a place like this, especially, where you have a different tenant every few months, and so many people coming and going anyhow, we don't go crazy trying to catalog them. We collected what we thought made sense."

"Going a little further, though," Hawke added, "I didn't get the impression that anyone but the woman lived there. For example, we did check the toilet flushing valve and didn't find a print of his there. Same for the rim, just in case he'd taken a leak. We didn't find any droplets."

"Jesus," Willy said.

Lerner's laughter was genuine this time. "You men may lift the seat, but you never wipe the rim."

"I do," Willy blurted out.

The whole group fell silent.

"Really?" she asked appreciatively.

Willy stood up, red-faced, and glared at Gunther. "Are we done?"

Everyone laughed, happy for the embarrassment of a man who so routinely put them through the wringer.

Nevertheless, Joe also rose, keeping Willy company. "Yeah, we're set for the moment. One reason I asked, though, was that if you think Castine was on the inside, and Liz Babbitt's right about remembering she locked the door, then how did he get in?"

Willy opened his mouth to answer, but Joe stopped him with a raised hand. "An additional detail: Liz told me the lock wasn't new. It hadn't been changed since the previous tenant."

"That's what I was going to say," Willy commented sourly. "I already talked to the landlord. He said it would cost too much, and that nobody gives a damn anyhow." He looked at Joe balefully and added, "And no, Castine never rented the dump. And yes, that does mean we need to find out how he got his hands on a key, and so, yes again, I did get a list of all the people who've lived there over the past couple of years."

Joe smiled and addressed the entire group, bowing slightly. "And people ask me," he commented, moving carefully through the crowd toward the door that Willy was already holding open, letting in a blast of hot air, "how I can stand working with the guy. He's a genius. We should all be so lucky."

They both left to a chorus of boos and groans.

CHAPTER 6

Joe loosened his tie an inch and stood before the fan with his arms slightly held out, letting the wash of warm air suggest a passing breeze. At least it was finally night, and the heat had dropped a few degrees. This kind of weather didn't hit the region often or for long, and he knew people had it worse in a hundred other places, but that didn't make him feel any better. It was like being in a sauna with no controls and no door.

"Right," said Willy, walking in. "Block the fan so the rest of us can die."

Joe reluctantly moved out of the way, saying with sarcastic sweetness, "I'm so embarrassed, Agent Kunkle. Would you like a few moments in front of the fan?"

Willy glowered at him and headed instead for his desk, which was wedged into the corner facing the rest of the office—a perfect reflection of the man himself.

"Fuck you."

Joe pushed his lips out and murmured, "Indeed," under his breath.

Sammie Martens and Lester Spinney entered the office, chatting amicably. They were the two most level-headed members of this small unit, of which five others—similarly sized—were sprinkled across the state, not including the director at the Waterbury headquarters—headquarters being a single cubbyhole office on the top floor of the Department of Public Safety building.

Joe had a soft spot for Sam, which was in part only a reciprocal tenderness nurtured by her clear adoration of him. Whether he was the father she'd never had or the mentor she'd always craved, Joe could do no wrong in her eyes—which made her a difficult person for him to fault.

She could be a handful, however, which he only privately admitted. Her shaking Eddie Novack like a rag doll this afternoon was a good example of her short fuse. More clinically, her choice of Willy as a lover was a shrink's fantasy of unmitigated self-destruction, at least on the outside. In fact, they'd both made it work for longer than anyone anticipated. Like twin halves of a devilishly possessed pair of scissors, they functioned best—if sometimes destructively—when joined together.

"How's the noggin?" Joe asked Lester as the latter settled down behind his own desk, liberally festooned with stork memorabilia.

Les touched the back of his head. "Not a vital organ, as it turns out. Docs were amazed when they looked inside."

"No gerbil?" Willy asked.

"Several," he came back, typically self-deprecatory, "but all fully functioning."

"Seriously," Joe persisted.

Spinney gave him a thumbs-up. "Seriously—clean bill of health. Ask my nanny."

"True, boss. All true," Sam said, dumping a soft briefcase onto her desk and partly collapsing into her chair.

Joe took up one of his usual positions, sitting on the edge of the windowsill, although not before the fan, and addressed them all. "Okay—long day. You've worked hard and I don't want to keep you much longer. Everyone's earned a good night's sleep. I did want to compare notes very quickly, though, so we know what to start on tomorrow morning. Sam? Give us a rundown, allowing everyone else to fill gaps as they pop up."

"Like, who dun it?" Willy suggested.

"If you've got that, now would be the time."

Willy smirked, but remained silent, getting the message.

Sam, yielding to a propensity for notes and lists, opened her case and laid out a few sheets of paper before starting in. "Wayne Castine—autopsy to come, computer analysis to come, along with his phone records and interviews with coworkers, whatever family we can find, and the shrink Joe discovered he was seeing. Castine was presumably beaten and/or stabbed to death by someone who appeared at the door of an apartment he was using without permission and for reasons unknown."

"What kinds of reasons?" Joe asked. "Just for what-the-hell."

During the pause following, Lester suggested, "Discretion?"

"He wouldn't know when Babbitt might all of a sudden come home," Willy argued.

"He had his own place," Sam pointed out, "and he lived alone."

Joe had also thought of that. "I know he brought at least one child there," he shared. "But it is a dump-and-a-half."

"Suggesting the need for a more upscale love nest?" Les finished for him, and then added, "Why not a motel room?"

"The thrill," Willy proposed.

The others looked at him.

He flushed slightly. "Come on—put it together. Guy's a pervert, lives on the edge, probably sees himself as a real daredevil. Why not use a borrowed bed, and risk being exposed? Probably gave him a bigger hard-on."

The image all but killed the discussion.

"Did we ever find the key we think he used to get in?" Lester asked after an awkward silence.

"In his pocket," Willy answered shortly, clearly irritated.

"Meaning," Joe suggested, "that there're at least two keys in circulation."

"Anything special about Wayne's?" Lester asked.

"Willy?" Joe asked, but was testily interrupted by the man himself.

"It's just a key. I interviewed the landlord and got a list of previous renters. I'll find out who Wayne got it from. I been busy, okay?"

Joe held up both hands in surrender. "We got it, we got it. You're hot on the trail. Sam, what did we get from the canvass and what do we have left to do?"

"I took up Ron on his manpower offer, so we got a pretty good sweep in before everybody started talking to everybody else and muddling up their stories. The consensus on Liz is what you'd expect—she's new to the neighborhood, does her grocery bagging and hooking and barhopping on her own, and keeps to herself. She probably has as many friends as everybody does, and we can chase them down when the time comes, but from what I'm getting, she is what she says she is: an innocent bystander who just happened to have the wrong apartment at the wrong time. I'm not leaving it there—I know what I said is a huge assumption. But for the time being, I suggest putting her on the back burner."

"Fine with me," Joe agreed. "What about Wayne?"

"Totally different story. A lot of people knew him, even though he *didn't* live on the street. I'm building a who's-who list. A bunch of them swear he went after kids, but no-body's seen anything."

"Hold it, hold it," Joe requested. "There were that many kids he abused on Manor Court?"

"No, no," Sam reassured him. "Sorry—that kind of ran together. A few of those we canvassed said he was a snapper, but I couldn't get a single kid's name from any of them. It was all, 'So-and-so told me he'd done what's-his-name.' Super vague right now."

"A snapper?" Les asked.

Willy held up his wrist. "Comes from them using rub-ber bands—when they get the urge to fuck a kid, they're supposed to snap a rubber band they wear around their wrist. Pain equals lust, so lust goes away. That's the the-ory. Typical shrink crap. A bullet would make the lust go away quicker—cheaper, too."

"Thank you for that," Spinney said, shaking his head but smiling. "Short and concise, as usual."

"I found a box of rubber bands in his apartment," Joe told them.

"Bet they weren't used much," Willy commented.

Joe had to admit he was right—there'd been no rubber band on the body and the box had been full. "I'll talk to his shrink tomorrow," he said. "A word to the wise, though, before we go too far down this path. Right now, this snapper stuff is purely anecdotal, unless you know some-thing, Willy, that you're keeping in your pocket."

Willy raised his eyebrows innocently. "Not me. I just heard the guy was dirty—like Sam did—again and again."

"Meaning," Joe resumed, "that he probably is. But he doesn't have a record, which means we don't have proof."

"You worried about a stiff's reputation?" Willy chal-lenged, his face darkening again.

"What I'm worried about," Joe explained, "is getting blinded by this. Somebody killed him—maybe because he went after kids; maybe for some completely different reason. I don't want to lose this case because we got too focused, too fast."

He looked over at Spinney. "You dug into Castine's records. Anything you didn't mention earlier?"

Lester pulled out a couple of notes. "Wayne Castine, aged thirty-two, born Hardwick, Vermont, of Shirley Evans, since deceased, and an unknown father. Evans married when Wayne was five, and a few years later, Wayne cropped up as a person-of-interest in a child abuse case filed against the stepfather. I called a friend at child services and was told that Wayne was the victim. This conversation was off the record, of course, but it told me what you might expect—mom dragged a growing bunch of kids around the state, never making ends meet, and fell in with one loser after another. The abuse was repeated with another of mom's boyfriends a few years later."

Lester, the father of two, sighed and concluded, "You get the idea—he was done for from the start."

"But no criminal record of his own?" Joe asked incredulously.

"No *adult* record," Les corrected him. "I made another call to Parole and Probation and got the skinny there. Usual bad-boy stuff—underage drinking, criminal mischief, assault, B-and-E. He messed up a lot. He spent time in juvenile detention, was finally taken away from mom and passed around to a few foster homes. But it looks like he learned not to get caught after he reached maturity, 'cause that's where the legal trail runs out of gas."

"Except for the person-of-interest computer entries you mentioned," Joe added. "I hate to say it, but that's where you're going to have to spend some time, talking to those POIs, just to see what might pop up."

Spinney looked slightly glum. "I know."

"At least you can start from the present and work

backward," Joe added cheerfully. "Take the most recent entry; chances are that whatever got him killed stemmed from some fresh-out-of-the-oven insult."

He paused to rub his eyes. "God—it's getting late. Why don't we wrap this up . . ."

Sam had raised her hand, like a schoolgirl. "Anything specific you want me to do tomorrow?"

"Wayne's coworkers," he told her succinctly. "Also, a Bratt PD cop—a new guy named Gary Nelson—interviewed two of Castine's neighbors, one of whom saw Castine with a young girl he claimed was his niece. Reinterview that witness and see if you can't get a fix on the girl. Also, there was one neighbor Nelson missed—could be the one who knows something."

Sam didn't look up from the notes she was taking. "Got it."

Joe stood up. "All right. That's it. Keep in touch. Reconvene here tomorrow at sixteen hundred, but send up a flare if you find anything hot before then."

Everyone gathered their belongings—except Willy, of course, who merely sauntered out the door. Joe moved to his desk, pretending to settle in for some late-night paperwork, and waved good night to the last person to leave.

But he wasn't interested in paperwork. What was on his mind had been plaguing him all day—and building for the past few weeks.

With a New Englander's ingrained respect for personal privacy, he hadn't intruded on Lyn's request to be left alone. He had broken the news to her of the lobster boat's discovery during a hike up Mt. Wantastiquet, across the river from downtown Brattleboro. The view had been spectacular, the weather perfect, her welcome of him earlier encouraging. He'd recognized the burden he had to share, guessed at the magnitude of its effect, but had hoped it might be tolerably borne, at least after the initial shock.

But it hadn't been. It had crippled her, and then the two of them. He had tried to keep her company, quietly, supportively. She'd become almost mute, distracted, as if lost in an immense and all-consuming calculation. He had sensed himself changing in her eyes from someone she could just stand to a downright nuisance, before she'd finally affirmed the fact by asking him to keep his distance. She needed "space," she'd told him, and he'd rarely hated a word more. At first, his distress had been all about her, enhanced by the guilt that he'd been the bearer of her bad news. With time, in her absence, missing her, his emotions had turned more selfish.

He didn't doubt that this latest case had ratcheted up his desire to see her. Major investigations took time, cut into sleep, and destroyed all previously scheduled events, especially leisure ones. Weekends vanished, nine-to-five had no meaning. But it was also when the job became intoxicating, driving the brain into high gear, allowing adrenaline to replace sleep—and making him crave both a good sounding board, and some company in bed.

He envied Sam and Willy most now, and Lester with his wife, Susan. They all had someone with whom to share the odd thought that comes unexpectedly, over dinner or while taking a shower, the one that sometimes blows a case wide open. More importantly—even with Sam and Willy, who worked together days—such sharing could counterbalance the tension of the investigation with the need to fill a grocery list, or take out the trash, or make love and welcome oblivion.

Whatever his motivation or its timing, Joe missed her. Lyn had reignited a love of companionship he hadn't experienced in a long while. Things with Gail had hardened over time, often becoming couched in discourse and debate, disguising that their minds had gradually been asked to handle what had faded from their hearts.

The time Joe had spent with Lyn reminded him of how natural and uncomplicated a relationship could be.

And right now, he was longing for that enough to break his promise to her and act upon it.

Lyn's bar on Elliot Street, like a reminder of the trouble between them, was named "Silva's," which she'd told him once was more in honor of her father than a reflection of her own last name. It was better than a going concern—it had been the proverbial right place at the right time. Opened just recently, it was jammed nightly with appreciative patrons, drawn by the music, the crowd, and, of course, the need to be seen where it counted, for some reason.

Lyn had been a bookkeeper for years, as well as a bartender. She and Joe had met in Gloucester, where he'd been on a case. The attraction had been mutual, if initially chaste. Indeed, by the time she found a bar up for sale in Brattleboro, he'd placed her in a backlog of very pleasant but distant memories. Her reappearance in his life had been surprising and extraordinarily welcome. Right place, right time.

He climbed the concrete steps to the bar's carved wooden door, and left the swelter of the darkened street for the air-conditioned bedlam of a night spot in full swing.

Joe was no lover of bars. He barely drank, found no pleasure in drunks, disliked loud music, and hated crowds. Still, he had a regular seat here, when Lyn was on duty, which she was several times a week, both to support her staff and to keep an eye on the business. Many a night, Joe would park himself on the last bar stool against the wall and nurse a succession of Cokes as he watched her ply her trade, impressed by her natural ease with people—all the more so since he knew her to be an introvert at heart, happiest alone or in his company. Until recently.

"Joe," came a woman's voice. "You want the usual?"

He looked over the tops of the heads lined up at the bar and saw a young woman's face glimpsing out from between them—the night's barkeep, Holly.

"Not tonight, thanks—was hoping to catch Lyn."

Holly's brow furrowed. "You been away?" She gestured to the far end of the bar, where they could have some semblance of privacy. He squeezed in between his usual perch, now occupied, and the wall.

"Kind of," he told her. "Why do you ask?"

She was leaning far over the bar, with her ear almost pressed against his mouth. She now straightened enough to face him and shout, just inches away, "She left for home, about three, four days ago. Family emergency."

"She all right?"

"Yeah, yeah. She's fine. It's her mom, I think. Her brother, Steve, called. Is she all right, by the way?"

He was able to hear about every other word. "All right?"

"Yeah," Holly spoke louder. "She's been really weird lately. I mean, before the phone call from home."

"A different piece of bad news," Joe explained vaguely.

Holly knew better than to ask. "Well. I hope it gets better. We miss her. Give her our love when you see her. You going there now?"

He considered the idea. He hadn't thought of it—merely rued his bad luck when he'd heard she'd left town. But for a man with his needs, and who often went sleepless for days, a night of travel to and from Gloucester sounded feasible and possibly restorative. To hell with her "space," he suddenly thought.

"Yeah," he yelled. "I think I am."

CHAPTER 7

On the map, Cape Ann, of which Gloucester is the dominant town, forms the top of a capital letter "C" that cradles Boston Harbor in its embrace, with the bottom arm being the Hull/Cohasset area. As a result, where it isn't a working-class fishing port, Gloucester is a Boston playground, hemmed in by Martha Stewart mansions and country clubs. During the summer, during the day, and certainly during weekends, it is a recreational madhouse, filled with Type-A urbanites charging through their supposed time off like a bunch of drunks at a liquor store sale. Not fun to watch, and even worse to experience, especially in heavy, SUV-clogged traffic.

Fortunately, Joe had none of that to concern him. He drove through the middle of the night with his windows down, his air conditioner off, and his radio barely murmuring—virtually the only car visible on the entire 150-mile trip. As he crossed the Annisquam River onto the cape itself, swung around the Grant traffic circle, and headed south on Washington Street, he could fully appreciate the salt-tinged quiet of the maritime breeze that had enwrapped this quintessential fishing village for over 350 years. Approaching the center of the town—incongruously decorated by a statue of Joan of Arc—he felt the hyped-up, modern tensions of Boston's extended commercial crush yield to something more permanent and stubborn. Perhaps Joan wasn't so misplaced after all, he thought. She, too, persevered against reason and all odds, just as the fishing fleet in this town had defied both financial and ecological dread.

Of course, he only hoped that Gloucester would end up better off than Joan.

Like many of its ilk, the town has two faces—a glossy one for tourists, offering lobster meals, boutiques, ocean tours, and overpriced latté; and the time-tested working-class reality, with its docks, factories, bars, and a cluster of churches offering whatever solace the bars lacked. In a town from which, over its history, some ten thousand people had died at sea, any kindness, from any quarter, was worth consideration.

Joe turned east, leaving the photogenic Gloucester for its grittier back bay, crested a small hill, and drove into a scene of boats, docks, and processing plants, garishly isolated from the black of night by a scattering of sodium lights, hung on high.

Working from strained memory, he left the primary street and entered a cobweb of narrow lanes—Webster, Friend, Elwell, and more, all riding a hilly terrain like boats on a rolling sea—in search of the address he knew Lyn's brother shared with their mother, Maria.

Eventually, no longer sure where he was, he suddenly recognized the building—small and tired—and pulled over to the curb. In both directions, he was boxed in by rows of similar homes, mostly painted white, crowded together as if warding off wind and cold. It seemed they knew, like the generations they'd sheltered, that despite the balmy weather, bad times were just over the horizon.

Joe craned his neck to see the house's dark facade,

recognizing Lyn's car parked before it, and pulled his cell phone from his belt.

A sleepy, quizzical voice answered after the sixth ring. "Hello?"

"Lyn? It's Joe. I'm sorry I woke you up."

A long pause was followed by, "It's okay. What's wrong?"

"I'm all right. I know this sounds crazy, but I wanted to hear your voice again."

He could hear her shifting, no doubt rearranging a pillow behind her head. "Jesus, Joe."

"I know, I know. Stupid . . ."

"No, not stupid," she interrupted. "I'm glad you did."

"Really?"

Another silence, followed by, "I've been a little jammed up, not sure what to do. I thought I had to figure that out alone."

"And now?"

She sighed. "I don't know. It's still pretty confusing."

He nodded in the darkness, sharing the feeling. "How's your mom doing?"

"You know about that?"

"I dropped by the bar. They told me Steve had called, and that you'd gone home."

"Yeah. She's doing better. She just had a meltdown when I told her about the boat being found, and Steve couldn't handle it on his own. He's a little beaten up, too. With his history, I figured I better head down."

After his father and brother had been declared lost at sea, Steve had caved in, first indulging in drugs, and then dealing them. He'd just recently emerged from prison, barely in time to help his quasi-catatonic mother in her last years. It was no wonder they'd both been shaken by Joe's discovery.

"I don't know how you'll take this, Lyn," Joe admitted, "but I followed you down."

He could almost see her astonishment. "You *what?*"

"I drove to Gloucester. I'm parked outside your house right now."

No response.

"There's no obligation to it, Lyn," he said quickly. "I can leave just as easily. I yielded to impulse."

"It's okay. It's okay," she said, to his relief. "I'm sorry. I had to get my head around it. I'm still half asleep. Let me come down."

"You don't have to."

She laughed, albeit less with delight than at the stupidity of the comment. "Of course I do. Hang on."

It didn't take two minutes for her to appear, dressed in jeans and a light sweatshirt, and dart across the street to slide into his passenger seat. They hugged awkwardly across the center console, making him regret that he hadn't waited for her on the sidewalk.

"You really are crazy, you know that?" she told him, settling back in the corner and shaking her head. "This is pure high school."

"I know," he conceded. "It was just getting under my skin. I feel so guilty about all this."

"That you stumbled across the *Maria*?" she asked. "How's that work?"

He gazed out the windshield, appreciative of the way even stationary cars allowed for conversation without eye contact. "I was worried I was being held to blame a little."

She didn't answer directly, but joined him for a few seconds, studying the dark street ahead. "Maybe you were."

"What do I do about that?" he asked slowly.

"Maybe you just did it."

He wasn't sure what to say.

She crossed her arms and tucked her chin in slightly. Now it was her turn to avoid eye contact. "Look," she said, "I know this has been weird. You probably had no idea you were hooking up with such a psycho."

"That's not what I'm seeing."

"Because you only see what I show you."

He couldn't say much to that.

"Joe," she said in a stronger voice, shifting in her seat and looking straight at him. "When you first told me you'd found the *Maria*, I didn't give you a chance to explain. I mean, you told me it was way up north and in some bad guy's boathouse, but then I shut you down. Can you give me all of it now? I promise I won't get weird again."

Joe nodded, happy to talk about something concrete. "It was your brother, Steve, funnily enough. He was telling us how your dad would take the whole family up the coast of Maine, pretending to be on vacation but actually picking up tips on the lobster trade."

"I remember that," she said.

"Well, he mentioned how, when you were in Jonesport, you and your mother went off shopping or something, while he, José, and your dad went to the docks to talk shop with a boat captain."

"Okay," she said, her excitement building. "I didn't know what he was talking about. Yeah. It's coming back."

"Well, both things stuck in my mind at the time," Joe continued. "That the captain did some smuggling on the side, and that his name was Wellman Beale."

"*He's* the one who had the *Maria*?" she asked, astonished.

Joe nodded. "And the smuggling involved prescription drugs from Canada. Beale was up to his neck in that case in Maine, with the Customs task force and all the drug cops. He wasn't a major player, but he was part of the overall scheme to use fishing boats to import the goods."

Her expression saddened and her gaze shifted to her lap. "And Dad was involved, too," she stated listlessly.

"I didn't say that," he emphasized. "According to Steve, your father didn't even know Beale back then, much less about his smuggling. The way he told it, your dad and brother just happened to meet him on the dock and they talked shop while Steve climbed all over Beale's boat."

Lyn looked at him sourly. "Joe, he was a kid, and he loved them. What do you think he was going to say?"

"What are *you* saying?" Joe asked.

She hesitated before avoiding the question. "Did Beale explain how he got the boat?"

"That part I told you in full, since there wasn't much to it—he said he found the *Maria* floating abandoned at sea and brought it home. Since 'home' in this case is an island he shares with nobody else, no one was the wiser. It just sat there from then on, collecting barnacles and seaweed. You got it back, didn't you?"

"Yeah," she admitted vaguely. "Steve runs it like a taxi service now, for Realtors with offshore property, or rich people wanting groceries . . . Whatever. He renamed it *The Silva Lining*, which I hate. But it gives him something to do and keeps him out of trouble. Maybe."

"Maybe?"

Her face hardened. "Well, think of it. You're a cop. Here's a guy with a rap sheet and a boat going out to sea at all times of the day and night for vague purposes. You just told me about drug runners using fishing boats. Steve did time for dealing drugs. I even had an obnoxious little chat about that with a local cop, who was insinuating the same thing."

"Based on anything?" Joe asked, and instantly regretted it.

Lyn stared at him through narrowed eyes, and then threw open the door.

"Wait. Lyn," he said, getting out, too.

He circled the front of the car and met her on the sidewalk. He didn't touch her, and she refused to look at him, but she stayed by the open door.

"Lyn," he said quietly. "You started this. You were the one expressing doubt."

Her arms were by her sides, her hands forming fists. She swung them in frustration and then crossed them tightly before her. "Fuck."

He let her breathe for a few seconds in silence.

"He's not the most stable guy in the world," she finally said, adding, "and he screwed up before. I'm worried, too."

"But not based on anything solid," Joe suggested.

"No," she agreed.

"Well, then," he tried comforting her, "that's all it comes to right now: a concern. Right?"

She nodded, and then changed topics. "You talked to Beale, didn't you?"

"Yes, for what it was worth."

"Did he say he worked with my father?"

"Denied even knowing him."

"When did he get the *Maria*?"

"He claimed it was just a few days before we busted him. Total bullshit, of course, but we couldn't prove otherwise, and his sternman, Dougie O'Hearn, said the same thing. So, we were stuck."

She raised her arms above her head and clasped her hands behind her neck. "Oh, *God*. I hate this. Can we walk a little?"

He looked around them, taken off guard. "Sure, I guess. Where'd you want to go?"

She pointed vaguely ahead. The street angled uphill

and around a slight curve. "Up there. I feel like I'm about to explode."

They fell in side by side, the only moving things on an empty, silent sidewalk.

"Is Beale in jail at least?"

"I don't think so," Joe admitted. "Last I heard, he was about to cut a deal with the prosecutor. They didn't have much on him."

"Typical. What do you think happened, Joe?" She absentmindedly slipped her arm through his, which sent a warm flood through his chest.

"I wish I knew," he told her. "That's why the Mainers allowed me a crack at questioning him, even though I had no legal footing. The boat, whether found recently or long ago, had clearly not been used since the storm you all thought drowned them both. Did you see it after it was returned to Steve?"

"Yes. It looked perfect, except where all the identifiers had been painted over."

"That was another thing," Joe remembered. "We took a close look at that paint. You could tell it had been applied a long time ago. I mean, we *knew* Beale was lying—no doubt about it. And the guy is a total lowlife. But even with the paint, he would've said he just found it that way."

"Anyhow," he continued as they reached the end of the block and Lyn steered them gently left, now slightly downhill, "I was left with several possibilities: Your father and brother did drown at sea, the boat did survive, and Beale did find it, just like he said."

"Right," she almost spat out.

"Or," he went on, "they survived the storm, which may not have been a factor, anyhow—since the *Maria* was found two hundred miles north of its home port—and they ran into trouble some other way."

She didn't comment for several steps. Ahead of them, the maze of tightly clustered streets showed signs of opening up. He could see the glow of the harbor and plant lights faintly brushing the sides of the buildings in the distance.

"That's very delicate," she finally said. "What're you really saying?"

He stopped to face her. "You know, they may not even be dead."

She studied his features for a moment, and then tugged at him to keep walking. "Enough."

"What?"

"Maybe they weren't who we thought they were. Or maybe they were. Who knows? But I know in my gut that if they weren't dead, one of them at least would have contacted us. They're dead. That much I'm sure about. I just don't know how or why."

Joe bowed to her clear-sightedness. "All right. Did you ever get an inkling that either one of them was into smuggling?"

"No."

"A few minutes ago, you implied that Steve might've lied when he said your father didn't know Beale when they all met at the dock that time."

She laughed bitterly. "Jesus, Joe. I don't know, but look around you. People on the coast have been making ends meet any way they can for hundreds of years. Short lobsters, booze, cigarettes, marijuana back in the seventies, pills nowadays."

She stopped and pointed ahead, since by now they could see a bit of the harbor's inky water below, shimmering in the harsh industrial lights.

"People do what they have to, Joe. It's not right or wrong all the time. The big rules are followed—most of the time—no killing, stealing, or cheating the people you know. But there's a lot of gray worked into it."

She resumed walking. "Did José and my dad wink and nod now and then? Probably. Did their friends? Sure. But were they drug runners?"

She left the question unanswered.

Except to Joe, her omission spoke volumes, along with her grim, almost angry tone of voice.

If Lyn was unhappily adapting to the idea that half her family might have run drugs, he knew she'd have to settle it for sure. She had a history of seeing things through to the end.

What was left for him to consider, therefore, was how she'd pursue that quest—and what it might cost.

And that had him worried.

CHAPTER 8

"You look like shit."

Joe looked up from his paperwork. "Thank you, Willy. Always good for a shot in the arm."

"Didn't you get any sleep?" Willy persisted, dumping a thick report on his desk and pawing through one of his drawers.

"Not much," Joe conceded. "Drove to Gloucester last night to see Lyn. Her mother's under the weather."

"Jesus," Willy commented. "True love. If any of Sam's relatives got sick, I'd be more inclined to help 'em get it over with."

"I'm sure you would. Aren't you supposed to be out interviewing people?"

Willy scowled at him. "Ah, the micromanager finally surfaces. If you have to know, I need to find out who's who before I talk to them. Of course, I could just wander up and down the street . . ."

Joe cut him off, "I got it. I got it."

Willy finally found the tattered black notebook he was after, shoved it in his pocket, and headed back toward the office door. "Roger. Don't piss off too many people out there, boss. One of 'em may shoot you. Hot weather, you know? They're not all sweethearts like me."

He was gone. Joe stared at the empty doorway. It *was* hot, and it was barely eight in the morning. Willy was right, of course, if indelicately so. Joe would have to monitor how his weariness affected his manner.

He rubbed his eyes, shut down his computer, shuffled his papers together, dumped them into a drawer, and followed Willy's example, heading out the door.

The Brattleboro Retreat was one of the town's oldest institutions, dating back to the mid-1800s. It was a mental health and addictions treatment center, a major area employer and landowner, and was housed in what outsiders commonly mistook for a picturesque small college campus, overlooking the lakelike confluence of the West and Connecticut rivers. Dr. Eberhard Dziobek, the name on the card Joe had found at Castine's apartment, had an office there, and had agreed to a meeting.

At times, business at the Retreat had been good enough to sustain a substantial operation, and the campus—from the roadside—stood as testimony to that. But closer inspection revealed the current subterfuge—the cracks and peeling paint here and there, the roofs in need of repair, the windows intact but sheltering only hollow voids. The Retreat, although perfectly healthy, with full parking lots and people wandering about, was operating on partial power, and while some of its structures were modern and alive with activity, others, immediately adjacent, stood oddly still, like awkward reminders of a heady past.

Joe proceeded through the lobby, along a couple of nondescript passageways, and up a flight of battered stairs, all familiar from years of exposure to the place's inner workings, until he abruptly found himself in a contrastingly elegant corridor—carpeted, gently lighted, accented with artwork, tasteful armchairs, and potted plants. It was an office wing, quiet and far from the hurly-burly of the lockdown ward, and presented the vague aura of an up-scale, nineteenth-century, robber-baron hotel.

He walked to the door Dr. Dziobek had described on the phone and knocked gently.

"Come in, come in."

The theatrical setting shifted once more. The fancy hotel became a scholar's den—all books and prints and faded Oriental carpets anchoring a scattering of heavy, comfortable antique furniture in need of a dusting.

Joe crossed the room to greet a man rising from be-hind a century-old partners' desk.

"Mr. Gunther?" he asked. "I am Eberhard Dziobek. Delighted to meet you."

He was bearded, white-haired, with bushy brows and a kindly smile. Sharp blue eyes overlooked a photogenic pair of gold reading glasses. Joe noticed he even wore a herring-bone tweed jacket, which was not completely ludicrous, given both the setting and the central air-conditioning.

Dziobek ushered him over to a couple of worn leather armchairs in a far corner of the room. On the table near-est one of them was a framed photograph of a pretty, smiling young girl, inscribed, "To the best Daddy in the whole world—Hannah."

Dziobek smiled as he followed Joe's glance. "My daughter. A very precocious nine-year-old. Please, have a seat. Would you like some tea?" The man's accent was faintly Germanic.

Joe thought that Hannah was perhaps not the only pre-cocious one in the family. "No. Thanks. I'm all set."

They settled opposite each other, Dziobek chuckling. "Just as well. My wife tells me my tea is so awful that I really shouldn't offer. I'm here, after all, to heal, not to poison."

Joe nodded noncommittally and smiled politely, trusting that, for the moment, he was only to receive such polite preliminaries, and not prolong them by actually responding.

He was right. After crossing his legs and sighing happily, the older man broadened his smile and commented, "So, you are after a little information about Wayne Castine. How was it that he died?"

"We're thinking he was knifed," Joe said bluntly. "The autopsy's this morning."

Dziobek nodded, his face thoughtful. "I cannot say that I am surprised."

"Oh?"

"I do not mean the weapon," he corrected himself, adding, "although even that seems right. It is a personal thing to use, no? Is that not what you have found?"

Joe agreed, "Yeah, I'd say so. Of course, he was also beaten. To call it a crime of passion is a no-brainer. But you were saying that the mere fact he was murdered doesn't surprise you."

"Correct," Dziobek said. "Mr. Castine was an almost classic psychopath, with a very strong mean streak. It seems reasonable to me that someone without Castine's elevated verbal and social skills might have resorted to a more primitive means of communicating."

Joe couldn't resist a short laugh. "By killing him?"

Dziobek smiled slightly. "Yes. It is one way of telling someone you don't like them, correct?"

"True enough," Joe conceded.

"And if violence is what you know, and language comes awkwardly for you, then a knife will stand in better than an argument."

"Castine was that good?"

"Not the word I would have used," the old man faintly chastised. "But I see your point. Yes, he was highly developed verbally, given his indifferent education. Critically, however, he was effectively manipulative, which is also a hallmark of psychopathy."

"What are the others?"

Dziobek tossed his head slightly and waved a hand. "Oh, goodness. There is a menu of them, some of which we all share. It is a slippery thing to reduce such complexity to a simple list."

"Still . . ." Joe suggested.

"They have charm without warmth," he answered, holding up a finger. "Self-delusional grandiosity—they often speak of great schemes for which they have little training; a lack of remorse and empathy; the manipulativeness I mentioned; a short, explosive temper. They are also impulsive, thin-skinned, easily bored, and abusive of others. Very unpleasant, seductive people," he concluded, shifting in his seat and tacking on, "and they love to prey on the weak."

"Was he a child abuser?" Joe asked.

Dziobek shrugged. "I do not know. It would not be a long reach for him."

Joe pursed his lips momentarily. "Why did he come to you?" he asked.

The therapist's eyes widened. "Ah, yes. He only came as part of an agreement with the prosecutor. As I'm sure you know, sometimes, when people get into trouble for anger issues, rather than being sent to court, they are encouraged to offer reparation to the injured party and seek therapeutic aid. That was the agreement here."

Joe knew of the process—a hopeful, kinder, gentler alternative than saddling people with a criminal record for minor crimes. It wasn't unheard of for someone like

Castine, with a bad but sealed juvenile record, to appear far more benign than he was.

"What was the nature of the case?" Joe inquired.

"An altercation at a restaurant across the river, in New Hampshire—name calling, a shoving match. On the face of it, not much. That's why I was startled when I met him—not at all what I was expecting. It's one of the great benefits of my occupation."

The New Hampshire reference explained why they'd missed this in their background search.

"How many times did you meet?"

"Only what was required. Four sessions—not really enough to do much. And totally useless for the likes of Mr. Castine."

"That hard to reach?"

"Psychopathy, especially in someone his age, is not like bed-wetting with a child," Dziobek explained. "The modern expression—one I rather like—is 'hardwired.' Wayne was very much that way."

"Did you read the paper this morning?" Joe asked.

Dziobek nodded. "Yes, so I wasn't wholly surprised by your call. You contacted me faster than I'd anticipated, however. My hat is off to you. He was discovered in a flat not his own?"

"Yes. We wondered about that—why he'd run the risk of being caught there. He had a key to the place, but the current owner didn't know him."

The other man smiled knowingly.

"What?"

Dziobek's eyes brightened. "Ah—well, of course, one can never be absolutely certain, but I suggest that you consider the element of thrill. It fits rather well, unless you have an alternate theory."

Joe shook his head, swearing to himself that he would never tell Willy what he'd just heard. "We're just starting to dig. I barely know about the man. The rumor on the street, though, is that he abused kids."

"I gathered that, from your earlier question."

"Why did you say that wouldn't have been a stretch for him?"

Dziobek considered the question before answering. "Childhood predeterminants coupled with this particular psychopath's being drawn to weaker victims. He wasn't a big or imposing man and his own early years were, I'm sorry to say, an all-too-familiar nightmare. It makes sense to me that he'd have been attracted to children. Males or females?"

Joe was caught off guard. "I'm not sure—both, maybe. Why?"

"Simple professional curiosity. Both would be unusual, but not unheard of, and—again—given this man's degree of intelligence, perfectly possible. He might even have seen it as a worthy challenge."

"Ouch," Joe said softly.

The old man smiled supportively. "Yes. Well, the word 'psychopath' isn't so heavily laden without good reason. These are very unpleasant people."

Joe nodded. "Good point. Speaking of people, though, who were the ones in his life?"

Dziobek chuckled. "Normally, given that the patient is deceased and the nature of his demise, I would help you in any way. But while I heard about his mother and an abusive stepfather and a number of stories from his youth I had no way of verifying, Mr. Castine told me nothing of value about the here and now. He was well-mannered and put on a great show of openness, but in fact, all he shared were details I would only consider with great caution."

Gunther smiled at the erudition of the reply. "Meaning he lied his butt off?"

This time the doctor laughed outright. "Precisely."

Joe stood up, crossed over to his host, and shook hands, saying, "Don't get up, Doctor. You've been a great help, and I really appreciate it. Could I call you if anything else comes up?"

Dziobek stayed seated and nodded genially. "Absolutely. It sounds fascinating, what you do, and I wish you all the best. A psychopath being brutally murdered, against an implied background of child abuse—I can't imagine that a little psychological consulting wouldn't be useful."

He reached into his jacket pocket and extracted a card. "I keep this for occasions exactly like this. Do not hesitate to get in touch. I would be delighted to help out."

Joe thanked him again, pocketed the card gratefully, and took his leave. While the doctor's parting comments were as much politeness as genuinely offered, Gunther was getting the feeling that he would be needing all the help he could get before this was over.

CHAPTER 9

Lyn Silva paused on the sidewalk, looking up at the sign over the door. This was Gloucester's most notorious bar, where the police contended there were as many patrons with aliases as not. The cops were certainly the ones to know, since they dropped by more often than some of the regulars, either to break up a fight, or because this was the first place to begin rounding up suspects.

Lyn knew this from having served here as a bartender for years, before leaving for Brattleboro.

It had been a crazy job in ways—sometimes dangerous, and no place for a woman if she couldn't fend off men. But it had trained her in the art of nonmartial self-preservation, and how to handle situations that, from the outside, might have seemed far too threatening to approach. It had given her confidence, self-worth, a hefty amount of tax-free money, and a sense of ease around people the rest of society simply labeled as pariahs.

Not that she'd returned now for old times' sake. She knew a smelly dump when she saw one, and this had always been a classic.

But it had its purposes, which, in fact, was what had brought her back.

She pushed the door open and walked into a thick wall of sweat, stale beer, bad perfume, and loud jukebox music. There are bars in which to socialize and be seen by one's peers, and others, grim and silent, in which to get hammered as efficiently as possible. This one fit a middle ground—you could meet your equals, equipped with tattoos and names like Spike, and you could get so drunk that, for a few hours at least, no pain in the world could reach you. But you could also get laid, buy some drugs, feed and receive information, and otherwise pretend that you weren't the total loser you suspected you were in the daylight.

In the old days, Lyn had used the actual physical bar as a barrier. She strutted her stuff, wearing revealing clothes and giving men lip, but all the while remaining resolutely in place. No matter what fracas broke out on the floor, she stayed put—a look-but-don't-touch surrogate for many a patron's roving fancies.

She wasn't dressed provocatively now. She'd known to wear painter's jeans and a light turtleneck, despite the heat, but she was still surprised by her own vulnerability merely entering the place. It reminded her of how much of a role she'd played back then, often parodying early on a self-confidence she'd only hoped might be hers.

She scanned the room, looking for any familiar face, but for one in particular, too—a man who claimed this dive as his office.

"Oh, my God," she heard behind her. "Be still my heart."

She turned to face a middle-aged man with a full black beard and a nasty scar running near one eye.

"If it isn't the best-looking barkeep on the whole East Coast."

She smiled, reached out, and patted the man's upper arm. "Hi, Benny. How've you been?"

He was carrying a mug of beer, but reached out nevertheless and gave her an awkward bear hug. She immediately began to feel more at home, if still aware of the general potential volatility.

"I thought you'd left forever," Benny told her. "Someone said you went to California, or something."

She laughed. "Hardly. Maybe they were talking attitude. I moved to Vermont. I own a bar there."

His eyes widened. "No shit? I never been to Vermont. I never been anywhere 'cept out there." He jerked his thumb in the direction of the sea.

"You ought to give it a try," she encouraged him, knowing it would never happen.

Sure enough, he ignored the comment. "And you *own* a bar? Good for you. I thought you'd want nuthin' to do with bars after this hole."

"Hey," she said with a smile, "sometimes, it's what you know that you go with."

He looked up at the dark ceiling. "Oh, Jesus. Do I know what you mean. You come back for old memories?"

"I'm looking for Harry Martin, actually," she admitted.

Benny straightened with surprise. "Harry? What would you want with an old fart like that? Stick with me, girl. I'll show you a good time."

She patted his chest with her open hand. "I bet you could, Benny, but I got business on my mind right now, and Harry's the man for that."

Benny didn't argue. Lyn had said the magic words. Of the many unclassifiable jobs that people claimed in this bar, being a "businessman," in the literal sense, was Harry Martin's. Harrison Martin, as only his birth certificate knew him, was the type of man forever found between two others hoping to do a deal. He might have introduced them, or have never met them, but somehow he would know what they were up to, and—better still—

how to end it unless he was kindly included. He never overstepped his bounds, and always made sure to be more help than a hindrance, but he was always where he needed to be at the right time.

Lyn made her farewells to Benny and plowed deeper into the crowd. Since her departure, there'd been a management change, and special event nights were now standard. Tonight, it was discount beer and limited free pizza—and, she suspected from experience, something more in the back room. The place was as packed at midweek as it used to be only on Saturday nights. The noise was deafening, the smell awful, and the number of hands on her butt and elsewhere as she navigated through too many to count. In the distance, seen only occasionally through the press, the bartender glided behind her barricade, flashing a broad, empty smile.

Lyn found Harry Martin parked in his spot of choice—a corner table beyond the pool players, his back to the wall and a bottle before him. An anxious man was sitting in the single seat beside him, his body bent at the waist like a supplicant's, a sheet of dog-eared paper near his hand on the tabletop. Harry was staring out over the crowd, not showing any sign that he knew the man was there.

Harry had chosen his post carefully. Even with the place this full, he wasn't overly hemmed in, the pool players needing room to move. He was also on the far end of the worst of it, meaning anyone had to travel to get to him. And, lastly, immediately by his side was the dim hallway leading to the restrooms and the rear exit. The drunks needing to pee—or the half-blind couples needing a little privacy—were well worth the defensive advantage such a position discreetly supplied.

After all, not all of Harry's deals went as smoothly as desired.

Lyn waited for the pool players to migrate to the far

side of the table before she emerged from the mob and walked into Harry's view.

His weather-lined face broke into a broad smile at the sight of her. "I'll be damned," he said as she drew near. "If it ain't Abílo's little girl. Have a seat. Take a load off."

He reached out and poked the man in the shoulder. "Beat it," he said without emphasis, making the latter fade away without complaint. He didn't act that way often—he could be a supplicant, too, after all—but right now, he was feeling top dog.

There was no question of hugs in this case, though. That wasn't his style, and Lyn was here for a favor.

"Hi, Harry," she said simply. "Long time."

"I heard your mom's not too good."

That was to tell her his sources were on the job—a small running up of the flag, in case it mattered. Harry liked to prepare the ground before him—it wouldn't have surprised her if he knew her current companion was a cop.

"She's doing better now."

"The bar business treating you okay in Vermont? You like being the boss?"

She shrugged. A waitress she didn't know appeared by their side. She ordered a beer no one would be paying for.

"It's okay. It's something I know. Makes it a good starting point."

Harry nodded. "You always had a head on your shoulders. Your dad was happy about that. How's Steve doin'?"

It was not a casual question. "You probably know better than I do," she said.

He took a pull on his bottle and wiped his lips with the back of a gnarled hand. "Probably."

"Is he going to stay out of trouble?" she asked him.

"That why you're here?"

"No," she admitted.

"Probably," he repeated, adding, "if he minds his manners."

She wasn't sure what to make of that, but knew he wouldn't tell her. A large part of his livelihood depended on people thinking he knew more than he did.

"I am sorry about Maria," he said without prompting.

Maria was her mother, and the comment made her wonder if he was fishing, which she hoped would be to her advantage.

"It's been a rough time," she said vaguely.

He shook his head mournfully. "That water out there. It's made a lot of widows."

Lyn purposefully didn't answer, forcing him to ask after a pause, "She's still a widow, isn't she?"

Lyn tilted her head and raised an eyebrow. "Why wouldn't she be, Harry?"

He laughed softly, his gaze wandering to a young woman in a miniskirt who'd taken up a pool cue and was lining up a shot.

"Why're you here, little girl?"

Her beer arrived. She took a swig before asking him in turn, "Why do you think?"

His eyes returned to hers. "I think it has something to do with your brother running a boat we all thought was at the bottom of the ocean."

"You picked up on that, did you?"

"What happened to Abílo and José, Lyn?"

"You interested as a friend or an old business partner?"

She took another sip to hide the tension within her. This was going to the heart of her visit here, and to questions that she'd never shared with anyone—questions that had to do with how all the Silvas had eventually turned out, including the two who would never again speak for themselves.

"Your father and me went back a long way," Harry said ambiguously.

"So do you and I," she said, smiling.

He thought about that. "Fair enough," he said. "So, maybe we know why you're here. The question is, what do you want?"

She leaned forward, watching him closely. "What was my dad up to, Harry? What was he doing?"

Harry dodged at first—a creature of habit. "The day he disappeared? Fishing, I thought. He was a lobsterman."

"And when he wasn't?"

Harry pressed his lips together momentarily before answering vaguely, "They all dabble a bit. You know that. Didn't Abílo ever put a short lobster on the table?"

"No," she said pointedly.

"Huh," he muttered.

"Short lobsters wasn't his game," she said.

"Right," he agreed.

"So, what was?"

Harry rubbed his index alongside his nose. "The man's dead. Who cares?"

Lyn kept her eyes on him. "You're looking at her."

"Why?"

"My family's in the toilet and I want to know why. I have a brother who thought he never could live up to his brother and father, and now he's not sure if they weren't worse than he ever was. My mother's like a walking dead woman because the fantasy she buried at sea has come back to bite her in the form of a perfectly preserved boat. As a kid, I worshipped my father, Harry. He was everything a man was supposed to be, and maybe because of that, no man I could find as a young woman ever measured up. But now . . ."

He reached out and grabbed her forearm, his expression hard. "Don't you go back on that. Abílo was one of the best of us."

"Not toward the end," she insisted stubbornly.

"Maybe not," he relented, "but that's not how he should be judged."

She put her hand on top of his. "Then *tell* me, Harry. I mean, for Christ's sake, the genie's out of the bottle. You're saying the truth's not as bad as what's going on in my head, but I don't know the truth. And my mom and Steve don't, either. And if you're right about Steve, what he thinks is liable to get him into really hot water, 'cause he's got no heroes left."

She shifted in her seat. "You wanted to know what happened to José and Dad. I can't answer that, but I do know the boat was found two hundred miles up the coast, on a privately owned island, hidden in a boathouse, with all its markings painted over."

"Whose island?"

"I wasn't told," she lied. "I have a friend who's a cop, and that's all he told me. Why was the boat that far away, Harry? What were they doing, almost in Canadian waters?"

He wavered, staring at the bottle before him. "If you don't know that, you're not as smart as I thought."

She let him go and sat back, her face ashen. "Drugs?"

This time, he leaned toward her, his expression intense. "*No.* No way."

One of the nearby pool players glanced at them. Harry gave him a glare, making him move away.

Harry lowered his voice. "Your father was no drug dealer."

"I didn't say he was a *dealer*," she reacted.

He waved a hand angrily. "I don't give a flying fuck, okay? He wasn't into that shit."

"So what was it, then?"

"Stuff. What do I know?"

"You *know*, Harry," she said in a forceful whisper. "He would've come to you, like I'm doing now. You're like my uncle, for crying out loud. You two were the brothers neither one of you ever had. My dad came to you and asked how he could make ends meet, right? Isn't that what happened?"

Harry merely nodded, studying the tabletop.

"But what I don't get," she continued, "is we never saw any of that. He and José kept going out, and they kept catching lobster. Where was the money going, that they needed more?"

Harry sighed and rubbed his face with both hands. "Jesus," he muttered.

"What?" she pressed him. "I need to know."

"Nobody tells nobody nuthin', you know? It's no wonder there's no trust."

She forced herself to show no reaction. Such a comment, from this of all men. She stayed silent, letting him work through his own inner process.

Eventually, he passed a hand through his thinning hair, took a long pull on his bottle, and sighed again, finally saying, "I don't really know what they were doing, just why. It had to do with smuggling, though."

Her shoulders sagged. "I knew something was wrong, for months before they disappeared. Mom did, too. I think that's why losing them hit her so hard. She must've guessed they were up to something and it got her nervous. Then, afterward . . ." Her voice trailed off.

Harry made no comment.

"You have no idea what went wrong?" she asked.

"No," he told her. "I heard they were supposed to pick up a load before the bad weather, then maybe lay low for a few hours, to ride it out. I never knew. It was like the

Bermuda Triangle or something. They just vanished. It wasn't the storm, though—I'm sure about that."

"Heard from who?" she asked.

He shook that off. "You don't need to know, but a solid guy. I go back with him, too. Somebody else got 'em. Who or why, I don't know."

"That leaves the question you didn't answer, then," she told him.

He frowned. "What?"

"What was going on? You said you knew why they started doing this."

He shook his head as if warding off a bee. "Jesus, Lyn, what is the point? Leave the dead be."

Suddenly furious with all the verbal sparring, she half rose from her seat to push her face close to his. "Fuck you, asshole. Somebody *made* them dead. You think I'm going to let that go? You must have shit for brains. I'm not my father's daughter for nothing, and if Dad were here right now, he'd take you apart for that crack."

He sat back under the assault, and for a moment she feared her outburst would cost her what little he had left.

But he smiled finally, and even reached out and touched her cheek with his hand, saying quietly, "You're right. I'm sorry. I was kidding myself. I felt bad when they disappeared, and made myself think it was better left alone. I let you all down."

She seized her opportunity. "Who is it you know? I have to start somewhere. Maybe he can help."

Harry closed down. "I asked already. He's as clueless as I am. They just disappeared—that's all he knows."

She wasn't going to give up. "Then tell me what started it all."

"It was José. Abílo was just looking out for him. He got deep into gambling and owed big time. He finally went to Abílo for help. It was bad. But your old man had his pride—he figured they could pay off the debt and keep all of you in the dark."

"But the people he owed were crooks, no?" Lyn asked incredulously.

Harry smiled. "Technically, maybe—he's the guy I've been talking about. More of a middleman businessman, really. But Abílo was going to settle the debt anyhow, so it doesn't make much difference."

She sat there for a while, absorbing a set of images she'd never before imagined, fighting her disappointment.

Looking up at him one last time, she then asked, "What's this businessman's name?"

She expected more resistance, but apparently Harry Martin had run out of steam. Without hesitation, he said, "Brandhorst. Dick Brandhorst. Lives up north. Used to be Portland, Maine. I'm not sure now. We always talk by cell phone. That's all I know."

"You think he killed them?"

He shook his head. "No reason to—they were playing ball. The guy's like a banker for the down-and-out, Lyn. He's not the one José laid the bets with—him I don't know. Dick's the moneyman; call him the collection agent, but not a leg-breaker like in the movies."

Lyn nodded and stood up, shaken and drained. "Thanks, Harry."

He caught hold of her hand, in an oddly gentle gesture, given the setting. "Lyn," he said to her earnestly, and in contrast to the placating words he'd just uttered. "Please be careful. You're all your family's got now. Think of the living."

She squeezed his hand back and then let it drop. "I am," she said, and headed toward the back door.

CHAPTER 10

Joe paused at the bottom of the stairs, adjusting to the darkness. He knew where the light switch was—the municipal building's basement was as well known to him as his own, housing as it did the police department's cells, booking room, old case files, lockers, and sundry other areas. But it was cool down here, resonant only with the dull mechanical rumblings of most nineteenth-century hulks, and he wanted to savor the soothing silence. He was reaching the limit of how many hours he could stay awake and still be effective, and was therefore finding every cold drink, trip to the men's room, or moment of respite like this to be an oasis amid the exhaustion.

But for the time being, they couldn't be overly indulged. He hit the lights and walked down the ancient, gloomy corridor to a door with a combination lock. This he typed in quickly from long memory, waited for the audible click, and pushed the door open.

Ron Klesczewski turned from the table he was overseeing, deep in thought, and greeted his old boss.

"Hey, Joe. You look like you could use some sleep."

Joe half smiled. "I might grab a little just to kill off all the comments."

Ron laughed. "Oh, oh. Sorry."

Joe flapped his hand dismissively. "No—you look like death warmed over, you should expect it. I can't fake it like I used to. After this, I'll lie down for a while."

He gestured toward the table—actually one of three that had been shoved together to carry all the items seized from Castine's apartment. "You find anything?"

"We're getting a feel for his habits," Ron told him. "His garbage hadn't been tossed yet, so we got a mother lode there. That job," he admitted with a laugh, "I assigned to somebody else."

He crossed over to a neat display of soiled and wrinkled receipts. "We got these to add to the ones you found," he explained. "And I have people talking to merchants all over town, flashing his picture and asking if he's been seen with a kid—or anyone of interest, for that matter. Maybe we'll get lucky. It's a small town, especially the circles he traveled, and nobody likes what he was doing."

"Plus, he's dead," Joe added.

"Never hurts," Ron agreed. "Nobody's gonna come knocking at night."

"What about the computer?" Joe asked.

"Sheila's got that," Ron said simply. Sheila Murphy, one of his detectives, had recently gone to school to get certified in high-tech forensic autopsies, as Joe thought of them. "Don't know what she's found yet."

Joe was staring off into space, seemingly miles away.

"You okay?" Ron asked him quietly.

Joe shifted his gaze. "Yeah. Sorry. Daydreaming a little."

"Troubles?"

"Could be," Joe conceded. Ron was an old friend, they didn't work on the same squad anymore, and certainly Ron had bared his soul to Joe a time or two in the past.

"Lyn really took it to heart when I discovered her father's boat in Maine."

"I heard about that," Ron said. "She's not blaming you, is she?"

"Not rationally," Joe agreed, "but it's not rational territory. The family disintegrated when the old man disappeared. It was an old-fashioned patriarchy."

"I don't get it, though," Ron argued. "Why's finding the boat a big deal? I mean, not to be indelicate, but he and the son are still dead, right?"

"It implies they didn't die in a storm," Joe explained. "And in that culture, where smuggling is like a historical prerogative, the next reasonable explanation ain't too cheery."

Ron grunted softly. "I see what you mean. You get the local authorities on it?"

"On what?" Joe countered. "They know about it, but there's nothing to work with."

He paused and surveyed the belongings scattered across Ron's three tabletops. "Anyhow, that's not what we're here for. What else have you got?"

Sam stood in the shadows, her body loose and relaxed. Over the years, initially coached by Willy—a past master at this—she'd learned to stay on surveillance, immobile and nearly invisible, for hours on end, denying any desires for food or drink, or even the need to pee. She knew she was probably slowly ruining her kidneys in the process, but her prowess had gained her a reputation she perversely enjoyed.

She was standing outside Castine's now emptied apartment, unknowingly where Gary Nelson had stood guard when Joe had told him to interview the neighbors.

Nelson had met two of the three, and gotten the story

of Castine being seen with a young girl, but that's where it had ended.

Sam thought she might improve on that. For one thing, she'd run the occupants of all three apartments through the Spillman data bank—shared by ninety percent of all the law enforcement agencies in the state—and had come up with some interesting tidbits on the one missing tenant.

Andrea Halnon, nicknamed Andie, had not chosen the straight and narrow. A thief, a drug mule, a check forger, she had several pages of references attesting to her criminal acumen—from consorting with known felons, to supplying kids with cigarettes, to being the driver at an armed robbery—the list was a veritable primer on how to violate the law. And she was only thirty-three years old.

The point of interest to Sam, however, wasn't her easy way with rules, but her negotiating skills after being caught. Andrea Halnon had become a master in judicial deal making. In exchange for selling everything and everyone down the river, she'd either bartered her way straight back onto the street, or at worst spent a few months in one of the state's less-than-lethal lockups.

To Sam's mind, that made her someone who was not only willing to deal, but who made sure she always had something to trade, just in case.

Halnon also had a weak spot. She was a two-time loser in cases where it counted, and she'd been officially warned that the habitual offender statute was dangling right over her head. Even for able, fast-footed runners, there was an end to all roads eventually.

Sam knew something else: that all her research had only revealed the crimes for which this woman had been caught. That meant, especially given her record, that Halnon had done much more than the law knew, and was most likely still hard at work—if cautiously. Finally, she was on the last legs of a probationary stretch. If she messed up now, even slightly, she'd be back in jail.

Sam heard noises in the distant stairwell—quiet talking, some muted laughter—before two figures appeared at the far end of the hall. They paused while the shorter of them toggled the light switch to the bulb hanging halfway down the corridor, and which Sam had unscrewed earlier.

"That dumb fuck," she heard a woman exclaim. "The light's out again. Jesus. What a rat hole."

The taller shadow stayed quiet.

They proceeded slowly, the woman leading, still talking. "Every week, something craps out in this goddamn building."

"You should move," the male suggested quietly.

Halnon laughed. "Yeah. Fuckin' A. I should have a million bucks, too."

She reached the apartment door and pulled a key from her jeans, fumbling to fit the lock. When she pushed open the door at last, the light inside shot into the hallway, catching them like a theatrical spot. Sam immediately recognized Halnon's companion as Tanner Fitzhugh, recently released from jail on a federal weapons charge, and someone that Halnon's probation prohibited her from contacting.

It wasn't quite what Sam was expecting. She'd hoped to put the squeeze on this woman after a late night out, while she was possibly drunk, tired, doped up, or all three. Sam hadn't considered a possible companion.

By protocol, she had several choices: give up until the odds improved; retreat and call for backup, preferably from Parole and Probation, since they had the real clout in this game; or simply forge ahead and be the cowboy that her boss kept stressing she should never be.

Without hesitation, she stepped forward, gun drawn, and ordered, "*Police*. Get down on your knees, cross your ankles, and lock your hands behind your necks. *Now*."

Luckily, her rashness didn't cost her this time, as it had in the past. Both people simply followed orders and dropped to their knees, only Halnon muttering the obligatory, "Fuck me."

"Tanner Fitzhugh," Sam addressed the man, approaching slowly.

"Yeah," was the tired response. "I know you?"

"Keep looking straight ahead," she ordered. She crouched behind him and quickly patted him down, looking for weapons and finding none.

"I'm the cop who actually reads all the faxes about recently released federal inmates, and the fact that they're not to consort with known criminal elements. That phrase ring a bell?"

"Yeah," he admitted with a sigh.

"Well," Sam informed him. "She's what they were talking about."

Halnon varied her delivery only slightly. "Fuck you."

Sam grabbed Fitzhugh's interlinked fingers from behind and yanked him to his feet. He let out a short cry of pain.

"You come here to get laid?" she asked. "Dope? Do some planning for the next bank heist?"

"I don't have to talk to you," he said, but without great effort.

"That make you feel better?" Sam asked him, picking up on his weariness. "Good. You're wrong, by the way. I could have you mailed right back to Rahway. You feel like testing me?"

"No."

She let go of his fingers. "Drop your arms and walk down the hallway. Ten feet."

He did so, and stood still, peering into the darkness ahead.

"Okay, Fitzhugh," Sam told him. "Now that we've met,

you can take a hike. But don't forget the favor. I'll come knocking someday."

Fitzhugh half turned on his heel and glanced back at her, the surprise clear in his voice. "For real?"

Sam, still watching Halnon, waved at him. "Bye-bye. Don't forget."

He didn't answer as he quietly retreated, but she saw the half nod of his head in the gloom.

She waited until the sound of his shoes had stopped resonating on the stairs.

"Can I get up?" Halnon complained from her position.

"Not yet."

Sam moved over to her and repeated the pat-down she'd conducted on Fitzhugh. Finding a soft, slightly crunchy bulge in the woman's back pocket, she ordered, "Straighten up."

Halnon raised herself slightly on her knees, alleviating the pressure against the butt of her pants, and allowing Sam to reach in and extract a bag of weed from the pocket. Halnon half twisted around at the gesture and said angrily, "You can't do that. It's not a weapon."

"Wrong, legal-eagle—read Terry versus Ohio. Plus, you're still on probation, and I've already got you on consorting. Do you really want to dick around like this?"

Halnon resorted to what she knew. "Fuck."

Sam stepped away and holstered her gun. "Okay. Get up."

Halnon slowly rose, dusting off her knees. She was dressed in jeans that should have cut off her circulation, accessorized by a tank top so tight and so brief, Sam wondered why she'd bothered. On the other hand, it was pretty clear what had lured Fitzhugh up here.

Sam pointed to the open door. "Go. Straight to the couch and sit."

Again, Halnon followed orders, but now aware that

something more was afoot than a simple opportunity arrest. She settled in comfortably, crossed her legs, and asked, "Okay if I smoke?"

Sam was standing to one side of the now closed door, her back against the jamb, so she could see the entire room. "You got 'em?"

Halnon gestured to the table beside the couch. "Right there."

"Okay."

While her hostess extracted her cigarette, Sam asked her, "You hear about your neighbor?"

"Wayne?" Halnon reacted instantly, flicking her lighter. "I heard he got knifed. That what you mean?"

"You know something else?"

She drew in a lungful of smoke and slowly let it out in a sigh, wreathing her head in a temporary cloud. "Jesus," she said simultaneously. "You rousted me for Wayne? Who cares?"

"Yeah," Sam conceded. "We're getting that a lot. Tell me about him anyway."

Halnon took a stab at taking control. "Why should I? I'm no snitch."

Sam burst out laughing, making the other woman smolder. "*What?* Andie, for Chrissake. You just practicing, or do you actually think I'll buy that?"

Her lips pursed, Halnon dropped the unfinished cigarette to the floor, stamped it with her shoe, and crossed her legs. "Fine. What do you want me to tell you?"

"Interesting wording. The truth, Andie. Just the truth. I take it you knew him."

"Kinda. Sure."

"You were friends?"

This time Halnon laughed, albeit bitterly. "I was a little old for him."

"So, he was exclusive that way? Only liked kids?"

"Far as I know."

"Both sexes? Boys and girls?"

"Girls."

"You ever witness that?"

Halnon flared up. "What do you think I am? I wouldn't watch that shit."

"Then how do you know what he was doing?"

Her expression was wiltingly condescending. "How did you know what Tanner and I had in mind when you busted us?"

"You saw Castine bring kids to his apartment?"

"That's what I'm saying."

Sam left her position by the wall and crossed to the couch, sitting on its edge to imply an intimacy she didn't feel. "Andie," she said feelingly. "I'm sorry I came on so strong. I really hate this stuff. It gets to me—with the kids. But you know how it can be, being a girl and having a scummy guy like that come after you."

Halnon reacted immediately, as if warding off a bad memory. "I wouldn't know. Even as a kid, I woulda cut the balls off anyone trying that."

Sam nodded thoughtfully. "I know, I know. That's not what I'm saying. I just want to nail this down. Could be whoever killed him was a competitor—another snapper. May not be just good news, like you said."

Andie's eyes widened. "For real? Holy shit."

"I'm not saying it's a fact," Sam said quickly. "Just that it's possible."

"Sure, sure." Halnon nodded her head, having clearly not heard the built-in denial.

"So," Sam continued, "I'd really appreciate anything you can give me—what you heard; what you saw. There must've been something."

"Oh," Andie now freely volunteered. "He was a total pig. I hated having him next door. I'm glad he's dead, 'cause I was wondering how to do it myself. You know?"

Sam nodded sympathetically. "Did you tell someone about it?"

"I didn't need to. People knew about Wayne."

The continual vagueness was getting to Sam. "Like who, Andie?"

"I'm not gonna rat out my friends. What if one of them did do it?"

Sam scratched her forehead, considering her options.

Out of the blue, Halnon then volunteered, "I knew one of the girls, though. Becky Kerr. I saw her running out of here once, crying. I knew in my gut what had happened."

Sam sat forward. "You saw her running from Castine's apartment?"

"Down the stairs when I was coming up. Same thing."

"She could've been visiting one of your other neighbors?"

"Those bitches?" Halnon asked incredulously. "I don't think so. It was Wayne. I'm telling you."

Maybe, thought Sam. "Any others?"

"Kids?"

"Yeah."

But Andrea Halnon shook her head, undermining the accusation she'd previously made against Castine.

Still, this was something to pursue. A thread.

"How do I find Becky?" Sam asked.

"Beats me. Ask her mom—Karen Putnam."

Sam rose and crossed back to the door. "I think I will." She then pointed a finger at Halnon and added, "And remember: You owe me one."

Halnon's familiar expression of contempt resettled in place. "Yeah, whatever."

CHAPTER 11

Willy Kunkle checked the list of ex-tenants that Liz Babbitt's landlord had given him, and then consulted his
watch. He wasn't bored, or longing to get home. He'd
been known to work for days on a whim, and knew Sam
was chasing leads anyhow, and that home therefore meant
an empty apartment. The thought made him smile ruefully. There'd been a time when the mere notion of having
a woman living with him was a fantasy, much less something to count on.

He'd been married once, long ago, and had completely
messed it up. An ex-New Yorker from a troubled family,
briefly an NYPD cop, also a former combat sniper, he'd
amassed enough psychological baggage to propel most
people straight to suicide. But he'd held off, perhaps out
of perverseness, as he claimed, or from a stubborn need
to simply defy the odds. Whatever the motivation, he was
still around, and looked like he might be enjoying the
best time of his life.

Besides, right now, he was doing what he loved most:
hunting, sitting in his car in the village of Bellows Falls,
by the curb, waiting for the next name on his list to appear.

This happened three minutes later. An older car with a

pizza sign magnetized to its roof went whipping by on its mission with a skinny, worn-out man at the wheel.

Kunkle pulled in behind him with surprising dexterity, given his one-handedness, passed him, and then cut him off, forcing him to either stop or become a lawn ornament.

He swung out of his unmarked vehicle, marched back to the delivery car, and thrust his face through the driver's open window, smiling widely at the terrified, sweat-covered face of one Terry Stein.

"Hi, Terry," he said. "How's tricks?"

The other man gaped at him. "Kunkle? You almost killed me. What the hell was that?"

"I want to talk. Shove over."

"What?" Stein stared from Willy to the pizza box beside him. "I have a delivery."

Willy opened the door. "Hold it in your lap. Move over."

"You can't do this. I'll lose my job if I'm late."

Willy shoved his face so close, it was barely an inch from Stein's, making the latter cringe. "*MOVE*," he shouted, forcing the man to obey.

Scrambling awkwardly, Stein tried to maneuver the large, hot box, as well as slide his butt over the console of the small car, muttering, "I didn't do nuthin'. This is wrong."

Willy slid behind the wheel and slammed the flimsy door, barely noticing the stink and heat of the car's interior. Terry had been known to use the vehicle as much to live in as for transportation, and was no advertisement for personal hygiene. In a phrase, he was one of "Willy's people," as Joe and many others referred to them— overlooked members of the occasionally working poor, given to life at the edges and to whatever opportunities arose, many of them illegal.

"You used to live on Manor Court," Willy stated.

Terry stared at him. "Maybe," he said tentatively, adding, "that was a while ago."

"What did you do with the key?"

The other man was trying to keep the pizza off his lap and not burn his hands. His employer was too cheap to buy insulated delivery bags. "I kept it on me."

Willy glanced out the window, sucked on his upper lip a moment, rubbed the side of his nose with his index, and tried again, his voice tightly under control.

"Not then, you moron. What did you do with it afterward?"

"After I left? Gave it to the next guy."

Willy reached out suddenly, grabbed the box with his large hand, and jammed it between the windshield and the dashboard, crumpling it in two and releasing an odorous cloud. He quelled Stein's predictable outburst with, "*Focus*, Terry. Listen to what I'm saying here."

It was a bluff, of course. Willy had no idea if it had been Terry who'd circulated an extra copy of Liz Babbitt's apartment key. He didn't even know if a duplication had occurred. That had just been a guess, if an educated one. But after having spent some time researching the theory—and interviewing others in the same manner—Willy had become comfortable thinking Terry Stein might supply him with what he needed to know.

He grabbed Terry's shirtfront and yanked him around to where the back of his head almost jammed against the dashboard.

"Terry," he said quietly, "who did you give the key to?"

It worked. Stein blinked up at him a couple of times, swallowed hard, and said reluctantly, "Some guy. He paid me for a copy—two months' rent."

"Why?"

"I don't know. He just said it wouldn't matter till I was

out of the apartment. I didn't believe him, course, so I put an extra padlock on for the rest of my time there."

"And?" Willy released his grip.

Terry straightened and smoothed the front of his T-shirt. "And nuthin', man. I never saw him again, nobody ever fucked with my stuff, and I got the money. It was a good deal."

"You ever read the papers?" Willy asked him.

"Sometimes."

"That murder in Bratt?"

Terry's mouth opened slightly. "Yeah?" he said hesitantly.

"Your old apartment," Willy stated.

Terry was already shaking his head. "I had nuthin' to do with that. Nuthin'."

"You read who the dead man was?"

"No."

"Who did you give the key to?"

The pizza man shrugged. "I didn't know him. Funny last name."

"Castine?" Willy asked.

"Maybe."

Willy pulled a cleaned-up postmortem portrait from his pocket and showed it to Stein in the streetlight.

"That him?"

Terry nodded, grimacing. "Jesus—yup."

"How'd you meet?"

The man lifted a shoulder. "You know—around town."

Willy poked him hard in the ribs, making him gasp. "And you sell him your front door key 'cause, what the hell, you want everything you own ripped off."

Stein licked his lips.

Willy leaned into him, making him cringe. "You are fucking with me," he said slowly and carefully. "I don't like that."

Terry caved. "So I knew him."

"How?"

"I sold him some dope; we shared a few drinks. You know, we did stuff, now and then."

Vague as that sounded, Willy knew it to represent an entire lifestyle of random, day-to-day interactions for a good many people. The Terry Steins of this world often functioned with the accuracy of bumper cars, never knowing where they were headed or who they might meet at any moment—including a one-armed cop during a pizza delivery.

"So, why did he want the key?" Willy asked him. "Even you would've asked that."

"He said he wanted to get laid."

"In your apartment, when you were at work or wherever," Willy suggested.

"Yeah."

"Who with?" Willy asked.

Terry made a face. "I don't know. Some broad."

Willy took hold of his hot, sweaty hand and bent one of his fingers back, making Terry flop around, trying to ease the pain.

"Oh, fuck. That hurts, man. Shit. Stop. You can't do that. It isn't legal."

"*LEGAL?*" Willy yelled in his ear. "You handed over an apartment key to a man who then got murdered there. You have any idea how deep the shit is around you?"

"I didn't know," Terry howled.

"Tell me what you do know. *NOW.*" Willy let go of him.

Stein sat piteously holding his hand, rubbing his finger. "You coulda broke it."

"I *will* break it, if you don't talk. Who was Castine seeing?"

"A married broad," Terry admitted. "Small place, lots of kids. They had to be quiet about it."

"You're not gonna make me ask, are you?"

Terry sighed. "Karen Putnam. Her hubby was in the can then. I don't know about now. Wayne and her had a thing."

"Where does she live?"

"West Bratt Mobile Park," Terry said without hesitation.

Willy smiled. "Suddenly, you're the goddamn Answer Man."

Terry merely nodded, still pouting.

"Then answer me this," Willy pursued. "Why your apartment and not his own?"

"He said she wouldn't go there—too much of a dump."

"They couldn't just rent a room?"

Terry lifted both skinny shoulders. "I don't know—maybe this turned him on."

Willy thought a moment. "Tell me more about Wayne."

Terry was sullen. "What about him?"

"He like anything besides married women?"

Terry stopped staring at his finger and looked at Willy. "What's that mean?"

"Boys? Girls? What else?"

Stein wrinkled his nose. "That's gross, man. I don't know nuthin' about that."

"You ever see him with Putnam?"

"I walked in on 'em once, by mistake."

Willy laughed. "You little pervert. This had to be after you stopped living there, unless you just lied to me about the padlock."

Terry's face reddened.

"How long did you wait around in the bushes, waiting to quote-unquote walk in on them?"

Terry laughed guiltily. "About an hour," he conceded.

He then stared at Willy intently. "But I didn't know nuthin' about anything else, and I wouldn't've helped him with that."

"Maybe," Willy told him. "Maybe not."

He reached for the door handle and swung his legs out, still speaking. "I know something, though. I know that you will not be leaving your place or your job or going anywhere on vacation without letting me know first, right?"

Terry nodded emphatically. "Right."

Willy slammed the door and poked his head in through the open window. "And I know you'll be calling me if you got any more to tell me about this."

"Right." Terry wiped his damp face with his open hand and caught sight of the crushed pizza box.

He groaned. "I am so fucked. I'm probably fired already."

Willy reached into his pocket, threw a twenty-dollar bill onto the driver's seat, and said with a smile, "Keep the change."

Terry's eyes were wide. "What about the customer? He'll be pissed."

"I am the customer, stupid," Willy explained.

CHAPTER 12

Lyn stood aside from the other pedestrians and consulted the map in her hands, trying to orient herself. She'd caught a glimpse of the Thomas Hill Standpipe—Bangor's picturesque, almost two-million-gallon municipal water tank, overlooking most of downtown from high on a hill—and had twisted the map accordingly, finally deciphering Hammond from Main from Central Streets. Entering the city by car earlier had resulted in total confusion, what with a flurry of one-way streets and up to ten bridges spanning both the Kenduskeag and the Penobscot waterways—a third of which she'd seen up close—and she was hoping for better luck on foot.

It was a good plan. Fifteen minutes later, she entered an older building—three-storied, brick-clad, and reminiscent of some of Brattleboro's bastions—aside from the refreshing, wall-to-wall air-conditioning—and paused in the lobby to read a glassed-in display case listing all of the offices overhead. She found what she'd been hunting since her conversation with Harry Martin, and hit the Up button of the old-fashioned elevator, marveling at how easy it had been to locate Richard Brandhorst—and wondering if that meant she'd merely found the wrong man.

Her doubts grew when she stepped onto the mosaic-tiled third floor and found herself staring into an eight-foot-square antique mirror facing the elevator.

She hesitated, looking around. There was a choice of offices, up and down the hall, each carefully hand-labeled in black paint on its glass door entrance. She felt like she'd stepped onto a 1930s movie set.

One of the doors advertised "The Brandhorst Group."

Lyn stuck her map into her purse, squared her shoulders, and turned the brass knob.

She found herself in a reception room with several comfortable chairs, a coffee table with some neatly arranged business magazines, and a young woman typing on a computer behind a desk. There was a blank wooden door directly behind her.

"May I help you?" she asked.

Lyn smiled brightly. "Yes. I'd like to see Mr. Brandhorst."

Frowning, the woman checked a book lying open beside the computer. "Do you have an appointment?"

"No. I'm sorry," Lyn countered cheerily. "I'm in town sort of by accident, and I was told by a mutual friend that if I didn't see Dick when I was here, I'd better have a good excuse." She laughed and leaned forward confidentially. "I guess he comes highly recommended."

The receptionist showed no reaction aside from a thin smile. "And your friend's name?"

Lyn pulled out what she hoped would be her trump card—to Brandhorst if not this woman. "Harry Martin, from Gloucester."

Her hostess rose and crossed to the unlabeled door. "And yours?"

"Lyn Silva—sister of José Silva."

She hesitated. Lyn was unsure if the names meant something to her, or if she was merely getting them both straight in her head.

"I'll be right back," was all she said, suggesting, "Why don't you have a seat?"

Lyn didn't bother. This would work or it wouldn't. She stayed standing in the middle of the room, trying not to anticipate what might come next.

The door opened a minute later and the young woman reappeared, carefully closing it behind her.

"Mr. Brandhorst will see you in just a few minutes, Ms. Silva. He's wrapping something up right now, but it won't be long. Would you like some coffee in the meantime?"

Lyn turned her down, and the woman went back to her typing. There followed several minutes of silence, punctuated only by the staccato of the plastic keyboard, during which Lyn imagined what Brandhorst was really doing beyond that door.

The buzzer by the receptionist's hand startled them both. The woman rose once more, without lifting the phone, and posed by the door, issuing the inevitable, "Mr. Brandhorst will see you now."

Lyn smiled at all this Alice-in-Wonderland banality surrounding her real reason for being here, and stepped uncertainly but boldly across the threshold.

Through her bartender training, among other places, Lyn had become a practiced observer of human nature. Pragmatically, it helped identify when someone was either about to fall over or get in a fight; more broadly, she used it to judge people's characters when time was short.

Dick Brandhorst's body language told her she had some hard work ahead. Though standing, he stayed behind his desk as she entered, gestured reservedly to a guest chair with two fingers of one hand, and barely managed a smile as he greeted her.

"Have a seat."

Had he been a dentist, she would have left; instead, she immediately knew she'd found the right man. She sat.

He did not. "What can I do for you?" he asked without preamble.

Not thinking, she came out with it directly, hoping a business angle might allow them more room to talk freely.

"I was wondering how much money my brother still owed you before he died," she said.

Brandhorst didn't respond. He stayed where he was, as if transfixed. She had to imagine that he was considering her motives—was she a cop? A crazed family member about to pull a gun? An even more crazed family member offering to pay off the remaining debt? The fine print under the company name on the front door had advertised "Financial Planning, Investment Advice, and Portfolio Management," which had seemed at once awkward and redundant, as when someone talks to excess in order to cover something up.

"Your brother being"—he paused for effect, swelling her suspicion—"José Silva, according to my secretary."

Lyn smiled thinly. "Look, I know this is a little weird—my marching in here and laying this out. But I wanted to be totally straight from the start. I'll tell you anything you want to know about me, or my family, or anything else, for that matter. I'm just trying to find out what really happened. I am not here to jam you up or get you in trouble."

At last, he reached back, found the chair behind him, and sat down, carefully crossing his legs. His eyes remained as watchful as before—a snake's on a mongoose, perhaps, or worse.

"Ms. Silva," he began. "What makes you think I know anything about this?"

She nodded, having expected the posture. This was going to be a cross between chess and a negotiation, with Brandhorst hoping to extract more than he gave, while pretending to know nothing at all.

Except that she wasn't going to play it that way.

"Because I know that you have a lot of irons in the fire and that some of them aren't legal. But that's what I'm saying: I don't care. My brother was a gambler. That's his fault. And collecting money from people like him is a service you provide. As far as I know, that contract was being honored, wasn't it?"

"Go on."

"So, the rest of the family didn't know this was going on. We just thought they were a couple of lobstermen doing what they do. Then a storm hit, they disappeared, and we moved on, thinking they'd been lost at sea. But they weren't, were they?"

He merely frowned and shook his head vaguely.

"The boat was found near the Canadian border, just a few weeks ago," she resumed, unsure of her headway. "Stored in a boathouse, all identifiers painted over."

"Does sound like a mystery," Brandhorst said blandly, but the legs became uncrossed and the pen he'd picked up idly froze in his hand.

"Where's the boat now?" he asked.

"That doesn't matter," Lyn told him, struck by the question. "The mystery is whether they were killed or not. I'll tell you something else you already know: In order to pay you, they were smuggling goods into the U.S. from Canada. That's a Homeland Security problem, meaning federal agents and U.S. attorneys and closed inquests and everything else. All that shit can land on you if you want it to, since we already know you're a link in this chain, but from my position, that's entirely your choice. I'm not here for that."

He scowled. "Hold it. Are you threatening me? I thought you wanted help."

"I do," she insisted. "But I want you to know I'm serious."

He kept on with the outrage. "That's a funny way of showing it. Help me out or I'll call the cops—especially when I have no clue what you're talking about."

She decided to play by his rules. She rose and crossed to the door. "Look," she told him. "You already screwed up. You agreed to talk with me. Not smart if the names I gave your secretary meant nothing. Cops don't need proof to start with; they just need it at the end. Till then, they run around interviewing people, staking out offices and homes, and getting court orders to dig everywhere." She pointed to a row of beige file cabinets lining the wall. "I can get that ball rolling, if you want. Even if it doesn't pan out, your clients might decide you've got a reputation they don't need."

She paused by the door, while he stared at her meditatively.

"Tough little bitch," he finally said. "You sure they didn't commit suicide just to get away from you?"

She placed her hand on the knob. "That the best you can come up with?"

He flapped a hand in the air, as if shooing away a fly. "Sit down, for crying out loud. Let's see what we can figure out."

She accepted his offer, genuinely curious.

He laced his hands behind his neck. "All right. Despite your being obnoxious and wrong—about everything—I can see you've had a rough time, and I'd like to show you I'm not the asshole you think."

"Meaning you know something?"

"Meaning I know people who know people. I deal in finances. That's a who-you-know kind of business. If I want to get in on a deal at the bottom, I've got to know what's going on in the street."

A comment welled up in her throat, but she kept it quiet so he could keep laying out a mythology he probably believed was being captured on a tape recorder.

"Okay," she said instead.

Brandhorst pulled a pad toward him from the middle of the desk. "Why don't you give me a few details? How to spell your dad's and brother's names, the name of the boat, where it's moored now, a few dates—stuff like that. I'll make some inquiries and get back to you."

She covered her contempt with a counteroffer, smiling as she spoke. "How 'bout this, instead? I'm at a local motel—what time should I come back tomorrow?"

His hand froze around the pen again. "That's not much time. I might not have anything for you."

"Then I'll come back the day after that."

He frowned, glanced out the window overlooking the street, as if composing himself, and then suggested, "Let's get to it, then."

CHAPTER 13

Sam slowed down at the entrance of the West Bratt Mobile Park, a name conjured up, she imagined, by a developer with a loathing for polysyllables and a marginal sense of subtlety. It was a middling place on the economic scale, neither high-class—with picket fences, concrete slabs, a central clubhouse, and aboveground pools—nor subsistence level. The roads were dirt but free of roots and car-sized potholes, and some effort had been made to preserve a few trees, instead of either clear-cutting them or wedging the homes amid a tangle of half-dead, mature evergreens destined to fall over and crush the nearest roof.

For that matter, it wasn't far from what Sam herself had called home as a child.

She glanced down at the printout she had cradled in her lap and drove down the road, killing the air conditioner and rolling down all the windows. She wanted to feel and hear what this neighborhood experienced daily, if only in passing.

It was incredibly hot, and very quiet, the temperature having either driven everyone indoors or reduced their activities to merely breathing, like iguanas on a rock. In fact, she did see a few people, sitting in the shade, moving as little as possible.

Sam reached the address and slowly rolled to a stop, the back of her shirt already sticking to the car seat.

She opened the door, got out, and looked around. The heat almost buzzed inside her head—echoing the sound of distant grasshoppers and the gentle hum of traffic.

"My mom's not here."

She tried locating the source of the boy's voice, but saw nothing moving.

"How do you know I'm looking for her?" she asked the surrounding air.

"You're a cop, right?"

"Your mom get a lot of visits from us?"

"Wouldn't you know that?"

Sam smiled. "Yeah, we probably would."

"So, you either know or you didn't check, which makes you pretty sloppy."

That made her laugh. "Ouch. Are you the family member who gets all the high grades?"

"I hate school."

"Maybe you're too smart for it."

There was no answer. For a moment, she wondered if that would be an end to it, and that she'd be left wondering if the conversation had ever taken place.

But the suspense was broken by a single word, "Here," and the tiniest movement of what looked to be a child's finger, wiggling from between the crisscrossed slats skirting the foundation of the trailer.

Sam crouched low by the latticework. "That your clubhouse?" she asked.

"I don't call it that," the voice answered. She could make out the faintest of shadows in the gloom.

"Right," Sam agreed. "Kind of dorky."

"Yeah. What's your name?"

"Sam."

"Really?"

"Yeah. It's short for Samantha, but nobody calls me that."

"Just Sam?"

"And Sammie, sometimes. I don't mind that. What's yours?"

"Richard. Nobody calls me that, though."

"Why not?"

"They like Ricky, or Richie. I hate those."

"Kid stuff," Sam agreed. "Okay if I call you Richard?"

She could hear the pleasure in his voice. "Yeah."

"What's your last name?"

"Vial."

She passed her sleeve across her forehead. She was squatting in the full sun and it was starting to bear down on her.

"You wanna be where it's cooler?" Richard asked.

"I wouldn't mind it. I'm cooking out here. Is anyone home?"

"Just me."

Suddenly, a section of the latticework popped away from its surroundings, revealing a narrow entrance. "Come in. You'll like it."

She hesitated. She only had his word for it that he was alone, didn't know when that might end, and also had to assume that the lair he was offering came with a decades-long accumulation of dirt, pet shit, and garbage—exactly what he would never notice, but which would force her to maybe throw out her clothes afterward.

But she liked him, and liked having even an underage ally on-site. Given what little she already knew of the address and its residents, this was not likely to be a onetime visit.

She pulled open the slat and slipped in beside the boy,

closing the latticework behind her. To her double surprise, she found herself on an old, fairly clean rug, and ventilated by a nearby oscillating fan.

She laughed gently, looking around. There were toys, books, bedding, and assorted childish accoutrements. "These are quite the digs," she commented.

He smiled in the gloom. "Yeah. I sleep down here sometimes."

"I bet," she said admiringly. "Lot of people know about this?"

"Not too many," he admitted.

She stuck her hand out for a shake. "Well, I'm privileged to be one of a small group, then."

He took her hand awkwardly, and only for a second. His hand was tiny, cool, and as muscular as a piece of liver.

"You been a cop for long?" he asked.

She studied him closely, now that she was out of the glare and could actually see him. He was thin, with a bladelike face and worried, watchful eyes.

"Yeah—years."

"You local or state?"

"Neither, really," she told him. "VBI."

She was about to explain, as was her habit, but his eyes widened. "No shit? The Bureau? That's really cool. I read about you guys. You do all the big cases."

She smiled and nodded. Leave it to a kid to nail it when half the adult population still had no clue. "Yup."

"That's gotta be neat."

She couldn't argue. "It's interesting. I get a charge out of it."

"I bet. You done murders and everything, right?"

"Right." She figured him for being about ten, precociously poised between childhood's receptive innocence and the vast expanse of the storm-tossed teens—at least according to her own experience.

He nodded thoughtfully. "I think I would like that."

She grabbed her opportunity. "What would you like the most?"

"To put things right," he said without hesitation.

She was struck by this choice from among so many. "There's a lot of that to do," she commented.

"I know."

She lay on her stomach beside him and took in the world beyond the latticework—the cars, the dusty, dazzling road, the other silent trailer homes. A couple of dragonflies were darting over the weeds near the bumper of her car.

"This is a really nice spot."

He rested beside her, his chin cupped on his fist. "Yup."

"Guess it's not always this quiet."

"Nope."

"What happens?"

He thought a moment. "Cars and fights, and people drinking."

"Bet that makes this hiding place pretty safe."

He glanced up at her and smiled. "Yeah. Most of the time."

She rolled her eyes to look overhead. "You live with a lot of people?"

He frowned slightly. "Don't you know?"

She laughed. "People think we know more than we do. We have records about some of them—mostly when they've broken the rules—but the computer's not great about keeping addresses up-to-date. The rest of them—like you? We have no clue. I didn't know you even existed, Richard."

That clearly struck him as interesting. He went back to gazing at the street. "Huh."

She didn't interrupt. She thought he might appreciate the time to think.

"There are six of us that're related, more or less," he finally answered.

"Wow. That's a lot. All at once?"

"Most of the time. When she's kidding around, my mom calls it a hotel. I think she likes it that way."

"Not someone who prefers being alone?"

He laughed, but it seemed almost private. "Nope."

"Just so I get it right," Sam asked, "your mom is Karen Putnam, right?"

"Yup."

"So, you have a lot of brothers and sisters."

He paused before saying, "Kinda."

"Like a mixed family?"

"That's it, all right," he responded freely. "None of us has the same last name; well, Nick changed his. Basically, I have two brothers and a sister—Nick, Ryan, and Becky. But nobody knows we're related. That used to be kinda funny sometimes, when we were little."

It sounded like the reminiscence of an old man.

"No dad?" Sam asked quietly.

But Richard wasn't so sensitive. He laughed. "I have more dads than I can count."

Again, the line sounded stolen from an adult. Sam wondered what the age gap was between the four siblings.

"Why're you here?" he suddenly asked.

Sam thought a moment before answering. From what she and Willy had separately gathered from less than reliable sources, Karen Putnam had been sleeping with a man who might have been also abusing her daughter. It seemed a dicey subject to dangle before a ten-year-old, even if he might be a bit of a philosopher.

"A name came up in one of my investigations," she said, instead. "I wanted to fly it by your mom."

The next question was a given, even if he seemed to understand its futility. "And you're not gonna tell me."

Sam abruptly changed her mind. "Wayne Castine. Why wouldn't I tell you, Richard?"

He smiled broadly. "'Cause grown-ups don't. What's your excuse?"

She laughed with him.

"I know Wayne," he admitted.

She watched his face. "And?"

He looked away—back toward the street. "I don't like him."

"Why not?"

She was about to rephrase the question when he didn't immediately answer, but then stopped, remembering his thoughtful tempo.

"He makes me feel dirty."

She kept her voice neutral. "Has he done anything bad to you?"

Richard shook his head silently.

"But he has to other people?" she asked.

His answer was small and fragile. "Yeah."

"Your mom?"

He nodded.

"Your sister?"

He turned his head so his cheek was resting on his fist and he was looking up at her. "Why're you here?" he repeated. "VBI only does big crimes, like murder and stuff."

"He was murdered, Richard," she explained. "That's why we're trying to find out about him."

He sat up and crossed his legs. "He was *murdered*? How?"

She hedged. "An autopsy's being done right now."

"Wow. Who d'you think killed him?"

Again, she chose carefully. "Well, we have a few ideas."

"Like my mom?"

She laughed, defeated, and laid her hand on his thin back. "Richard. I only heard your mom knew the guy, probably like a hundred other people. You knew him, too, right?"

She forced him to nod before she continued.

"And I don't think you killed him. But somebody did, and right now, we think it was somebody who didn't like him a whole lot—someone who was really angry at him."

"I just thought he was creepy," Richard stated, almost as an apparent alibi.

Sam leaned in slightly closer, sensing that some of her ground laying might be about to pay off. For, as sad as it was to admit sometimes, and as compassionate as she knew she could be, she remained a hunter, stimulated by the pursuit. "In what way, Richard? Why did you say what you did about him and your mom?"

But in a textbook example of one of those moments you repeatedly play over in your brain, her opportunity abruptly vaporized in the noisy, dust-shrouded, skidding-to-a-halt arrival of an older, rusty Town & Country van. Squinting through the brown, swirling cloud that rolled toward them and broke against their crisscross of slats, Sam and Richard watched a tall, slim, hard-faced woman in tight jeans and a spaghetti-strapped crop top emerge from the van, carrying a translucent grocery sack revealing two cartons of cigarettes and some beer. She stood motionless for a moment, studying Sammie's car, before she put the sack on the ground, crossed the narrow swatch of grass between the street and the latticework, and crouched down directly before them.

From sensing she'd gained access to an inner sanctum of security and privacy, Sam now felt like an adult trapped wearing a kid's costume, suddenly thrust into public view.

"Who the fuck're you?" the woman demanded, shading her eyes and squinting into the gloom. "Ricky, what the hell do you think you're doing under there? This is way over the line, you little jerk."

She began tearing at the slats, looking for the opening. "Get the hell out of there, you pervert. He's a fucking kid, for Chrissake."

Seeing no other way out, literally or otherwise, Sam tried meeting force with force. She pushed open the entrance, showing her badge as she awkwardly but quickly emerged, dusting herself off.

"Calm down. I'm a police officer. You weren't home, so I was chatting with Richard."

The woman straightened along with Sam, taller than her by half a head. "The fuck you were. You weren't invited in there, and don't tell me he did, 'cause he's a kid and you know better. You get the hell off my property."

"You Karen Putnam, ma'am?"

"You're damn right I am, and you're trespassing."

"I'm Samantha Martens, of the Vermont Bureau of Investigation, and I'd like to ask you a couple of questions."

Putnam reached out to push Sam's shoulder toward her car, but Sam caught the hand and held it in midair, halfway between merely stopping it in motion and swinging it around to throw the taller woman into an arm lock.

"Do not touch me, Mrs. Putnam," Sam warned her.

The hand was yanked back, as if from a hot stove.

"I don't want to even look at you, bitch. Now get the fuck away from here. *NOW*," she shouted.

In the corner of her eye, Sam saw Richard taking this all in, his expression tight and edgy. One of his hands was unconsciously scratching at the dirt, like a nervous animal's.

Sam kept her voice calm. "Mrs. Putnam. I am investigating a homicide . . ."

But Putnam cut her off. "I know all about that—Wayne. It was on the radio. Who gives a shit about that shitbird?"

"You knew him, then?"

Putnam gave her a withering stare. "Well, you're here, for God's sake. What do you think? Or are you just crawling under every trailer in town, hoping to get lucky?"

She distractedly finger-combed her long, tangled hair, glanced down at her son, and snarled, "Get out of my sight, Ricky. You and I'll talk later."

Richard vanished, pulling the slats tight behind him, reminding Sam of a pet bolting for cover.

Putnam then turned on her, her voice just under the yelling she'd maintained until now. "Okay—you. Don't get all twitchy now. I won't touch you. I'm poor, not stupid. And right now, I'm hot and angry. You feel like you have a real deep need to get in my face, I figure you'll find a way. But I'm going inside now, and you're not, so have a nice day and fuck off."

She made an exaggerated show of sidling around where Sam stood, both hands held up as if showing her passiveness, and then swooped down, grabbed her grocery bag, and stamped up the trailer's steps, slamming the door behind her.

There was a stunned silence for a moment, as if all of Nature took a breath to recover, before Sam became aware of the two dragonflies again, still darting about aimlessly, along with the distant sound of a lawn mower starting up.

She tucked her chin in slightly, so no one could see her mouth moving from the trailer windows.

"Richard?"

"Yeah?"

"You okay?"

"Yeah. She's got a mouth on her, doesn't she?"

Sam let out a snort. "I guess."

"She's a good mom, though. She just talks loud."

"I'm glad to hear it."

"She knows kids. Grown-ups are something else."

"I got that part."

There was a small giggle from the darkness under the trailer.

Sam opened the door to her car. "Take care, Richard. Hope I see you again soon."

"You, too, Sam."

Sammie smiled at him, slid in behind the wheel, and slowly drove off.

CHAPTER 14

"Hot, ain't it?"

Lyn turned away from studying the traffic clogging Hammond Street, running the gauntlet between Bangor's huge airport and a collection of industrial parks, and silently stared at the owner of the voice—a tall, mangy-looking man in jeans and cowboy boots, with tattoos decorating both sinewy arms.

He watched her expression, his smile slowly fading, along with his ambition. He shifted his few purchases from one hand to the other, said, "Have a good evening," and stepped outside into the gas station parking lot, heading for a semi.

She sighed and returned to the convenience store's counter, her own dubious dinner of a shrink-wrapped sandwich, a bottle of Yoo-hoo, and a bag of chips cradled in her left forearm.

The counterman didn't bother making eye contact. He stared at her choices, her breasts, and back again.

"Twelve ninety-eight."

She laid fifteen dollars on the surface. He did his auto-mated routine with the register, the receipt, the paper bag, and handed her change, telling her breasts to have a good night.

She'd left her motel on foot around the corner, on Odlin Road, in hopes of raising her spirits slightly, exchanging the offerings of the hallway vending machine for the wider variety at the gas station. She should have known better. The walk in this part of town offered no iota of rest for the eye, down to the burned grass by the curb, nor had it taken her mind off her earlier conversation with Dick Brandhorst.

He hadn't called her, of course. And she wasn't expecting much when she showed up at his office the next morning. What was truly dispiriting, in truth, wasn't the lack of progress, but the continued insinuation—from Joe to Harry Martin to Brandhorst—that her father and older brother had been neck-deep in illegal activities.

Lyn had a high tolerance for the realities of life, and the compromises they could spawn. But her father had issued the challenge of the high moral ground to all his children, and then embodied it to give it form. After his death, she'd held his example before her as she'd struggled being a wife and mother, a daughter and sister, and an overall human being, awed by how the Old Man had done it with such ease.

And only sometimes—in short, cynical spurts during challenging times—wondering *if* he'd been able to do it.

Because *that* had become the hardest aspect of Joe's discovery: that deep in her heart, she wasn't entirely surprised. Why else had her mother corrupted her younger brother, Steve, by involving him with alcohol to keep her company in her grief; and why else had Steve then followed that by becoming a drug dealer and getting arrested? How to now explain the depth of their mother's near paralyzing depression? Or even her own ready acceptance that both experienced men had perished during a storm deemed mundane at the time?

In Lyn's emotion-racked turmoil of the last few weeks, the common denominator had appeared to be personal weakness. Their father may have preached the high and mighty, but he'd practiced a nuanced pragmatism—apparently, his true genetic gift to the rest of them.

She headed back out into the hot and humid night, the store's air-conditioning evaporating from her clothes like a fog. The overhead summer clouds were stained with the city's luminous thumbprint and the lingering yellow afterwash of the sun's recent departure. The effect made passing headlights look ineffective and weak, echoing much of her mood.

She ate as she walked, without appetite or interest, her goal to have something in her stomach by the time she threw the rest of it into a roadside barrel she could see in the distance.

She thought also of Joe, albeit without much hope, low enough on herself to imagine that their relationship—once similarly held to high expectations—would inevitably founder as part of the disintegrating whole.

By the time she reached her motel room, down a dark hallway anchored by a stained patterned rug, she was deep in the dumps. Not even her own air-conditioning, tainted with the syrupy sweetness of room freshener, came as a relief.

She hit the lights, threw her plastic key card onto the dresser, and surveyed her small domain. A single queen bed, guarded by tiny night tables, a round table with a chipped edge, a single chair with a dirty cushion, and her bag, lying open near where she'd just thrown the key card.

The room was on the ground floor, which she generally didn't like, since it forced her to leave the curtains drawn.

Except, they were open.

She stood very still for a moment, studying her own reflection in the distant window. She had taken this room earlier, after meeting with Brandhorst, in full daylight. She always drew the curtains, and she definitely would have before heading for the convenience store. But had she? Her mood was so dour, she remembered being surprised by how the sun flooding the room had appealed to her.

Maybe she hadn't drawn them after all. The sunset had been spectacular, after all. But was that a memory from her walk outside, or because she'd admired it at the window?

Shaking her head, she closed them now, ruffling them to make sure they met tightly in the middle.

She then flopped down on the bed, piled up a stack of pillows, and reached for the TV remote, hoping to clear her head.

It wasn't where she'd left it.

She searched more carefully, frowning, swinging her legs back down onto the floor to check the dark crevice between the table and the box spring. Nothing.

"What the hell?" she muttered, checking the flowered bedspread, expecting to see the remote's small black rectangle lurking like a hiding lizard.

Failing, she glanced up at the TV, and saw it resting on top of the set. She froze.

First, the curtains. Now, the remote. Maybe she was starting to lose it.

She got back up and fingered the remote lightly without picking it up, as if it might have a pulse.

She studied the sparse room in detail, now questioning everything in it. Was her bag as she'd placed it, or slightly askew? Had it been open all the way, then, or just partly, as now? Hadn't she hung her clothes apart evenly? They were clumped together now. And that one, slightly cracked drawer . . . That wasn't like her.

She opened the drawer to reveal her underwear, neatly stacked, along with a folded blouse. Staring at the lingerie, she shivered, ever more uncomfortable.

Slowly, quietly, as if stalking prey through the woods, she moved up the tiny hallway, toward the bathroom. There, she stood for a moment, trying to see into its enveloping darkness, before finally reaching out for the light switch.

She screamed slightly as soon as the light flooded the room—not from any disarray; nor from some man standing before her. But one had been there, sure enough, and had left compelling proof of it.

Before her stood the toilet, its seat up, as only a man would leave it after taking a pee.

Lyn staggered back, physically shoved there by the realization. Fighting near panic, she grabbed a spare hanger from the open closet, and brandished it toward the drawn shower curtain.

"I've got a weapon. Come out *NOW*," she ordered, immediately feeling like an idiot. To cover her embarrassment, she slashed at the flimsy plastic with the hanger, whipping it aside and revealing the empty tub.

"Shit," she muttered, and tossed the hanger onto the floor.

Without hesitation, she threw her bag onto the bed, loaded it fast and without care, and stepped out into the hallway, all in under two minutes.

The hallway was silent and empty. She headed away from the lobby, toward the exit leading to the rear parking lot, and there emerged into the night air, like an underwater swimmer coming to the surface.

Her bag in one hand, she pressed her back against the rough wall of the motel, studying every aspect of the parking lot. It wasn't very full—most cars, including hers, being out front—and she could see pretty clearly into the interiors of most of them. They all appeared to be empty.

She tried telling herself that she'd pulled a fast one and gained the advantage—like a fox doubling back on the hounds.

Keeping to the shadows, she circled the building, until she'd placed herself in the shade of an evergreen bush, from where she could see most of the front lot, along with her own car.

Here the vehicles were too many and too tightly parked to allow her an unimpeded view.

She considered her options. That Brandhorst had ordered she be followed and checked out—or had done so himself—she had no doubt. Of his purpose she was less sure. In gross terms, it may have been simply to find out more about her, or at least get a look at any documents she might have; more subtly, it may have been a warning—I can get to you anywhere, at any time. The real question now was whether he was done, or just starting a process that included babysitting her to see where she went next.

That last part was the most ominous, making her think that tonight's scare was just the beginning of being under constant scrutiny.

She looked beyond the parking lot at the traffic, suddenly thinking of another option. She'd remembered something—a familiar logo—either while she was driving to this motel or while she'd been gazing about its lobby, waiting to register. It would mean a bit of a walk, but it could also sever the rope between herself and the people stalking her.

She discreetly backed away from her observation post, abandoned the parking lot and her car, and struck out for Odlin Road by cutting through a low barricade of shrubs. Once on the sidewalk, she transformed her bag's handle into a shoulder strap, fitted it comfortably onto her back, despite the instant heat it created against her spine, and set off at a fast pace. She was heading east, toward the airport terminal.

She'd readied herself for an hour or more of walking, but in far less time, damp with sweat, she found what she was after. She crossed another parking lot, pushed open the establishment's front door, and tilted her head back in relief as the air-conditioning engulfed her.

"Whoa," said the woman behind the Enterprise counter, laughing. "You've been putting in some exercise. Don't tell me: You want to rent a car."

Lyn laughed and approached the counter. "You bet I do."

CHAPTER 15

Lester compared the man in the distance to the mug shot in his hand. Usually, when people posed for these things, they weren't at their best, making the end result look more like a morgue photo.

But not this guy. He was his own worst photograph's spitting image, pale and dark-eyed with translucent, bloodless skin—a man death might actually improve.

He looked up and down the street, standing under a light on the stoop of his run-down apartment building, and lit a cigarette before crossing the sidewalk and getting in behind the wheel of a rusty, dilapidated Volkswagen Beetle of ancient vintage.

"Mr. Needham, I presume?" Les asked of his companions.

Ron Klesczewski was in the passenger seat; Sheila Murphy in back.

"The one and only," Sheila confirmed from the darkness. The alleyway facing Canal Street had no lights and no windows overlooking it—the perfect black hole in which to sit and wait.

They'd been doing just that for three hours, pinning their hopes on information Murphy had gleaned about a rash of salvage metal thefts, now the sudden rage in a poor economy. Copper tubing had gone missing from a building supply store, half a dozen catalytic converters from parked cars, and one homeowner had returned from vacation to find strips of copper roofing missing from his home. All in the last month.

Indications pointed to Ray Needham, and a check on him in Spillman's data bank revealed Wayne Castine as a frequent companion—until lately, according to Sheila's source.

That possible falling out explained Lester's presence here.

"There he goes," Ron muttered as the Volkswagen lurched away from the curb before winding down the street, heading west.

It was almost two in the morning.

Lester eased out of the alleyway and slid in far behind Needham, his lights off.

"You get a sense from your snitch that Ray was pissed enough at Wayne to kill him?" Spinney asked Sheila.

"He's pissed," she confirmed. "But murder didn't come up; just that Wayne had screwed him royally and Ray was looking for him. I can tell you Ray's a bad boy when it comes to temper."

"But you don't know the details?"

"Those are the details."

Lester smiled to himself. Sheila was old school—a Bratt detective for several years, comfortable within the community, with a teacher husband and two kids in local schools. She saw Lester as state police first, VBI second, and never a municipal cop. That made him suspect. And so it went, across the profession and throughout the state.

Ahead of them, the lopsided Beetle turned the corner without signaling and drove up Washington Street, its taillights looking like they were helping to push.

"What's he going after tonight?" Les asked.

"Not the ghost of a notion."

"We could pull him over for not signaling," Ron suggested lightly.

"Keep that in mind," Les agreed. "Might come in handy."

The car, however, left Washington at the top of the rise, entered a quiet side street free of overhead lighting, and slowly rolled to a stop in the middle of the road, as if out of gas.

"What the hell?" Sheila murmured from the back.

Ron laughed softly. "I think I get it."

"What?" Lester asked.

Ron pointed. He, too, had stopped, a hundred feet back, using a parked car as a shield, and they had a clear view ahead as Ray emerged from his vehicle holding a long, polelike object.

He stepped behind the Volkswagen and began poking at something in the middle of the road.

Lester put it together. "Unbelievable," he said. "Using a VW bug as a getaway car? Is he nuts?"

Sheila eased her door open and began getting out. "He was never the sharpest blade in the shed."

The two men followed her, spreading out to both sidewalks, and surreptitiously worked their way toward where Ray Needham was lost in his efforts. By now, he'd managed to pry up the manhole cover he was hoping to steal, and was trying to keep it balanced on edge and place the crowbar quietly on the road. Stealth, as the name implies, usually demands a certain amount of quiet, and this was clearly becoming a challenge. All around them, lining both sides of the street, were dark, quiet, sleeping houses, presumably filled with good citizens who would later resent losing an axle—or a small child—to an open manhole.

Noise wasn't Ray's only problem, though. As the three

cops, now so close they could hear him muttering, paused and watched from the shadows, he struggled to roll his prize to the side of the car—before discovering his second major hurdle. How to lift the thing inside?

He managed to rest it against the car, making the latter lean even more, and to open the door. But then, he was stumped. He stood there, panting, hands on his hips, his face dripping with sweat, staring at the VW as if asking for help.

The cops by now surrounded him, and on a signal from Ron, they calmly closed in from three sides.

"Don't know, Ray," Ron said conversationally, emerging from the gloom. "That's a real problem."

Needham's body stiffened, and for a moment, Les thought he might run for it, before Sheila added from a different direction, "Or maybe a couple."

Ray whipped around, saw Lester as well, maintained a startled gazelle imitation for a second more, and then slumped in defeat.

"Fuck."

They all circled Ray's project for the evening, as if about to lend a hand. Ron asked Murphy, "You bring the camera?"

She held it up.

He reached out. "It's your bust. You do the honors. I'll take the pictures before we put this thing back. I doubt folks around here would appreciate our taking it into evidence."

Spinney joined Ray Needham in the Municipal Center's holding cells a couple of hours later. The thief had been processed, interviewed, and locked up, pending his appearance before a judge in the morning. He was lying on the plastic mattress of his cot, his fingers locked behind his head, staring at the ceiling, when Les rapped his knuckles against the bars of his door.

"Hi again."

Ray slowly took his eyes off the ceiling, as if he'd been interrupted reading a good book, and fixed Lester with a stare. "Jesus. Don't you ever sleep?"

Lester laughed. "You should talk."

Needham shrugged. "I sleep days."

"I can see why." Les pulled up a chair and sat down on the other side of the bars. The rest of the cells were empty, so they had this part of the basement to themselves.

Spinney pointed upstairs. "They tell you what you're facing?"

"With my history? Years. Fuckin' manhole cover. 'Nother five minutes, I woulda left it there. Fuckin' weighed a ton."

Les agreed. "I know. I helped roll it back, remember?"

"Yeah. Well, life's a bitch. Least you were getting paid."

"Yeah," Spinney said. "And by the state, too. I don't work for these guys."

Needham's eyes narrowed. "I didn't think I knew you."

Lester showed him his badge. "VBI—we only do major crimes."

Ray studied him, reading behind the comment, before slowly saying, "Yeah."

"Like murder," Les suggested.

Ray remained quiet, but his hands unlaced from behind his neck, and his body lost its nonchalance.

"You hear about Wayne Castine?" Lester asked.

For a moment, he could see Ray's breathing stop.

"I heard he died," he finally said.

"You could say that," Lester said lightly. "He was butchered, more like it, by someone he really irritated."

"You don't say."

"Oh, yeah." Spinney raised his eyebrows, apparently thinking of something interesting. "Speaking of which, I heard you two had a falling out, just lately."

"I didn't kill him," Ray said, an edge to his voice.

Les sat forward. "You thought about it, though. Not much of a gap between those two. Gotta do one to do the other."

"I didn't kill him," Ray repeated, shifting to place his back against the wall.

"What made you so mad?" Spinney asked.

"Ripped me off, that's all. It was a business deal. I didn't like him, but I didn't kill him."

Lester smiled. "Yeah, so you say. Tell me about the business deal."

"We got hold of some scrap metal, Wayne said he'd sell it, and he never split the profits."

"Who'd he sell it to?"

"I don't know. He said he didn't, which is why he didn't have the money to split, but I know he was lying. He just took it all and figured I could go fuck myself."

"So, what did you do?"

"I went looking for him." Ray also sat forward, eager to sell his message. "That part's true. I was mad. I woulda torn him a new one, but I never found him. I'll swear that on the Bible."

He held up his hand. Lester nodded solemnly, if in fact unimpressed. The Bible usually came in too little, too late, in his experience.

"I read your rap sheet, Ray," Lester explained. "You pound on people you don't like."

"Not this time."

"You sent a couple to the hospital. Think you might've sent Wayne to his grave?"

Ray pressed his lips together before saying, "You

prove it, then I did it, but you can't do that. So, with all due respect, I gotta tell you to screw off."

Lester nodded. "Respectfully noted. So, since you had nothing to do with his death, when did you last see Wayne?"

"What's today?"

"Wednesday."

Ray shut his eyes briefly. "Then it was . . . Friday . . . No, wait. Thursday. Thursday last. Out back of the bowling alley. That's when he told me about the deal where he ripped me off after."

"On Thursday, you met so he could *tell* you about the deal? You didn't do it right then, too?"

Ray's brow furrowed. "Sure we did. We met, we did the deal, he ripped me off, and I went lookin' for him. That's it."

"When did you start looking?"

"Couple of days later. He said he had a fence."

"How did you find out that fell through?"

"I called him."

"At home?"

"Yeah."

"And after he told you, you went over there and killed him."

Ray's mouth fell open. He dropped his hands into his lap and leaned his head against the cinder blocks behind him. "Fuck you," he said tiredly.

Les laughed. "You telling me he stiffed you and you *didn't* go over there? You really do take me for an asshole."

Ray snapped forward and glared at him. "*I don't know where he lived,*" he enunciated.

Lester pretended to think about that for a moment. "Really? Your business partner? I know where my fellow cops live."

Ray became sullen. "Good for you. You think I whacked him, prove it."

"You're the one who was angry at the man, Ray. What were you doing Monday night?"

"Nuthin'."

"That the best you can do?"

But Ray was done. He crossed his arms and stared up at the ceiling—a variation of his posture at the start of the conversation.

Lester got the hint. He stood up, waved, and said, "Get some sleep, Ray. It's noisy in prison. I'll see you later."

"Whatever. You dumb fuck."

Lester climbed the stairs, at last feeling his own fatigue. At the top, just outside dispatch, he met Ron Klesczewski.

"You get it all?" he asked.

Ron nodded. "Yup. Sound quality was good—everything. I already cut a CD for you." He handed over a small envelope. "You think he did it?"

Les tilted his head to one side. "You think he didn't?"

Ron smiled and crooked his finger. "Come in here."

He led the way into dispatch, which had a standard array of radio consoles, TV monitors, tape and CD recorders. A woman was sitting at one of the two operator bays, talking to someone over her headset. Ron led the way to a CD player in the far corner.

"After Ray said he'd last seen Wayne on Thursday, I went back to some video footage we collected yesterday. Remember? Wayne had bought some fast food and thrown the receipts on the floor. To establish a timeline and see if he was with any kids, I had my guys pull the videos from all the stores on the receipts."

He pushed a few buttons on a player. The small TV screen before them lit up and Lester saw the back of a clerk operating a cash register. The camera was mounted up against the ceiling and showed everyone from a giant's viewpoint. Seconds later, they watched Wayne Castine step up to the counter, lay down a sandwich and a soda and a bag of chips, along with a twenty-dollar bill.

Next to him was Ray Needham.

"That," Ron explained, "was this Monday."

Lester grunted. "And he was dead Tuesday morning. Cool."

CHAPTER 16

"Where are you?" Lyn's voice asked over the cell phone.

Joe tried to see through the rain streaking the windshield. It was dark and the glass was old and slightly pitted, causing all points of light to flare.

He'd left the Interstate at Augusta, hoping the late hour would offset using Route 3 East instead of driving all the way to Bangor and then cutting south. Despite a downpour over the past hour, it still felt like a good decision, which mattered, given the urgency he'd heard in her voice three hours ago, and which remained still.

"I just left Searsport," he finally said, reading a passing sign. "I've got to be only about ten miles away."

"You'll go over two bridges in a row," she told him. "The first is over-the-top modern—a suspension bridge. It's right next to an old metal one that hasn't been demolished yet. The second is short and regular-looking. That one T-bones into Route 15. Take a left into Bucksport. You'll see the motel on the left, not too far afterward."

"Got it. See you soon. You're still okay, right?"

"I'm fine, Joe," she answered, her voice softer and calmer. "Thanks for coming so fast."

He hung up and concentrated on the road. As promised, he soon saw emerge from the gloom a ghostly, spot-lighted span to his right—its twin towers like obelisks, linked by a gleaming web of steel cables—accompanied by its older, peeling, stalwart, traditional predecessor, mere feet off to one side. This was the Penobscot Narrows Bridge, famous for its architectural innovation, and near the site of two unheralded naval battles, where the British twice creamed the Americans, during the Revolution and the War of 1812. As Joe crossed the soaring bridge, he glanced left and saw the harbor village of Bucksport, barely a mile off, gleaming through a curtain of rain. Almost there.

He had no idea what was coming. Lyn had called him, close to midnight, and told him she was in trouble. She was in Maine, she'd said, had met a guy who'd maybe sicced some people onto her—or maybe not—but, in any case, she was worried that she'd really stepped into it this time.

He'd asked her if she felt unsafe, to which she'd answered that while she was scared, she couldn't call the cops, since she had nothing to give them.

It had still been enough for him. Finally stirring from her weeks of emotional catatonia, Lyn had chosen to act. Maybe something had happened in Gloucester; maybe someone had spoken to her of her father and brother. Joe didn't know and didn't care. Despite Lyn's fear on the phone, he was oddly content that something had finally dislodged the status quo.

And he was pleased she'd called him for help.

The irony was that he could ill afford such chivalry, or the time it was costing him. Things were building in the Castine investigation. Ron's crew and his own were compiling suspects. The logistics of processing them effectively would be tricky and sensitive, the penalties being people either "lawyering up" prematurely or fleeing and/or destroying evidence.

But he was torn. His squad was experienced, competent, and skillful, while his feelings for Lyn were growing by the day. Besides—to his ear—her crisis sounded like the more pressing of the two.

He crossed the second bridge, turned left, located the motel, and rolled to a stop in the parking lot.

Almost immediately, a pale shadow appeared in his side window, as Lyn rapped her knuckles against the glass.

He opened the door and wrapped his arms around her. She was trembling.

"God, Joe. It's good to see you."

He rubbed her back and kissed her cheek. "It's okay, it's okay. Let's get out of the rain and you can tell me what's going on."

She led the way inside, to a room on the other side of the building, where the motel's appeal was immediately revealed. Facing him across the room was a large window overlooking the dark Penobscot Narrows and the modern bridge he'd just crossed in the murky distance. In addition, to the right, also spotlighted and spectral in the rain, was the restored Fort Knox, uselessly built in the mid-1840s against any future British drubbings.

"Pretty," he muttered.

She closed the door, bolted it, and came up beside him. The lights were out in the room, allowing the scenery to dominate.

"It is," she agreed. "Gives me a little peace in the middle of all this."

He turned to her. "Which is what, exactly?"

She sat at a small table under the window, so they could talk and enjoy the view at the same time. He joined her, sitting opposite, recognizing her need for at least a semblance of order and normalcy.

Slowly, occasionally correcting herself or retracing her steps, Lyn detailed her recent activities, from her first misgivings to her meeting with Harry Martin to her conversation at Brandhorst's office, and finally to her discovery that her room had been searched, or at least visited.

Joe mostly listened, asking questions only rarely, until he was sure she was done.

After which, he got up, leaned across the table, and kissed her. "I'm glad you're all right."

She smiled as he sat back down. "I am now. I don't know what to do, though."

"Okay," he offered. "Let's talk about that, if you're up to it."

Her eyes widened. "God, yes. I'm scared, but excited, too, you know? I feel like I really stirred something up. That's got to be good, right?"

"Tricky, but sure," he agreed. "Why not?"

Privately, however, he was less enthusiastic. Her approach up to now had been totally unorthodox—appealing, perhaps, but without controls.

"Okay," he began. "First off, you were right when you said you had nothing to give the cops. I could ask for a favor and have Brandhorst's record run, but that would be only marginally kosher, and probably not useful. I'd prefer to keep my powder dry until we've got something meatier on him, or maybe found out why he's so interested in you."

He held up a finger, adding, "Assuming he's even connected to the visit to your motel room. It sounds right, but we shouldn't shut any doors prematurely."

She was nodding. "All right. But what's my next move? Should I go back to his office like I said, and pretend I didn't notice about the room?"

Joe shook his head. "Let's go on the assumption that Brandhorst is dirty and that he sent a team to check you out. Why would he do that? You dropped in on him out of the blue, told him a wild story he claimed he knew nothing about, and told him you'd be back. So why go through your things? He could've just waited. It could be he wanted to see if you were a cop or a competitor. But maybe you did shake something up. Whoever went through your room might've been after something specific."

"What?" she asked, nonplussed.

"If we're right, that's what we need to find out, by turning the tables on him a little."

"How?" she said next.

He laughed. "This is where it can start being fun. I think we should let him stew for a while. He's got your cell number?"

"Yeah."

"Good. Don't show up at his office in the morning. He'll send his people to the motel and find your car there and your stuff gone. Maybe they'll even find the toilet seat up and have a dope-slap moment, realizing they goofed. In any case, that cell number's going to start burning a hole in his pocket. It'll push him to call you, which means the next meeting will be ours to arrange."

She frowned at him. "What's the advantage there? If we still don't know anything about him?"

"His meeting you on your terms," Joe explained, "confirms you've got something he wants. It's subtle, but a valuable next step. Also, he won't know about me, which means I can photograph him and whoever he brings along—that could come in handy later."

She sat back and studied him for a moment, her excitement shadowed by anxiety. "Sounds like a spy movie."

He smiled encouragingly. "Where do you think they get their ideas?"

A brief lull fell between them as they contemplated the near future.

Joe saw her face cloud with sadness. He came around the small table and took her into his arms. She turned toward him and held on tight, speaking into his chest. "I feel like an idiot—totally lied to."

She paused and added, "And I passed all those lies on to Coryn—lock, stock, and barrel."

"You passed more than that to your daughter. You know that," he challenged her, breaking her grip to look her in the eyes.

She didn't answer.

"You gave her your own example. That counts for a lot more than a few glowing memories of a dead grandfather. Look at what you're doing now, Lyn—searching for the truth, regardless of the consequences. That means something to a kid as bright as her."

She stretched up and kissed him, long and passionately, her face wet and her nose dripping. They both started laughing partway through and broke apart to wipe their upper lips.

"Jesus," she said. "What a mess."

He laughed and leaned in for more. "Hell. A minor obstacle."

They didn't have long to wait for Dick Brandhorst's phone call. By noon, barely ten hours later, while they were eating at a local restaurant, Lyn's cell buzzed on the tabletop. She studied the number on the small screen and gave Joe a meaningful glance. "We're on," she said, turned on the small recorder he'd set up for her, and answered it.

Listening to her end of the conversation, Joe could tell things were lining up as they'd hoped. In extremely short order, she asked Brandhorst, "You know where Bucksport is? Head down there at three o'clock this afternoon, park downtown, and wait for me to call you. Give me a cell-phone number."

She wrote it down on a napkin, hung up, and killed the recorder.

They looked at each other for a couple of seconds.

"He sound okay?" Joe asked.

"Far as I could tell. Why did you want him parked in the street? Why not send him straight to the meeting place?"

"'Cause then he'd send his goons there immediately and stake it out. Plus, I like him dangling a bit."

She reached out and took up one of his hands. "I'm worried about what to say when we meet."

Joe shrugged. "You don't have to say much of anything. He called you, after all. Let him worry about it. My guess is he'll try to play you."

"How?" she asked.

"By giving you some bogus contact. Without meaning to, that's what you asked for when you came to his office. He's never had the upper hand with you. The first time you showed up, it was straight out of the blue; the second time, he would've been ready, but you never appeared. Now, you're calling the shots. I'm betting he'll just give you a name and a place where all your questions will supposedly be answered, but they'll really be the equivalent of a dark alley somewhere."

"But why?" she asked, not for the first time. "I don't have anything for him."

Joe turned both palms to the ceiling. "He thinks you do, which is what makes this interesting."

He reached for his coffee, taking advantage of the moment to reconsider all she'd told him so far.

"Did you ever tell him Steve's got *The Silva Lining*, or where it is? He did ask you about it a couple of times, didn't he?"

"I don't call it that," she said, thinking back. "No," she then said confidently. "I remember thinking I'd tell him only what he needed to know—José's name, my father's; I mentioned the *Maria*, but not *The Silva Lining*. And I definitely didn't bring Steve into it, or where he had it moored."

"But you let it slip that you got it back," Joe pressed.

She acknowledged as much, if mournfully. "Kind of."

Joe touched the back of her hand. "Not to worry—perfectly reasonable. It's interesting that he cares, though."

"What?" she asked him as he furrowed his brow.

"Well," he explained, "you said they were paying off José's debt, implying they had more to go. If Brandhorst got hold of the boat and sold it, he'd probably see that as helping to balance the books."

She nodded. "Right."

Joe then gave her a lopsided smile, hoping to lift her spirits. "It is amazing, though, you know? In two days, you may end up popping the lid off of something the local cops're going to love. We're not there yet, but I got to hand it to you—you do good work."

Her response was rueful at best. "Even if I did scare myself half to death?"

The meeting spot Joe chose was both practical and an homage to more than a few cinematic forebears. The Penobscot Narrows Observatory is a two-story glass cube atop one of the towers distinguishing the new bridge. Access is via an elevator, where a ticket taker lets you on, and another employee meets you some four hundred feet higher up. From the observatory, which Joe and Lyn visited earlier, the view was absolute—of both the beautiful surrounding countryside, and the roads and parking lot servicing the tower. When Brandhorst made his approach, he knew he'd be under surveillance; just as he knew that this spot, with its restricted access, would be an awkward place to try anything violent or off script.

Lyn was in place early on, caught between earth and sky, feeling like a captive bird within the floor-to-ceiling glass walls, when her cell phone went off two hours later. Of Joe, she had no clue. Somewhere far below, he'd placed himself to wait and watch.

"Hello?" she said, feeling this would be the perfect time for a phone marketer to mess everything up. At the last moment, she remembered to turn on Joe's recorder.

"Ms. Silva?" came the unctuous reply, paradoxically setting her at ease. "I just got to Bucksport. There are a couple of good restaurants in town, especially if you like seafood."

"I'm not hungry," she answered. "Can you see the modern bridge from where you're parked? Over the Penobscot Narrows?"

He sounded quizzical. "Sure. The side-by-side bridges?"

"Right. The tower on the right has a glass top."

There was a pause. "Okay. I see that."

"Drive to the base of that tower and buy a ticket to the observatory at the top. That's where I am. And come alone."

"I am alone, Ms. . . . ." He was still talking when she hung up.

She crossed the small, exposed room, now feeling as if she were hanging from a string in midair, and looked down at the narrow span of the bridge far below. The massive cables stringing the two towers together ran in a single line down its middle, like a knife blade, rather than in the more traditional double row along the outsides, as with the smaller, rusting suspension bridge alongside. The result was to give her a totally unobstructed view of the road from Bucksport, and thus of Brandhorst's vehicle when it came. But she stared in vain at car after car scurrying along the bridge like bugs running for cover, before she finally gave up and moved to the window above the parking lot.

She was aware of nearby Fort Knox, the steam-spewing paper plant across from it, and the widening of the river, the mirrored image of picturesque Bucksport reflected in its waters. But just barely. At the moment, the charms of the observatory were more irritating than impressive.

This was taking forever. Joe hadn't given her any tricks about how to wait. In her real life, Lyn was prone to action and noise, at least while she was working. This stillness was driving her nuts. The observatory had been empty since her arrival, being a little unusual as tourist stops went, and she was beginning to crave a diversion—even a busload of busybodies.

She suddenly froze. A car had glided to a stop between the white lines of a slot near the walkway to the tower's base. She knew it was Brandhorst, even before he emerged and stared straight up at her roost.

He waved cheerfully, although she was obviously not visible to him. Still, she stepped back, as if caught in the open with stolen goods in hand. Unlike when she'd walked into his office the day before, she was now sweating and nervous, her brain teeming with possible mishaps. Innocent and headstrong then, now she knew too much, thanks to Joe.

It seemed like half an hour before the elevator doors hissed open on the first floor of the two-story cube, and footsteps climbed the stairs to the observation deck. Again, she readied the recorder, now in her pocket.

Dick Brandhorst was all smiles as he floated into view. "Ms. Silva. What a great idea. You had me going with all the cloak and dagger, but I never would've discovered this, otherwise." He paused on the top step to take in the panorama.

"My God," he continued, passing by her to press up against one of the glass walls. "It's incredible. You can see everything."

It occurred to her only then that he was probably still in role—playacting that he was doing her a favor by looking into her father's disappearance.

This was odd, given that at their last encounter, he'd called her a tough little bitch, but then she thought that being half a chameleon was probably an asset to a financial planner who was also a bookie—or whatever he was.

"So," he said suddenly, twisting on his heel to put the view abruptly behind him, reinforcing the personality sketch she'd just completed. "What's on your mind?"

She played it along the lines she'd discussed with Joe. "Same as last time—I want to know what happened to my family."

He looked pleasantly bewildered. "You couldn't have asked that on the phone, or by coming by the office, as agreed?"

"You or your goons dropping by my motel room made me leery," she told him.

"Really?" he asked. "Whatever that means, of course."

"Right. Whatever."

He moved right along. "Well," he said, "it so happens I might've found someone to help you out."

He reached into his pocket and extracted a slip of paper, handing it to her. "This is the cell number of a contact. I don't actually know much about him, but a friend of a friend recommended him as the go-to guy for such things."

She took the slip and glanced at it. "That's it? You don't even have a name?"

Brandhorst shrugged. "That's all I got."

She shoved the information dismissively into her other pocket. "I seriously doubt that."

"Believe what you will, Ms. Silva. I'm the one doing

you a favor, though, so don't get too bitchy. Speaking of which," he added, as if as an afterthought, "I ran the *Maria* through maritime registrations. They have it as lost at sea."

"So?"

He smiled. "I was just wondering what her new name was. I'm assuming you reregistered her."

She shook her head. "Decided not to. Too expensive, and not my area of interest. I put her in storage. Probably sell her eventually. I don't know . . ." She waved her hand as if the whole topic was a hassle.

Then she stared at him, eyes slightly narrowed. "Why? You want to buy her?"

Brandhorst actually took a half step back. "Not personally," he told her. "But you know, I keep an eye out for things like that. It's not bad money for a middleman— you can get a couple of hundred thousand for a halfway decent boat, even now."

"Right," she said, still watching him. "I'll remember that when the time comes—if it does. How much money did they still owe you?"

He smiled, heading toward the staircase. "Not a dime, Ms. Silva. I didn't even know them. Good luck."

She stood alone, listening to his retreat fading back toward the elevator below. Joe had been right. She pulled the slip of paper from her pocket and studied it again.

There was a sudden upwelling of noise from below, and she realized that at long last, a surge of tourists had finally discovered the observatory. She waited where she was, at the window, watching for Brandhorst to appear below, while a small mob of photo-taking, gasping newcomers joined her.

Finally, seeing him cross the tarmac, enter his car, and drive away, she eased through the crowd to the elevator and followed his example.

As previously arranged with Joe, she drove only a few hundred yards to the parking area servicing Fort Knox, before abandoning her car again, passing through the gift shop and museum, and climbing the grassy incline to the entrance of the fort itself.

Filing through a thin collection of other visitors, she made her way past several photogenically placed cannons, down a narrow staircase, along a darkened corridor—lighted only via whatever sunshine could squeeze through a row of rifle slits—until she reached a cool, black corner room, perhaps once an ammunition dump.

There, alone, she waited for about ten minutes before Joe joined her.

It was a place from which they could see and hear anyone approaching for a hundred yards in any direction, without being seen themselves.

She gave him a hug and whispered in his ear, "Jesus. Am I glad that's over."

He answered in a similar, barely audible tone. "It went okay?"

"Just like you said it would. He gave me the number of someone supposedly in the know, and again tried to get the new name of the *Maria*."

"What did you tell him?"

She handed him the recorder, which he put away. "The first thing that came to me—that it was in storage and that if I ever got around to it, I might sell it. I even offered it to him."

Joe chuckled. "And he didn't bite?"

"I guess he didn't want to be that obvious. I did ask him why he was so curious. He said he wanted to keep an eye out for a buyer, just for what the hell. How did you do?"

Joe patted a small camera bag hanging from his shoulder. "I got pictures of him, his car's registration, and two guys who couldn't have cared less about the observatory or the bridge, one of whom followed you after you left the bridge, but had to drop you in the fort because of the route you took."

"And the other one?"

"He left after Brandhorst. My guess is they won't pay you much attention till you contact the guy with the cell phone. You told Brandhorst you knew they'd searched your room?"

"Oh, yeah, not that he admitted it."

"That's okay," Joe said. "We just wanted him to know you were on your guard. You make a couple of fancy moves after leaving here, like we discussed, and you should lose that tail again, assuming he's still around. As I said before, I think Brandhorst was just playing it safe showing up with muscle, and maybe hoping to get lucky."

"Did you make it back to Bangor after lunch?" she asked.

He nodded. "Double-checked your motel room and moved your car to the rental place. You want to have dinner together, maybe in Augusta?" he asked.

"Don't you have to get back to Vermont?"

"Sure, but it's on the way, and it'll give me a chance to make sure you weren't followed."

She reached up and kissed him. "Deal."

He studied her carefully then. "So—are you going to stay put until I can get back out here—no running off on your own? We're only talking a couple or a few days, max."

She patted his chest and smiled. "I promise."

CHAPTER 17

Willy propped the heel of one shoe against the edge of his desk. "Where the hell is he?" he asked, scowling.

Sam glanced over to Joe's section of the office, empty and neat. "Told me he had to duck out for a personal day—that something came up."

Even Lester was caught off guard by that. "Something came up?"

"That's what he said."

"Fuck him," Willy recommended. "Let's do it without him."

"Thank you for your support," Joe said from the doorway as he entered, adding, "and sorry for running late. Small family emergency."

"Everything all right?" Sam asked, typically solicitous.

"Better not be," Willy threw in, "'cause Bill Allard was looking for you, too. Didn't sound happy. I had no clue what to tell him, so you better be dealing with a full-blown personal crisis."

Allard was the director of VBI, Joe's immediate boss in Waterbury, strategically located near Montpelier, the state capital. Bill Allard tended to let his people run on their own, but he did like to be kept in the loop, just in case he got bushwhacked by a bureaucrat with a need to know. Joe hadn't spoken with him since Castine had been found murdered—a definite and unusual oversight. He wasn't surprised to hear Bill was getting twitchy.

"Probably didn't help that you told him to drop dead," Lester suggested from his desk.

Willy smiled. "He's used to that from me—wouldn't expect otherwise."

Joe gave Kunkle a serious look, to which Willy waved his hand. "Just kidding, boss, just kidding. I was on my best behavior."

"Whatever that is," Sam muttered.

Joe dumped his bag beside his computer and perched on the windowsill behind his chair. Mercifully, the region-wide heat wave had broken during the night, and the weather was back to a pleasant high seventies—sunny and dry.

"Okay," he said. "Let's find out where we are."

"The way things're looking," Les volunteered, "we may be the only ones who didn't want this guy dead."

"Speak for yourself," Willy cracked.

Sam stayed on track. "It's getting complicated fast. Last night, Les grabbed a guy named Ray Needham who used to steal with Castine and split the proceeds. Castine screwed him on their last outing, and Ray claimed he hadn't seen him since—except that Ron found a store tape that shows them together the day before Wayne died."

"Did Ray know about the Manor Court apartment?" Joe asked.

"He says he didn't even know where Wayne lived," Les said. "'Course that doesn't mean he couldn't have followed him there, or anywhere else. If Ray lied about when he last saw him, maybe he was also the one knocking on that apartment door."

Joe opened his mouth to ask a question, but Les then

threw in, "And the last guy he tuned up, he used a base-ball bat. Damn near killed him."

Joe nodded instead and looked over to Sam.

She got the message. "Next on the radar is Karen Put-nam. She was having an affair with Wayne while her daughter—Becky Kerr—was maybe being abused by him, at least according to Wayne's neighbor, Andrea Hal-non. That would make me consider killing Wayne, and that was before I met Karen. She's got a real short fuse."

"What did she tell you?" Joe asked.

"Nothing constructive. I was actually talking to one of her kids—the only one at home—when she drove up and threw me off the property."

"You have a plan for her?"

"I'll talk to her again. I think she's expecting it. Maybe I started off on the wrong foot, interviewing her son first. For all her faults, she's a protective mother."

"You get anywhere with him?"

Sam shook her head. "His name's Richard Vial. A real sweetheart. Maybe ten or eleven; likes to live under the trailer. Sounds like life overhead gets a little crazy. I'm pretty sure I made an ally out of him, for what it's worth. But I need to do a lot more work on the whole family—figure out who's who. Could be Karen wasn't the only one who hated Wayne."

"Like Becky," Lester suggested.

"True," Sam conceded. "I'll be checking her out, too."

"Anything else?" Joe asked them.

"Just that we've barely started," Willy cautioned. "Ray, Karen, and Becky are already in our sights, but like Les found out, it could be anybody, this early into it."

"Okay," Joe conceded, "so, maybe we focus on a couple of the neon signs in this case, for instance the degree of passion in the attack."

"Or that it specifically happened in the apartment

Wayne used to get laid," Sam suggested, "instead of his place or down a dark alley."

"Speaking of which," Lester said, "when I went back to Manor Court to interview a few folks we missed during the first canvass, I found the guy who rented the apartment between Terry Stein and Liz Babbitt. He told me one reason he left was that he felt someone was dropping by when he wasn't there. There was never anything missing or screwed up; he said it was just a feeling. Gave him the chills."

Joe thought back to Lyn's story of having her motel room tossed.

"He never bitched to the landlord?" Willy asked.

Lester laughed. "Yeah. Right. He left instead. Anyhow, it does suggest that Wayne's use of the place started right after Terry left, and maybe involved people besides Karen Putnam."

Joe said softly, almost to himself, "We need to really dig into Wayne's history."

"We got his body," Willy volunteered. "What did your pal Hillstrom find out?"

Beverly Hillstrom was the state's medical examiner, and an old friend of Joe's, which, as Willy had implied, usually made her an early stop for Joe in such investigations.

"I haven't seen her yet," Joe admitted.

There was a stillness in the room as everyone absorbed the anomaly.

"You're slippin', boss," Willy suggested with predictable subtlety.

"We got the prelim," Sam suggested helpfully. "Basically said what we thought—blunt trauma and a sharp instrument, neither of which found at the scene."

"Hillstrom's always got more," Willy pressed. "Joe just needs to massage her a little."

Joe smiled. "Consider it done, for you, if nobody else."

But he was embarrassed by the oversight, tacking it onto a growing list of lapses that he'd committed since Lyn's departure. The thought reminded him, too, of his own boss's interest in having a talk.

"Guess I'll kill two birds with one stone and see Allard, too," he told them.

He slid off the windowsill and concluded, "All right. Sounds like we've got more than enough to keep us busy. Sam, you'll coordinate who does what while I'm upstate?"

She waved from her desk.

"Then wish me luck," he said, grabbing his bag. "I'll see what I can bring home."

The break in the heat allowed Joe to cross the state with his windows open, instead of wrapped in air-conditioning, which he instinctively disliked. Vermont has only two interstates—91, which runs up the eastern side, from Brattleboro to Canada; and 89, which intersects with 91 halfway up and cuts diagonally northwest, toward Burlington, on the shores of Lake Champlain.

The trip is a soothing, picturesque, graceful, two-and-a-half-hour offering of some of the best that Vermont has to offer, from serpentine rivers to granite-capped mountains. Fields, farms, covered bridges, low-head dams, railroads paralleling rocky streambeds—all of it rendered in a seamless slide show. Joe was a native Vermonter, the older of two sons of a Thetford Hill farmer. The values, traditions, and life lessons of that heritage always played in concert with the scenery to lift his spirits.

Today was no different. Smelling the cut hay and fresh manure from a nearby farm, as the road headed into the Green Mountains, Joe pondered the balancing act between his professional and personal lives—as different as the contrast he'd been appreciating recently between Vermont and the Maine coast. Or, more relevantly, the tug of war he felt himself battling between addressing Lyn's plight and tending to the Castine case.

But there were also some overlays, and the more Joe drove, the more he began to recognize them. He had forever appreciated the often lethal quirkiness of human nature—its drive to reach beyond its grasp, to resort to baser instincts, to assume the worst. His entire professional life had been spent in responding to these traits, and there was no reason to believe he was seeing anything new right now. They were just hitting him from two directions at the same time.

As a result of this insight, the longer he drove the less torn he became between either abandoning Lyn to her own devices or periodically leaving his team to fend for themselves. Instead, the two situations began to fuse into the practical concern to simply get both jobs done. There may be scheduling problems, and a few steamed-up people, but he slowly convinced himself that if he kept his own introspection at bay, and applied a little old-fashioned efficiency, he could still serve each taskmaster.

That he might be deluding himself never occurred to him.

In this artificially upbeat mood, he bypassed the Waterbury exit—and Bill Allard's office—to proceed directly to Burlington and the so-called Office of the Chief Medical Examiner, or OCME. If Allard was miffed at being left in the dark, it wouldn't hurt to meet him with the latest autopsy findings in hand.

On the list of "largest cities" for each of the fifty states, Burlington has the unique distinction of being the smallest of the bunch. As if in compensation, however, it has drawn to its outskirts and environs almost a third of Vermont's entire population. Joe therefore found himself easing away from his inner thoughts to pay closer attention to the thickening traffic.

He took the downtown exit, toward the broad, sweeping hill and the huge lake beyond, but cut right at the top, into the embrace of the sprawling, perpetually under construction maze of the Fletcher Allen medical center. The OCME was located—like an oft overlooked family heirloom—in the nearly inaccessible nether reaches of this complex. Every time he visited, despite his numerous trips here, Joe managed to get lost while strolling the corridors, passages, and hallways that bound Fletcher Allen together.

He was surprised, therefore, when he traveled from the garage through the labyrinth without a misstep, finding himself in short order not only standing before the properly labeled door, but just as it flew open to reveal a tall, slim, white-coated, slightly aristocratic blonde holding a file in her hand—the chief herself, Dr. Beverly Hillstrom.

She burst out laughing at the sight of him. "My God. Joe. Where did you pop out of?"

They embraced warmly, kissing on the cheek, two friends of such long standing that—just once—when each had coincidentally been in emotional turmoil, they'd even been lovers for a night.

"I was curious about Wayne Castine—or at least that's my excuse," he said with a smile.

She squeezed his arm. "You are a born romantic, even if I'm the only one who knows it."

In fact, that was truer for her, who addressed virtually everyone except Joe as "Mister," "Ms.," or their official title, to preserve propriety. If anyone had been told of what she and Joe shared, they never would have believed it, so convincing had Hillstrom been in creating her Ice Queen persona.

"Walk with me," she urged him. "I'm only going down

the hall to deliver this"—she waved the file—"and that's only because I wanted to stretch my legs. A day full of paperwork. Perfectly awful."

"How have you been otherwise?" he asked.

"Oh, wonderful," she admitted. "We've been getting out more. Bought a small sailboat that's become a complete life saver. I sailed as a youngster, and forgot how much I liked it. Life is good. How's Lyn?"

Beverly was married, with children, all older now and out of the house. She and her husband had briefly gone separate ways—that's when she and Joe had found mutual solace—so he was happy to hear that the suture was holding.

"A little shaky, to be honest. Her mom is worse, so she's in Gloucester right now, lending a hand." He left it at that, although he would have felt free to share more under different circumstances.

"I'm sorry to hear that. It is a curious cycle we humans travel, from cradle to grave. The whole parent/child connection has so many unexpected angles."

He smiled at the clinical language, typical of the woman, but it did bring him back briefly to his ruminations about both the Brattleboro homicide and Lyn's wrestling with the state of her family.

Hillstrom abruptly turned left, entered an empty office, and dropped the file into a slot cut into the far wall.

"That's it," she announced, turning around and retracing their steps.

"You did get the preliminary summary on Castine, correct?" she asked as they walked.

"Oh, yeah. Many thanks."

"It's funny," she then said, touching his shoulder. "I actually expected you up here a few days ago, not that I would have had much to say."

"I know," he agreed. "This thing with Lyn has me

driving back and forth to Maine. It's raising hell with my schedule. It wasn't for lack of desire, though."

She was amused. "Now there's a word. Actually, your timing is excellent, because just this morning, I got something extra from the lab. I think you'll find it interesting."

They reached the OCME door, which she unlocked with a card key before leading the way through a couple of small offices and a short hallway to her personal inner sanctum. Joe exchanged greetings and at least one other fast hug with various staffers along the way. The medical examiner's office, casually neglected and shortchanged by the powers above, had a familylike closeness about it which they liked to compare to survivor's syndrome following a boat hijacking.

Beverly settled behind her desk, as Joe selected a comfortable armchair, and perused a neat pile of files at her right hand.

"Here we go," she quickly announced. "Wayne Castine. Let's see . . . Yes, this is it. David Hawke faxed me this today; you probably have a copy waiting for you at your office. His lab lifted a small sample of blood not belonging to the victim. Not a huge amount, but perhaps consistent with a cut hand or finger."

Joe sat forward, making a mental note to call Sammie once he was back in the car, to let her know they should start collecting either volunteered or discreetly gathered DNA samples from the people in Castine's life.

"Male or female?" he asked.

"Male, and no, they didn't get a hit when they ran it through what data they have available. That's hardly surprising, though, given what you gave us."

Joe was caught off guard. "What's that mean?"

She reached out and dialed her phone, explaining. "I'll let David tell you that."

Three minutes later, following the standard amenities, Hawke was addressing them both over the speaker-phone.

"The weather served you poorly, Joe," he said. "It was a very hot day, my team had a long way to travel, and the scene was not air-conditioned. I don't guess you had much of a choice, and I remember mentioning this at the time, but the body—and therefore any blood residue—just sat in the heat too long. Any and all samples degraded more than I thought they had. As you know, for an acceptable DNA match, the legal standard is ten loci, minimum. We were only able to extract six."

Joe was downcast. "Damn. We tried rigging a shade. I should've just hauled the body out of there and told you all to deal with it."

"It's not all bad news," Hawke said supportively. "Six loci are better than none. It's still a one-in-millions statistic. If you can collect a match that comes this close, chances are good you'll have your man."

That was heartening. No homicide prosecution relied solely on DNA anyhow. What David had said was perfectly true.

Still, Beverly saw Joe's disappointment. "Tell you what," she told them. "As a gesture of interagency cooperation, I'll pick up the tab if you, David, send the sample out for a mini-STR analysis. If we're lucky, that might expand the number of loci from six to nine. Still shy of the magic legal number, but nothing to sneeze at."

That did lighten the mood. "You're a peach, Beverly," Joe told her. "Thank you."

She eyed him severely. "Either one of you breathes a word of this, you'll regret it."

"I promise, I promise," Joe swore, holding up his right hand. "I take it this doesn't happen overnight."

Hawke was still laughing. "I'll do what I can, but yes, it takes about a week. Maybe less."

Joe bowed to the inevitable. "Just now, you said 'man.' Does that mean you think the killer was male?"

They both stared at the phone as a pause betrayed Hawke's embarrassment. "Slip of the tongue," his voice admitted. "I have no official opinion on that. The one odd blood sample is male, though."

Beverly added, "From the angle of the various knife thrusts, I would say that the decedent and his attacker were within six inches of being the same height. Also, for what it's worth, I have never seen such a killing that wasn't associated with some level of mental instability, but that could stem as much from interpersonal rage as any generalized psychosis."

"Meaning Castine could just as easily have been knifed by a nutcase as someone he ticked off."

She smiled. "Someone he ticked off couldn't also be a nutcase?"

"Come on, Beverly."

She laughed. "Okay. Yes, you're right. This does bring to mind the old crime novels and their favorite, 'crime of passion,' though."

"Nifty. We reached the same conclusion. You find anything else?"

"Actually, I did," she told him. "He'd had sex just prior to death."

That brought him up short. He thought back to the apartment, and the crime lab's finding that Castine had been assaulted as he opened the door to let someone in.

"I'll be damned," he murmured.

CHAPTER 18

Bill Allard's office was on the top floor of the Department of Public Safety, one flight above even the commissioner and the head of the state police.

That having been said, it was a mouse hole, with a view of an opposite wall, in a building resembling the insane asylum many wags said it had once been—all brick and steel and concrete-hard linoleum. In fact, the main stairwell's empty middle space—with its sheer drop to the ground floor—was caged off from the stairs themselves, presumably to discourage any suicidal yearnings. This did make the wags more difficult to dispute.

Joe didn't actually know the history of the building. The remnants of the euphemistically named State Hospital were just across the driveway, which operation had been thriving mere decades earlier, but that's where his knowledge stopped.

What he did know was that his behavior had turned up the temperature under his boss's seat, which was already wedged between the VBI field force Allard tried to nurture and protect, and the bureaucrats and politicians who constantly pestered him about the expense and value of the new unit.

"I've had a few balls in the air, Bill," Joe explained disingenuously, after they'd exchanged greetings. "These cases don't always come when you're ready for them. But the squad's on top of it, I've just compared notes with Hillstrom, and we've got a growing list of solid suspects."

"What did Hillstrom say?" Allard asked, his demeanor studiously neutral.

Joe knew to expect that—the scientific stuff always got the attention. That's why he'd started with Beverly before reporting here.

"The lab lifted a foreign blood sample from the body. If we find someone to match it, that'll be a big help. Who's been leaning on you, Bill?"

The question was a diversion. Allard was no different than everyone else, preferring his own woes over listening to the other guy's.

Allard rubbed his eyes. He was sitting behind his desk with his feet propped up. "Oh, God, name it and he, she, or it's been pounding on my door. It's not all bad, though—we get a case like yours—all gory and sensational—and it's suddenly hand wringing from everybody, wondering what they can do to help. But I need something to tell them, Joe."

"Word on the street," Joe told him, "is we shouldn't even be running an investigation—it's good riddance to bad rubbish."

"What do you think?"

"My gut tells me we'll be digging up some nasty stuff before we're done, but that it'll be restricted to a small circle. I'm seeing this as a revenge killing that's over and done with, meaning you can tell the worriers that once we solve it, we'll be set."

Allard nodded glumly. "But it's too early to leak anything?"

"Yeah, for the time being. Sorry."

He sighed. "All right. It's better than nothing. But for Christ's sake, keep in touch, okay? I want to pick up the phone and find you on the other end. We got cell phones, pagers, damn near wires in our heads. I'm just asking you to keep 'em turned on."

Joe rose and moved to the door, a whole two paces. "Got it, chief. I'll make Kunkle my personal liaison to your office."

Allard rolled his eyes. "Get out of here."

But once he was headed unscathed down the hallway, Joe half regretted not having been entirely open with Bill, either about Lyn or the case. Both situations seemed so fluid as yet, like complex recipes only half worked out, so he was loath to overthink them. He already feared that he'd soon be facing a personal time management traffic jam; he didn't want or need any additional complications, even from a friend and ally like Bill.

Sam's second visit to Karen Putnam's trailer was less spontaneous, following hours of interviews, computer time, and phone calls to identify the backgrounds and habits of at least most members of the Putnam household.

It wasn't easy. Karen ran a loose operation, as her son had implied, to the point where Sam finally had to estimate that at least eight people called the trailer home, not six.

They were: Karen, of course, and her four children— daughter, Becky Kerr, and sons, Richard Vial, Nicholas King, and Ryan Hatch. Followed by Karen's husband, Todd Putnam; a girlfriend of Ryan's named Maura Scully; and lastly, a man seemingly unrelated to any of them named Dan Kravitz.

The common denominator, it turned out, and the way she'd figured this out, was that each of them appeared in the Spillman database, listing the trailer as a current home address.

Lester actually discovered this in a moment of pure frustration, as he and Ron were helping Sam out. Ron had already lost time consulting tax rolls, welfare lists, voting records, Department of Corrections, and the like, gathering little, when Les simply typed in the trailer's physical location and hit *Search*. The results stunned them all.

Not that every family member had a criminal record. Spillman's strength was that it gave room to almost everyone who'd caught the legal system's eye. If a patrol officer pulled a car over and wrote up the driver for an offense, he was urged to enter the names, dates of birth, and addresses of everybody else aboard, as well. Spillman was an equal opportunity recorder.

On the other hand, a good many of the Putnam clan had done more than simply ride in the wrong car, the worst of them being the nominal leader of the pack, Todd Putnam. He'd just been released from prison after being charged for assault and battery, destruction of private property, being drunk and disorderly, DUI, and resisting arrest—all from a single explosion at a local bar, albeit not the first. Thirty-six years old, Todd had spent half his life incarcerated for not controlling himself, and was, to Sam's thinking, an outstanding exemplar of Karen's poor taste in men.

This research wasn't just to identify who was who; it was also designed to get a handle on each person's habits, or at least reveal where the adults worked. None of the investigators wanted to haul people into the municipal building for formal conversations at this early stage. The trick was to meet with each of them quietly, casually, and preferably privately. Knowing where they might be and when was helpful.

That's why Sam was pulling to a stop at the trailer when she was pretty sure Karen was alone—barring, of course, young Richard, of whose whereabouts she had no clue.

The thought made her pause outside her car, crouch briefly beside the trailer, and gently tap against the criss-crossed slats skirting its foundation.

"Richard?" she asked gently. "You there?"

But there was no response.

Karen's worn-out minivan, however, was parked near the flimsy aluminum stairs leading up to the narrow front door. Sam took in a small breath, straightened her back slightly, and knocked.

The response was less explosive than she'd anticipated. With the resignation of a true veteran, Karen Putnam opened the door, gave Sam a weary look, and said, "I figured you'd be back."

"I was wondering if we could talk."

Putnam stayed where she stood, her hand holding the spring-loaded door open. "Like I got a choice?"

Sam took a chance. "Sure you do, Karen. This is a favor I'm asking. And for what it's worth, I'm sorry I upset you yesterday. Richard's a nice kid; we just naturally started talking."

Karen made a sour face. "He's okay. A little weird, if you ask me—living under the trailer."

Sam smiled. "He's made it nice under there, though. Pretty cozy."

"Yeah—if you're a dog."

There was a pause between them.

"So," Sam tried again. "Can we talk?"

Karen hesitated, finally sighed, and stepped back. "Yeah. What the fuck."

The home Sam entered reminded her of a storeroom with every available surface piled with clothing, boxes, toys, miscellaneous junk, and—finally—a few recognizable items like a TV set, a toaster oven, a phone, and the like. Some of it was precariously perched, the rest packed in as snugly as a lost sock between two pillows. The air smelled of dirty clothes, cat litter, decaying food, and mildew.

"Sit," Karen ordered, gesturing vaguely to a bench seat mounted under the window along the trailer's narrow end.

Sam looked despairingly at the offer. The carpeted floor was filthy, the walls grimy, and the bench already occupied by two bedraggled kittens in a nest of clothes. Sam had no idea what microbial swamp she was sitting in as she gently shooed the cats away, shifted the pile, and gingerly settled down.

"Thanks."

"Wanna drink?"

"No. I'm good."

Karen chose a kitchen chair with a partially ripped plastic cushion. "This is about Wayne, right?"

Sam accepted the offer to dive right in. "How well did you know him?"

Karen lit a cigarette. "What do you think?"

"You were lovers."

She laughed harshly. "Jesus. La-di-dah. I'll guarantee you we weren't that. We were a fast fuck—a way to scratch an itch."

"Your husband know about him?"

"Todd?" she asked, as if it were a trick question. "No way, and I'm a dead woman if you tell him."

"Could Wayne be a dead man because Todd found out on his own?"

Karen wasn't fazed by the suggestion. "Todd's not a killer."

"That's not what you just said."

Karen watched her through the smoke. "I know what I said, and you know goddamn well what I mean."

"Still," Sam pressed her. "Todd is a violent man. Things can start as a fight and go wrong by accident."

But the other woman was already shaking her head.

"He didn't kill him. He didn't even know him, for Christ's sake."

"Prison's the biggest rumor mill there is," Sam told her. "People coming and going all the time; everybody knowing everybody else. They gossip in there like a bunch of old grandmothers."

Karen's expression betrayed her growing boredom. "I told you, if Todd found out, he would've hammered me, not Wayne. Sure as shit, even if he had done Wayne, I would've heard about it, along with the whole neighborhood and every cop in town. Todd is not a man to keep things buttoned up."

Sam knew the type. "When did you last see Wayne?"

Karen laughed again. "It sure wasn't after Todd got out."

"When was that?"

"Two weeks ago."

"And where did you used to get together?"

"Depended. Sometimes it was my van, or his car. He had a friend's apartment we used a couple of times, until the friend walked in on us once. He tried to take me to his place once, but I wouldn't even go in, it was so gross."

"How did you meet the first time?"

Karen took a long, final pull on her cigarette and stubbed it out in an overflowing ashtray. "Wayne and me? At a bar. I was lonely. We got loaded. You know how it goes."

Sadly, that was true. Before Sam and Willy became a couple, she, too, had spent a good many nights at bars far outside Brattleboro, looking for companionship, and usually making the wrong choices.

"How long ago was that?"

Karen looked thoughtful. "Todd went up for a couple of years . . . I guess maybe half that. A year, a little less."

"You get to know him well—I mean socially? His

family life, where he came from, any kids? Things like that?"

She became irritated. "You don't get it, do you? We fucked." She dragged out the last word. "That means not a lot of chitchat. I didn't know and I didn't care. Same for him."

"But he came over here," Sam countered.

That stopped her. Karen studied her for a couple of seconds. "Goddamn Ricky," she then said. "He told you that, right?"

"Not actually," Sam said, hoping to cover for him. "I took a shot and you just confirmed it."

Karen dug around in her pack for another cigarette. "Yeah, he came over a couple of times. I didn't invite him, and I wasn't happy about it."

"You basically just told me one son met him. Did the other kids, too?"

The answer was made mid-inhalation. "Maybe a couple. What do I know?"

"Just curious. But it makes me wonder if you didn't squeeze in one last fast one with Wayne, even after Todd got out."

"Why do you care? I told you I didn't kill him. I didn't have a reason to."

"Maybe someone else did. Do you know of any other girlfriends?"

"Didn't want to know."

Sam decided to leave it at that for the moment, pending additional research. "Okay," she said. "That works for me."

She made her voice more upbeat and conversational. "How many people live here? It's got to be tight."

"The kids, me and Todd, a few others."

Sam already knew of Dan Kravitz and Maura Scully. "Who? I didn't realize you had guests."

Karen waved her cigarette in the air vaguely. "They're

not guests. It's a guy and his daughter—Dan Kravitz and Sally."

Sam nodded, as if completely up to speed. In fact, Willy had told her he actually knew Dan, but there'd never been mention of any daughter. "Oh, yeah. We've bumped into them. How old's Sally now?"

"Fourteen."

Sam shook her head in amazement. "God. Where do you put 'em all?"

"Here and there. Some of them double up."

"Sally and Becky?" Sam asked, mentioning Karen's daughter for the first time.

Karen puckered her mouth. "Becky? No way. She's way too stuck up for that. We put Sally in with Nicky. They seem to like it," she added with a dirty laugh.

"I bet," Sam went along, knowing Nicholas was thirteen. "That work for Dan, too?"

"He's got nothing to complain about."

Sam covered her surprise with a knowing smile. "Damn. You're good, girl. How often do you get it on with him?"

Karen brushed it off. "Now and then."

"Even with Todd back?"

Karen chuckled, rolling her eyes. "Oh, yeah, right. Let's say that Dan's on his own for a while."

Sam returned to an earlier theme, holding up her fingers to count. "So, wow. That's you and Todd, Dan and Sally, the four kids. Eight of you, all in here? Even with Richard camping in the basement, that is something else, especially with Becky not cooperating."

Karen's face darkened. "It's nine, and it's not like we have a choice, is it? You make ends meet—that's something you fucking cops never get, always harassing us for pissant shit."

Sam held up both hands. "Not me. I grew up like this.

That's why I'm asking. This is like home-sweet-home. You do what you gotta do, right?"

"Fucking right."

"But who's the ninth? I miss a kid?"

"That's Maura," Karen said dismissively. "Maura Scully. Ryan's girlfriend. She's kinda one of the family, ever since her own threw her out."

"You're kidding? What's the story there?"

Karen looked disgusted. "It was Maura's stepdad. I don't know the details. Her mom went along with it, though. Worthless piece of trash—do that to your own flesh and blood."

It was a revealing comment. Sam knew too well that women like Karen, for all their faults and self-indulgences, could be fierce when defending their children against threat, even if such protectiveness was wanting day-to-day. It also implied that Karen knew nothing of Wayne's involvement with Becky.

"So, is Becky a bit of a handful?" Sam asked.

As if on cue, Karen's relaxed manner slipped away. "What's it your business?"

Sam raised her eyebrows. "You said it yourself—her sleeping alone, being kind of aloof."

Karen studied her cigarette after taking another pull. "She's a good kid. Just sensitive. Needs more peace and quiet than most."

"Where is she now?"

"In back."

This time, Sam's surprise got the better of her. "She's here? Now?"

"That a crime?"

"No, no. I just thought we were alone, and it's a beautiful day. I noticed Richard was out and about somewhere."

Karen appeared to settle down a notch. "Yeah, well.

You never know with him. He likes pokin' around. Becky keeps more to herself."

"Kids can be that way, sometimes," Sam agreed diplomatically. "Especially if they've had a rough time."

It was another chance for Karen to flare up, but instead she merely grunted. "No shit."

"That's too bad," Sam said softly, her curiosity sharpened. "I'm sorry to hear it."

Karen tossed her head back. "Well, you know what they say, life is shit and then you die."

Sam pushed at the boundary a little, hoping to get lucky. "Sounds like life is shit for Becky, all right."

Unfortunately, she would never know Karen's reaction, for as the latter opened her mouth to speak, a loud, explosive rattling shook the thin walls as a motorcycle with earsplitting pipes pulled into the dooryard.

Karen segued into a broad smile instead, and slid off her chair to open the screen door.

Sighing with disappointment, Sam stood up and waited.

Karen called out as the obnoxious clatter abruptly died, "Ryan. You get that prescription like I asked?"

A querulous male voice shot back. "What do you think? Whose the car belong to?"

"A cop."

"Fuck," came the response. Sam readied herself to leave, recognizing the inevitable.

There were a couple of additional sounds from outside, before a scowling, muscle-bound teenager in a white T-shirt appeared, a dirty canvas bag in one hand and a drugstore sack in the other.

This he thrust at his mother, muttering, "You owe me ten bucks." Then he glared at Sam and demanded, "What do you want?"

"Just having a conversation with your mother."

He looked like he'd just caught a whiff of something noxious. "Don't let the door slap you on the ass," he said, turning left and heading for the back of the trailer.

Karen smiled. "Like father, like son."

Sam nodded, having no doubts about that. She approached the door and her hostess. "I better head out, Karen. I really appreciate the time. Like him or not, Wayne was murdered, so we got to go through the motions. Walk me out?"

Karen looked torn, but didn't say no.

Sam stepped off the stairs and walked to the outside corner of the trailer, five feet from her car, where they were mostly out of sight from both the trailer's windows and the closest neighbor. She didn't want to be interrupted again and figured this was now or never.

"I've got one last favor," she said. "Something you see on TV a lot."

"What?" Karen was cautious.

"Well, part of what we do is rule people out—that's why all the questions. We start with everyone who might've had it in for the dead guy, and then we take them off the list, one by one."

"So?"

"I was just wondering if you'd like to have your name taken off the list for sure."

"You haven't already done that?" she protested. "I keep telling you I didn't kill him."

"I know," Sam agreed, "but I never got to ask what you were doing the night he died."

"I was here," Karen answered, her mood darkening once more. "I got half the family that'll swear to it."

"Cool." Sam rummaged in her bag and extracted a small tubular case. "Then here's the favor. If you'll give me a quick DNA sample—just a swab from inside your cheek—I'll run it by what the crime lab collected, and that'll be that."

Sam pulled a long-handled cotton swab from its sterile container and held it up, her eyebrows raised questioningly. "Takes three seconds and is totally painless."

Karen hesitated. "I don't know . . ."

"It'll sure cut down on our bugging you all the time," Sam suggested.

Karen finally yielded. "What the hell."

Without further comment, Sam had her open her mouth, quickly swabbed inside both her cheeks, and returned the sample to her bag.

"That's it," she said. "I really appreciate it."

Karen was running her tongue around inside her mouth. "Well, I don't. That fucking dirtbag deserved what he got. You should've nailed him for some of the shit he pulled, instead of hassling all of us because someone had the sense to finally kill him."

"What kind of shit?" Sam was caught by the sudden bitterness, and immediately thought of Becky.

Karen pressed her lips together briefly. "He was a bad man. There wasn't nuthin' he wouldn't fuck around with."

Eager for more, Sam still hesitated before asking, "Look, I know we already covered this, but if that's true, then why did you sleep with him?"

"Some of us get what we can," Karen told her resentfully. "I'm not looking for Mr. Right. That's all bullshit. I take what I'm handed, and I took Wayne a few times. My guy's in jail; I just wanted a little comfort now and then, you know? It's not like I was lookin' to marry the man."

Sam shrugged, faking nonchalance, wondering about what seemed hidden just out of sight. "I got it. Just so long as he doesn't bring his shit inside the family, right?"

"He didn't," Karen said reactively. "I saw to that. I

mean, yeah, he came here a couple of times, but not because I invited him . . ."

The door banged open behind them and Ryan appeared on the top step, glowering.

"God damn it, Ma, give it a rest. She's a cop. Every fucking word she says is to fuck you up. Don't you know that? Get your ass in here, for Christ's sake."

He glared at Sam. "And you get the fuck off our property. What're you doin' here anyway?"

Sam stared at him levelly, hiding her disappointment. "I'll tell you if you come down. We'll need to talk anyhow."

He glowered. "I don't got to talk to you."

"Not now, you don't, but you will soon."

"About what?"

Karen had been watching them like a spectator at a tennis game. Now she contributed, "It's Wayne Castine. He was murdered."

Ryan looked disgusted. "Who cares? The guy was a pervert. I hope they tortured him first."

"Where were you Monday night, Ryan?"

"None of your business, cop," he spat at her, and then ducked back inside, yelling, "Ma, get in here. No kidding."

Karen smiled awkwardly. "I better go." She then volunteered, "And Ryan was here Monday night."

Sam nodded, defeated for the time being. "Okay. Take care of yourself. Call me anytime, for any reason, deal?"

All fire gone, Karen lifted her hand halfway and wiggled a couple of fingers in farewell. "Okay. Thanks."

Sam got in behind the wheel of her car, knowing for a fact that she'd be back. There was a lot going on inside that trailer. The problem was going to be puzzling through who knew what—and what they'd done as a result.

CHAPTER 19

Lyn looked up from her magazine as the door banged open in the kitchen.

"Steve?" she called out, surprised.

"Yeah," came the sullen reply.

She pursed her lips. He was in a mood again. She checked their mother, Maria, who was staring, transfixed, at the TV set, its sound reduced to a murmur, and rose to her feet, the magazine still in one hand. As she passed by, her fingers caressed the older woman's frail shoulder, to no reaction.

"Be right back, Mom."

Steve was still in the kitchen, rummaging in the fridge. He straightened, bearing a can of beer. It was nine in the morning.

"What're you doing?" she asked.

"I'm having a beer, all right?" he said belligerently.

"Why?"

" 'Cause I feel like it." He took a swig.

Steve was an alcoholic. Sadly, their mother had seen to that, making him her teenage drinking buddy after Abílo and José had been taken. But he'd never attended AA, had taken only whatever prison counseling he'd been obliged to, and had otherwise relied on Lyn and his own reborn sense of responsibility to stay straight. It had been a lumpy, uneven ride, even if lately she'd believed he'd put the worst of it behind him.

Until now.

She reached out gently and laid a hand on his wrist, stopping him from taking another drink. "Talk to me, Steve," she urged quietly. "What happened?"

"I was ripped off," he said angrily. "I got to the boat this morning to make a delivery, and it was trashed—totally torn apart. What the hell is up with that, huh? What the hell did I do to anybody?" He pulled away from her, tried to drink from the can and missed, spilling some of it onto his shirt.

"*Fuck*," he yelled, and threw the can into the sink. It bounced back out, hit the cabinet overhead, and landed on the floor. Lyn quickly grabbed it and dropped it back into the sink, where it seethed like a school science project.

She took a paper towel and knelt down to clean the floor, not showing how worried she was by his news. All she could think of was Dick Brandhorst and his goons.

"Was it vandalism, or did they really steal something?" she asked the floor.

Steve leaned against the wall, his arms slack by his sides, dejected. "I don't know. I didn't see anything missing."

"So the electronics are okay?" she asked. "The gear? Toolbox?"

He cut her off. "Yeah, yeah. It's there."

She rose from her knees and threw the towel out. "What did the cops say?"

"Nuthin'. I didn't call them."

She looked at him, recomposed for his sake. "Steve, why not? How're we going to collect on the insurance without a police report?"

"They're not gonna do anything," he protested. "They'll just use the chance to search the boat and see if I have any drugs on board."

She walked up to him and took hold of both his shoulders. "Do you?" she asked, her face inches from his.

He stared back at her angrily. "No, I do not."

She nodded, her mind in a turmoil. "Then let's call them, go down there right now, and get this settled. To hell with their attitude. We need to get you up and running again, as quick as we can. What did you do about the delivery you were supposed to make?"

"I gave it to Bobbie. He screwed up his wrist and can't fish for a while."

"Good." She pulled him off the wall and pointed him toward the door, already extracting her cell phone. "Let's go."

"What about Mom?" he asked over his shoulder.

"She's fine. The morning-show airheads're on. She'll be good for hours."

At the dock, she prepared herself for the worst as they approached the boat, but it wasn't until they drew abreast and could see into it that she saw the extent of the mayhem. Charts, logs, equipment, and even some wood splinters lay scattered about from shattered cabinetry, as if someone had thrown everything they found over their shoulders as they went tunneling on a scavenger hunt.

"Jeezum," she muttered. "What a mess."

"Hey there, Lyn," an artificially jocular voice said from behind them.

They turned to see a bearishly built detective from the Gloucester PD coming down the dock. "Hey, Brian," she said.

"Sergeant Wilkinson," Steve joined in, reserved.

Wilkinson smiled at her, but eyed Steve more coolly as he drew near. "Long time no see."

"Yeah," Steve said quietly.

Wilkinson addressed him directly. "Been keeping out of trouble?" Wilkinson had played a direct role in arresting Steve the last time—which hadn't been the latter's first encounter with the law.

"That's not the issue right now, Brian," Lyn said clearly. "Somebody trashed our boat."

Wilkinson let his eyes stay on Steve just a second longer than necessary before turning to Lyn and smiling again. "Yeah, so I can see. Any ideas?"

"None. Steve came down around nine to get ready to make a delivery and found it like this."

Wilkinson placed one foot on the boat's rail and peered inside. "Anything missing?"

"We don't think so, but we didn't want to disturb anything till you got here."

Wilkinson nodded, his professional interest gaining the upper hand and veering him away from Steve, at least temporarily.

"Good thinking." He snapped open the black case he was carrying and extracted a camera and a tape recorder. "Well, let's get started."

Across town from where Sammie Martens was collecting DNA from Karen Putnam, Willy Kunkle parked to the side of a local trucking company's row of loading docks and emerged into the pleasant embrace of a quintessentially New England summer day—sunny, not too hot, a gentle breeze, and the sky a brilliant blue. In other words, for him, a total bore—not that he missed either the recent heat wave or the looming winter months. Those were a pain in the ass.

Frowning, he scanned the scene before him—a broad,

flat, cinder-block warehouse, a scattering of tractor-trailers to one side and empty boxes to another. At one end of the building was an office with some men loitering outside.

The group quieted at his approach, a couple of them knowing who he was. At this level of the employment pyramid, law-enforcement encounters tended to increase, especially during Friday and Saturday nights.

"Detective," one of them said, nodding.

"Alvin Davis," Willy acknowledged, his encyclopedic memory unhesitating. "Everything good at home? Your mom okay?"

Davis's wariness softened a notch at the unexpected question. "Yeah. The chemo kicked the crap out of her, but she's doing good. Thanks."

One of his friends asked, "Your mom sick?"

Alvin merely looked at him pityingly before asking Willy, "What's up? You shopping for bad guys?"

"Nah," Willy reassured him. "Just doing homework—looking to talk to Dan Kravitz. I heard he was working here."

"He in trouble?" one of the men asked.

Willy waved it away. "Not even close. He around?"

Alvin looked a little vague. "He sort of comes and goes, you know? Not like he's really on the books."

The other man said, "He's in the maintenance shed, working on that pile of shit in the back room—probably find a Model T at the bottom of it." He pointed to another concrete building across the yard.

Willy nodded his thanks, told Alvin to give his mother his best, and ambled over to where Dan Kravitz was purportedly practicing archaeology.

Kravitz was the oddball in the Karen Putnam household—he and his daughter Sally. Only an occasional customer of the local PD—mostly for vagrancy—Kravitz kept a low profile, minded his manners, and either stayed out of trouble or never got caught. For Willy, that made him an interesting character, and a valuable informant, which he'd been for over ten years, if only sparingly used.

The shed was cavernous, and—with cinder-block walls and a metal roof—like the inside of a drum. It was also, aside from the resonant clangs of heavy objects being thrown about, empty of life. Adjusting his eyes to the gloom, Willy searched in vain for whoever was making the noise.

He walked farther inside the building, ducking under large pieces of machinery and sidestepping piles of tools and discarded truck parts, until he spied a small opening in the back wall, which was acting like a loudspeaker for all the clatter.

He paused on the threshold to get his bearings, the description from the group at the office suddenly taking form. A pile of unmitigated junk reached halfway to the ceiling, high enough to completely hide anyone in its midst.

The lighting didn't help. A couple of yoked floodlights, screwed into a single overhead outlet high above, threw a ghastly, angular glare across the jagged peaks of accumulated debris, leaving the corners and the floor shrouded in gloom.

Willy quietly entered and followed a narrow path between precariously piled walls, eventually discovering a thin man in work clothes, clean shaven and close-cropped, who was standing like a mythical combatant in the only cleared space between metaphorical good and evil—a mountain of trash on one side, and a smaller pile of salvage on the other.

Both men froze and stared at each other in the abrupt silence, Kravitz with a bent piece of rebar in his hand.

"Hey, Dan," Willy said, his voice sounding orphaned in the stillness.

"Mr. Kunkle," Kravitz responded.

"It's been a while."

"Yes, sir."

"You taking care of yourself?"

"Won't complain."

Willy looked around. "Got a little project here, don't you?"

Kravitz nodded. "Guess I do."

Willy studied him for a few seconds, reacquainting himself with the man. Even in these surroundings, Dan was neat, tucked in, and relatively clean, aside from his hands, of course. His appearance spoke of his demeanor. Reserved and quiet to the point of being withdrawn, Kravitz could hold his own. Of unknown origin, he had slowly, almost invisibly, become a part of Brattleboro's social fabric, if only at its edges, but it was his work ethic and moral stamina that made him stand out. He stuck to every job given to him, worked hard, and—most remarkably—had raised a daughter in the process. This despite a driving personal code that made him refuse all offers of steady employment, or stay at any job beyond its immediate completion. It was a guarantee, given this, that once the contents of this shed were sorted out, Dan Kravitz would move on. No one of Willy's acquaintance knew what made the man tick. He wasn't handicapped, by any means, but he certainly wasn't part of the mainstream, placing him beyond categorization.

"I'm not here to jam you up, Dan," Willy told him. "But I'd like to talk to you for a bit—outside."

Kravitz considered that for a moment, before nodding and placing the rebar carefully on the floor. "Sure."

Willy stood aside to let him pass, again noting his cleanliness—a virtual hallmark. Willy hadn't dealt with him much, and certainly didn't know him well, but he liked the man, in part—not surprisingly—because of his nonconformity.

They wended their way to the main room, and beyond that to the truck yard. There, Willy led them to the relative privacy of the building's far side, where they found seats on a stack of discarded wooden loading pallets.

"I need to ask you a few questions, Dan," Willy began, "but not because of anything you've done—or Sally, for that matter."

Once more, Kravitz nodded. "Okay."

"It's about your living situation," Willy continued. "I hear you're both staying with Karen Putnam."

"Yes."

"Is that working out?"

"Yes."

"No frictions between you and the others? It's pretty jam-packed."

"No."

Willy tried for a little more eloquence. "And Sally?"

He failed. "No."

Willy scratched his neck, rethinking his strategy.

"Okay," he said. "Do you ever say anything except yes and no?"

"Sure."

Willy got up and stepped in so close, their faces were inches apart.

He glared at him until Kravitz allowed for the tiniest of smiles.

Willy sat back down. "I thought so, you asshole. You done fucking with me?"

Kravitz finally conceded. "Yes, Mr. Kunkle."

"Describe the family to me, then, member by member."

Kravitz didn't say a word for a moment, and Willy wondered if his request might actually be challenged. After all, he'd not explained why he was here.

But apparently, Dan was merely thinking. "Karen and Todd are the parents," he began mundanely. "Todd is a frustrated bully. He scares a lot of people by lashing out, but he lacks ambition and brains. He doesn't know how to organize that energy and so can't earn respect except from other losers like himself. Karen is loving, caring, and needy. She doesn't know how to protect herself, and so she turns creature comforts like booze, sex, and cigarettes into temporary shelters from reality."

Willy was staring at him. "Are you shitting me?"

Dan smiled a little wider this time. "What?"

"You know goddamn well what, you little prick. Why do you pretend to be such a dummy when you got all that shit inside you?"

"I don't pretend. That's where people put me because of my lifestyle and my manner."

Willy was fascinated. He sat forward. "Dan, get real. Who do you talk to like that? I mean, a lot of people know you. I have *never* heard anybody say you were anything other than a yup-nope kinda guy. Christ knows, that's all you've ever given me."

"Are you going to blow my cover?"

Willy straightened back up, caught off guard by the question. He thought carefully before answering. "No. That's your point, isn't it?"

"We're alike in some ways," Dan told him. "People think you're a crippled asshole who acts like a Nazi; they think I'm a retarded bum with good manners who knows how to shower. They're wrong, but they do buy what we're selling."

Willy shook his head. "Holy Christ. I thought I'd seen it all. Why open up now, after all these years?"

Dan shrugged. "It was time."

"Damn." Willy spoke wondrously. "I met an accountant like you once, living in a tent by the river. A real mental case, of course, but he'd gone to college, had a home and a family once. He just couldn't handle it. Liked the simple life, as he called it. 'Course, he was a roaring drunk."

Kravitz merely shrugged. "There but for the grace of God," he said softly.

Willy understood all too well, his own disabilities looming large in his mind. "But you ducked the bullet," he commented.

"I may have seen it coming," Kravitz said more fully.

Willy stared off into the distance, wishing he'd had such prescience. "No shit."

He then looked at his companion. "Okay. You're right. I won't tell anybody. But thanks for telling me. That means something. Maybe someday, you'll tell me who you used to be."

Kravitz smiled again. "Sure."

Willy straightened, back on track. "You read the papers at all?"

"Some."

"You hear about the murder?"

"Wayne? Yeah. That's a little beyond just the papers."

"Okay, okay. So, you'd have to be brain-dead. But you knew the guy, right?"

"I met him."

"At the trailer?"

"Yup. He came by once, sniffing around Karen, among others."

Willy eyed him carefully. "Meaning?"

"She wasn't his only interest."

"The kids?"

"The younger ones."

"Any in particular?"

But there, Kravitz shook his head. "Not that I know of. I saw him window-shopping when he came by. My priority was my daughter, but she's too old."

Willy pulled out a notepad and consulted one of its

pages, listing the inhabitants of the Putnam trailer. "So, we're talking Becky, Richard, Nicholas—or is he too old, too? He's thirteen, right?"

"Yes, but he's also pretty immature. Physically, he looks younger. Emotionally, he's got problems. I know more about him because my daughter sleeps with him."

Willy raised his eyebrows. "No shit?"

Kravitz shrugged. "He's a good boy, and Sally takes care of him. He gets the mother going in her, and she's not looking for anything in return."

Willy paused, not wanting to stray too far afield.

"Moral opinions aside," Kravitz volunteered, settling the dilemma, "I'm a lot happier living with people who're off the social radar. They have standards like everybody else, but they can be a lot more generous and less judgmental. Like Karen and her needs."

"And yours?" Willy asked, since the subject was in the air.

"Because she and I share a bed sometimes?" Kravitz asked. "You think I'm taking advantage of her?"

Willy realized he'd been blindsided after all by his own prejudice. He held up his hand. "Okay. My bad. I shouldn't have gone there—and I get your point, or maybe I do. Todd would probably kill you if he knew, so you could argue that Karen's actually taking advantage of you."

Kravitz smiled. "And maybe he wouldn't."

Willy laughed. "You're kidding, right?"

Kravitz joined in. "Yeah, I am."

"Okay," Willy said afterward. "Keep on going. What about the kids?"

"Ryan's the oldest. Last name Hatch. He's seventeen, hates Todd but uses him as a template, and is therefore heading down the same slope fast. You probably already know that, since I'd bet he's all over your computer files."

Willy couldn't disagree. "You think he could kill someone?"

"Now you're pulling my leg," Kravitz commented.

"Point taken. Was he around when Wayne came by?"

"I only saw Wayne once, so I can't say. He wasn't there then."

"Was Wayne ever talked about?"

"Nope."

"Do you know what he was doing with Karen?"

"I assume they were sleeping together."

Willy looked up from his notepad. "How did you feel about that?"

"Jealous?" Kravitz asked. "No. But I did tell her once to watch herself."

"Why?"

"The body language from the kids made it clear none of them liked him. Kids are like animals that way—good warning bells, if anyone's listening."

"How did Karen react?"

Kravitz chuckled. "Same as you. She said I was jealous."

Willy kept going, glancing at his list. "Ryan got a girlfriend?"

"Maura Scully, aged sixteen. Nice girl, bad taste in men, likely to end up like Karen. I don't see her as a killer, if that's your next question."

"Actually," Willy corrected him, "I was going to ask if you think Ryan would confide in her."

Kravitz straightened slightly. "Huh. Good question. I don't know."

"Nicholas?" Willy asked next.

"Nicholas. Right. Last name, King—none of the children are Todd's. Aged thirteen, as mentioned. A good, quiet boy, but differently wired from the others. Sally likes him a lot—tells me that he has nightmares sometimes, and won't tell her what they're about. In fact, he won't tell her much of anything—he's reserved that way; he'll accept what she offers, but doesn't give anything back, which works for her, luckily. I like him, too, but he sets people off—he's pretty compulsive, and does weird stuff, like stands too close, or walks out in the middle of a conversation. He's manically neat, obsessively reads about baseball, is very smart but not interested in good grades. I've seen it before in something called subthreshold autism, but that probably doesn't mean much."

"He a special ed kid?"

The other man tilted his head to one side, considering the question. "He is special, all right, but not diagnosed, as far as I know. His big problem is Ryan—the father substitute, at least in his own eyes. He and Nick fight a lot, with Ryan usually winning. That puts Nick out of the house most of the time, and—if you ask me—probably doing a fair amount of drugs. Throw Todd into the mix and you've got a ton of masculine, Alpha-dog, rub-your-nose-in-it nonsense going on between those four walls, and none of it dealt with well."

"Richard," Willy intoned, moving on.

Kravitz smiled. "Ah, the exception to all that. Richard, the Dreamer. Actually," he interrupted himself, "I should call him Richard, the Thinker, or the Wise Man. Eleven years old, last name Vial, hates being called Richie or Ricky and is called nothing but. There's the most solid of Karen's kids." He added, "And no, I don't think he's a killer."

"What about Dan Kravitz?" Willy asked.

The man in question rose and stretched—his lean, wiry body half a parenthesis. "Could be, I suppose," he answered. "Given the right encouragement. Not this time, though."

Willy pulled out a buccal swab from his pocket and held it up. "Mind if I collect some DNA?" he asked.

"Knock yourself out." Kravitz opened his mouth, un-asked.

Willy got up and quickly collected the sample. "Guess we're almost done."

"For now," Kravitz agreed. "I gotta get back to work."

"You didn't tell me about Becky."

"You didn't ask. Why did you save her for last?"

Willy was surprised, again. This man had a way of sneaking up on him, which Willy took pride in making difficult. "I don't know."

Kravitz let it go. "She's in trouble," he said bluntly. "The only friends she has are Richard and Nicky. Sad to say, she's outgrowing the first, and only interacts with Nicky when he's around or receptive, which isn't often. Her mother thinks she's just being a hormonal kid, but she needs help. Something happened there."

"Like Wayne?"

He tilted his head to one side thoughtfully. "Maybe. I'm not in a place to know, and she covers it up with a smoke screen of standard preteen crap that's worked on Karen—the clothes, the hair, the accessories, the attitude."

"But you think something happened, why?"

"She's not just a preteen. She's withdrawn—repressed, like a ticking bomb, but I've got nothing concrete to go on. How I am is because of my own choice. She's the way she is because I think someone made her that way. Big difference."

Willy nodded, reviewing the conversation in his head before he let Kravitz go. "Thanks, Dan. And I won't spill the beans about you not being a dummy."

"I know." Kravitz walked away from the pile of pallets, heading back to the shed's entrance around the corner.

"Set things right, Mr. Kunkle," he said before disappearing.

"I will."

Willy stayed put for a few minutes alone, half a dozen possibilities rattling around inside his head. Including the question: If Dan Kravitz was the smartest man in that trailer, wouldn't that make him smart enough to steer Willy wrong?

CHAPTER 20

Joe fumbled at his waist, wrestling to extract his pager from behind the car's seat belt, without also steering into the ditch. Keeping the road in sight, he raised the device before his eyes and squinted at the number on the screen. Sammie Martens had text-messaged him, "In case you think all is quiet, your cell phone died."

"Damn," he muttered, and went through the same contortions to free his phone from its clip. Sure enough. He plugged the recharger into the car's cigarette lighter and tried again—no bars.

He glanced at the passing countryside, recognized where he was, and calculated where he'd be able to find a public phone. Cell phones might have been around for a while, but across large swaths of Vermont, poor reception still made sure they were occasional luxuries at best—assuming they'd been recharged.

Fifteen minutes later, he parked across from the pumps of a Mobil station and walked into a minimart.

The clerk glanced up from behind the counter. "Coffee's fresh; bathrooms are in back." He pointed to the far wall.

"Just need a phone," Joe told him, already heading that way.

Sam picked up on the first ring. "Vermont Bureau of Investigation."

"Hey there," Joe said. "Got your page. Sorry about the phone."

"Yeah," she said. "Thought you'd like to know."

"Anything cooking?"

"We're collecting interviews and DNA swabs from the Putnam trailer tribe, doing pretty well. Willy hit a home run with Dan Kravitz, who turned out to know a lot. He gave us a good picture of everybody under that roof. Where are you, anyhow?"

"'Bout an hour out," Joe told her. "I saw Hillstrom and smoothed Allard's feathers a little. Did you just page me to let me know the phone was flat?"

"Not only," Sam reassured him. "It's Lyn. She called a couple of hours ago, then about an hour ago, and a third time just now. Never left a message, but she was pretty worked up the last time. You guys okay?"

"Yeah," Joe said absentmindedly, his brain already racing. "She's got some family problems I've been helping with. No big deal. I guess something blew up. I'll give her a call."

"You got it," Sammie said. "See ya soon."

Joe hung up, pulled out a small address book, and looked up Steve's number in Gloucester.

His voice was tense. "Yeah?"

"Steve? It's Joe."

"Where you been, man?"

"My cell phone died. What's going on?"

"Somebody trashed my boat. Ripped it all to hell."

"Is everyone okay?"

"Yeah. It happened last night."

"Did you call the police?"

"Lot of good that did. Wilkinson spent more time looking for what I might be smuggling than trying to find out who did it."

"Brian Wilkinson?"

"Yeah. You know him?"

"Back when I first met your sister. So he didn't give you much hope?"

"He didn't give me much anything. Guy's a loser."

Joe didn't pursue that. "I'm really sorry, Steve. Is Lyn there?"

Steve's voice grew more anxious still. "That's the point, Joe. She's gone. She tried calling you a bunch of times, and then she split."

Joe gripped the phone tighter. "What do you mean? Where?"

"I don't know. She just said she had to give somebody a piece of her mind and she took off. Why didn't you have your phone on, man?"

Joe didn't bother explaining himself again. Lyn's brother was no monument to rational stability, despite his recent improvement, and Joe knew that the additional pressure of their mother's condition was already challenge enough.

"Steve," he said. "How's everything else? Is Maria okay?"

"She's fine. She's got the TV."

"And other than the boat, you haven't been harassed?"

"No. Why should I be?"

Joe ignored him. "Why do you think you were targeted?"

"I don't know that, either. I figure some of the assholes I used to hang with. If that's true, they're gonna pay."

That told Joe that Lyn hadn't explained anything to him. "One step at a time, Steve," he counseled. "Was anything missing? Maybe it was thieves."

"No way. It was weird. They tore stuff apart, like some of the cabinets, but they didn't take anything."

"They were looking for something, maybe?"

"Could be. The boat was with a drug runner for years. He mighta stashed stuff on board."

Joe checked his watch. "All right. I'll call Lyn on her cell and . . ."

"Won't work," Steve interrupted. "She didn't take it. She couldn't find it when she was leaving."

Naturally, Joe thought. "Okay, not to worry. I have a vague idea where she might be headed. I'll see if I can't find her—right now. I'll have my cell recharging in the car, so you should be able to reach me if she calls or anything develops. In the meantime—and I don't want to alarm you or anything—but I think you and Maria should go somewhere to stay for a while. Just a couple of days."

"What? Why?"

"Just to be on the safe side. I'm mostly thinking of Maria," he lied. "You don't want her shaken up any more than necessary."

"By what?"

"I'm just being cautious—since we don't know what they were after on the boat."

Steve moaned softly. "Oh, shit."

"Steve," Joe spoke with authority. "Don't get worked up. Just do it, okay? I'll pay for it later, but for the moment, go to a motel and stick her in front of a TV there, all right?"

"I hate this."

"I know, but it'll make me feel better knowing you two are in a safe place. So, do this, okay? No screwing around?"

"Yeah. Okay."

"Good man. I'll let you know as soon as I get hold of Lyn. What motel will you go to?"

"The Clipper Ship, I guess."

"Got it."

Joe hung up and flipped through his address book one last time.

"Maine Drug Enforcement Agency. How may I direct your call?" a female voice asked him a minute later.

"Cathy Lawless, please," Joe told her. "Tell her it's Joe Gunther, Vermont Bureau of Investigation."

In a style not unlike Sammie's, Cathy picked up the phone almost immediately. She'd been working the same drug case where Joe had stumbled across the Silva lobster boat.

"Joe," she said. "Don't tell me you're headed this way again?"

"Not officially, Cathy, but I am fishing for a favor."

"Shoot."

"I'd like whoever's out there to keep an eye peeled for an '02 Honda Civic, dark blue, with Grateful Dead and Planned Parenthood bumper stickers next to the right taillight. Vermont registration." He gave her the plate number.

"Who is this?"

"Name is Lyn Silva."

Cathy didn't miss the connection. She had a cop's memory and a suspicious mind. "Your girlfriend? What's going on?"

"It's long and complicated and I have to get going," Joe told her. "This is more along the lines of a protective thing. Somebody trashed the family lobster boat; we don't know why, and I'm afraid she might be in danger."

"This tie into Wellman Beale?"

Joe surely hoped it didn't. "I don't know, Cathy. Anything's possible. What happened to him?"

"He's out," she said bluntly. "Back on his island, and probably back to running drugs. Is this a case yet, Joe? I mean on the books?"

"No. The Gloucester PD has the vandalism of the boat, but that's it, and they probably think it's teenagers."

"And you know it's not?"

He demurred. "My instincts say it's not, but I don't know, and I gotta go. I'll call you when I hit Maine, Cathy. I promise. I'm aiming for Bangor, which is where I think she's gone, in case that helps. Just spread the word to keep an eye out for her and let me know if anyone gets lucky. You still have my cell number?"

"Oh, yeah."

"Okay. Thanks. See you soon."

Her response was suitably ironic. "I can hardly wait."

Lyn was not headed for Bangor. That had been her initial thought, but the farther she drove up the interstate, the more she began rethinking the idea. Dick Brandhorst, who was clearly behind the vandalism of *The Silva Lining*, was no doubt looking for her to react exactly the way she was—or had been. The better idea, Lyn saw now, was to stop playing his game. Joe had suggested turning the tables by getting him to expose why he was interested in her. But with the vandalism of the boat, and the implied threat to her family, Lyn was more inclined to embark on a plan wholly her own—something direct, unequivocal, and which right now was feeling immensely more satisfying.

She'd tried several times to share this new idea with Joe, but failing in that, she'd yielded to impatience and an oddly stimulating sense of higher mission. Perhaps something of her father's and brother's reckless spirit was lurking inside after all, but whatever the source, she was going for straightforward retaliation. And not against Brandhorst, either; she had no clue what his actual role was, nor was she sure she cared. She was shooting higher. Joe had mentioned that Wellman Beale lived on an island off of Jonesport, Maine. As far as she could figure, Beale was the one solid connection to José and Abílo's disappearance, even if the authorities hadn't been able to act on it.

She unconsciously reached out to the passenger seat beside her and felt for her father's old nine-millimeter pistol she had tucked into her bag.

Well, she wasn't an authority. And she wasn't bound by their rules.

CHAPTER 21

Lester was waiting in his car outside Parole and Probation. The parking lot overlooked a restaurant and a small marina, while the Department of Corrections had chosen a bright pink building that had once housed a chocolate factory. All told, it was an unexpectedly pretty spot, at the confluence of the West and Connecticut rivers—a shallow flooded area called the Retreat Meadows—a favorite of anglers and boaters in the summer, and skaters during the cold months. Les himself had driven the family down from Springfield a couple of times for winter outings, enjoying how Brattleboro, unlike his hometown, continually found ways for its populace to engage in its rural surroundings, often just a stone's throw from the business district.

Now, of course, it was warm and sunny—a far cry from skating or ice fishing weather—and he had the window down to enjoy the breeze, waiting for his unsuspecting interview subject to appear from a scheduled meeting with his parole officer.

Les had been here for under ten minutes, and was just starting to unwind and let the sunshine sink in, when he saw a big man in a T-shirt step into the bright light.

Karen Putnam's husband, Todd, fresh from jail, squinted as he fumbled for the dark glasses hooked into the crew neck of his shirt. He was a muscular man, dressed in clothes one size too small, but he'd slacked off enough to ruin the overall effect—the gut struggling not to hide the belt buckle, the back of his tattooed arms flapping just a little as he moved. The cheeks beneath the glasses were slightly gaunt, the big shoulders a bit drooped. While clearly still the bull in his own mind, he appeared to be drifting toward the edge of the pasture.

Curious about what all this fading testosterone might become during a delicate conversation, Les opened his car door, hitched his gun more comfortably under his jacket, and strolled across the lot to meet the man.

"Hi," he said, drawing near. "You Todd Putnam?"

Putnam hooked his thumbs in his belt, swelling his arms slightly. "Maybe."

Les didn't offer his hand, but kept his tone friendly. "Lester Spinney, I'm from VBI."

"Good for you."

"You got a minute?"

"I got a choice?"

"Sure," Lester said agreeably. "You want to set up a better time?"

Putnam put on a show of considering the offer, glancing off into the distance as if contemplating some calendar in the sky.

"Okay," he finally said.

Spinney pointed to a weather-beaten wooden picnic table at one end of the lot. "Let's sit."

He didn't give Putnam an option, leading the way. He wanted the man sitting, his legs trapped between a table and a bench seat, and far from his own car, which was now parked beyond Lester's. Spinney was tall and could be fast, but this man had thirty pounds on him, and a reputation for using them—any signs of aging notwithstanding.

"You aware of the Wayne Castine killing?" Les asked after Todd had settled in place.

Putnam pulled a crumpled pack of cigarettes from his jeans pocket and extracted one of its mangled denizens.

"Yeah."

"You know the man?"

A lighter appeared from the other pocket. "Nope."

"You ever hear about him before he was killed?"

The cigarette was carefully placed between his lips before Putnam ignited the lighter and deeply inhaled the first pull.

"Nope," he exhaled.

Lester smiled. "How'd you hear about his murder?"

"News."

"Not at home?"

That made him pause. He moved his gaze from the smoke coming off the cigarette's tip to Lester's face. "What?"

"You didn't hear about it at home?"

His eyes narrowed. "Why would I?"

"He's been to the trailer. I assumed there'd been some discussion about it."

Lester's instincts worked faster than his brain, making him lean backward before he even saw the fist coming. As a result, Putnam's swing fell short, just grazing Lester's nose as he tipped over and fell off his bench.

"You son of a bitch," he heard the man snarl, and fully expected him to come vaulting over the table.

Instead, Putnam added, "I'll kill that whore," swiveled away from the picnic table with surprising ease, and started to run.

"Damn," Lester muttered, "not another one."

He rolled to his feet and gave chase, pulling his radio free at the same time.

The parking lot was located on a flat stretch of land, between the water and Brattleboro's busy "miracle mile," named the Putney Road. Putnam headed for the latter, straight up the embankment.

Slipping on the grass in his city shoes, Spinney breathlessly gave dispatch a quick call for help, amazed at both his luck at not getting clocked this time, and the stupidity of parolees who were prone to hitting cops and then running for it.

"Putnam," he shouted. "Stop, for Chrissake."

It didn't do any good. Putnam reached the Putney Road and a solid line of traffic, and cut right, parallel across the bridge and toward downtown, Spinney a hundred feet behind him.

Lester considered simply letting him run. Todd Putnam wasn't a public menace, hadn't done any damage to Les, and would be easy to find, given his parting words.

But that, of course, was the catch—Putnam was guaranteed to harm his wife if he found her before he was caught. Plus, Spinney had to admit, he was officially irate.

They pounded down the length of the bridge, Spinney's better condition and lighter weight shortening the distance between them. Sensing this, and perhaps hoping for better luck over broken ground, Putnam took advantage of a small break in the traffic to cut between two cars and switch to the east side of the road, closer to the railroad tracks running parallel.

Lester did the same, loping along at a steady gait, pacing himself more to outlast the other man than to actually catch up to him. Spinney had been in enough chases to appreciate everyone being too tired to fight in the end.

But Putnam was clearly aware of his own flagging energy. At the end of the bridge, still hugging the road, he saw a chance to improve his odds. At a pull-off equipped with a war memorial and a flagpole, Putnam again cut left, and headed directly east, this time straight for the railroad tracks perched on an elevated berm.

"Shit," Lester muttered, hearing sirens approach. He retrieved his radio and issued a quick update as he followed suit, now fifty feet to the rear.

"God damn it, Todd," he then shouted. "You got nowhere to go."

Putnam ignored him, his feet digging into the slope bordering the tracks above.

Neither one of them saw or heard the train.

It was on them, out of the south, like a mechanical nightmare, in the proverbial blink of an eye. All noise and blur and heart-stopping surprise.

Todd Putnam had both hands resting on the near track, lifting himself up off the embankment, when he saw it just to his right—a monster bearing down.

As the engine's air horn exploded in warning, he threw himself backward, straightening briefly like a man surrendering, before being blown back down the slope onto Spinney by the passing gust of wind.

Both men, in a tight embrace, rolled to the bottom just as two patrol cars came skidding to a stop nearby.

For a moment, numbed and deafened, everyone froze, suspended in time.

And then, it was over. The short passenger train vanished across its own bridge headed north, and Lester and Putnam were left sprawled like two tired wrestlers.

As two uniformed cops approached with guns drawn, Lester reacted first, pushing Putnam away from him.

"Todd, you sorry son of a bitch. What the fuck were you thinking?"

Putnam just lay there, staring up at the sky, blinking.

"Did you see that?" he asked quietly.

Lester rubbed his face with both hands and got to his feet. The cops holstered their weapons and began chuckling nervously.

"Yeah," Lester conceded. "I did. And you're under arrest."

Never fond of using a phone while driving, Joe was becoming a master at it. With the cell plugged into his cigarette lighter, he step-by-step shepherded Steve and Maria Silva through the move into a local motel, all the while aiming his car toward Bangor. Lyn had remained out of touch, and Joe was by now convinced that—angered and adrenalized—she'd returned to Bangor to beard Dick Brandhorst in his den.

With that in mind, he also called Cathy Lawless back, as promised, and more fully explained why he was headed to Maine. He mentioned the name Dick Brandhorst.

He heard her typing into a computer on the other end.

"We have him as a person-of-interest on a bunch of cases," she reported. "Always on the money side of things."

"No record?"

"Nope, which is probably how he can function as a financial advisor. I don't know that side of the law very well, but I'd guess getting a license for a job like that would be tricky with a rap sheet. You really think Lyn's headed there to confront him? You don't have any proof he trashed the boat, do you?"

"Not that I know of," Joe conceded. "And I know what you're thinking."

She laughed. "That would be a first for almost anybody. What's that?"

"That Lyn's the one likely to get arrested if she hands the guy his head."

"It crossed my mind," Cathy agreed. "How 'bout I call

in a favor and have one of Bangor's finest keep an eye peeled for her at Brandhorst's office door?"

Joe hesitated, fearful of the reaction once Lyn found out. He equivocated. "Just to watch and not stop her? You got a deal. Have them call me as soon as she's spotted and we can go from there."

"Right." Cathy's voice was ironic. "Just in case she's carrying flowers instead of a sledgehammer? I'll tell them to use their own discretion."

Lyn killed her engine in a parking lot near the Coast Guard station at the base of the Moosabec Reach Bridge in West Jonesport, and slung her gun-weighted bag over her shoulder before stepping out into the evening's salt-scented warmth.

She was tired and nervous. Her first stop, in Jonesport proper, had predictably been a bar—akin to the one in Gloucester—where, true to expectations, she'd found the local version of her own Harry Martin, and asked him how to find Wellman Beale.

That part hadn't been difficult. Her veiled rationale had been commercial, which no one in that setting was going to obstruct—especially coming from an attractive woman.

However, she also understood the potential fallout of her approach. She might get what she'd come for—a meeting time and place, arranged by a go-between—but it was guaranteed to be accompanied by a follow-up phone call she'd never witness, concerning details she wished she knew.

She looked around, half expecting a dark-windowed sedan with its engine idling, but all she got was a variation on the scenery she'd grown up with—water, boats, gulls overhead, islands in the distance, and that near cloying odor of most working-class maritime harbors, of rotting fish, diesel oil, and brine. The one striking variation was the bridge, leaping from the mainland to an island, two football fields offshore—a single slab of concrete, supported by a string of support piers.

At long last, perhaps because of the absence of any threat, she also began to experience real fear settling in.

There was a pay phone by the railing overlooking the docks. Without hope of success, she crossed over to it and dialed Joe's cell number.

"Hello?"

Her eyes widened with relief. "Joe. You're there."

He sounded equally relieved. "Thank God. Lyn. I'm heading your way. I'm already in Maine. Where *are* you?"

"At a pay phone in Jonesport, near the Coast Guard station. What's been wrong with your cell?"

"It died and I didn't notice. I'm really sorry. I talked to Steve and got the lowdown, but he had no idea where you'd gone and said you'd lost your own phone. I had him take your mom to a motel for a while, just to be safe, but what happened? Why're you in Jonesport?"

"I got mad," she admitted, at once embarrassed and relieved. "The whole thing with Steve's boat finally pushed me over the edge. It was like a violation."

She could almost hear him trying to connect the dots. "And so you called that cell phone? The number Brandhorst gave you? That brought you to Jonesport?"

Now that she was admitting it out loud, she almost cringed as she explained, "No, I decided to blow off the whole Brandhorst gambling debt thing—that sort of misses the point, anyhow. I'm here to meet Wellman Beale—try to settle what happened to my dad and José."

She half expected an explosion from the other end. Instead, there was another measured silence, followed by his calm, almost soothing voice asking, "Lyn, have you hooked up with him yet?"

"No, I just got here."

"He's a bad guy," Joe said quietly. "And I can't be but an hour or two out by now. How 'bout some company?"

She smiled at his wording. It was like he was coaxing someone back off the edge of a windowsill.

"It's a deal," she said gratefully. "To be honest, I was having second thoughts."

"I'm on my way," he told her. "Just stay put and keep low till I get there. See you in a bit."

Comforted, she replaced the phone, just as a voice said behind her, "You Lyn?"

Startled, she whirled around to find a large, bulky man with a broad face, bland to the point of caricature. His hint of a smile struck her as utterly threatening.

"Who're you?" she asked.

"You're looking for me," he answered her. "You stupid, or trying to be smart?"

"Mr. Beale?"

His eyebrows rose. "Mr. Beale? I like that." He reached out and took her elbow.

She immediately pulled away. "What're you doing?"

The smile faded. "You wanted to meet? I got a boat over there; couple of comfortable chairs. But time's money, and now's the time. Now or never, like they say."

She pointed to a bench by the railing overlooking the docks. "How 'bout there?"

"How 'bout you kiss my ass?"

She stared at him. A pretty bad guy, Joe had said. She had no doubts now.

Surprising her, Beale took a step back, turned, and began walking away, saying only, "Suit yourself."

"Wait," she blurted, before she could stop herself.

But he didn't, forcing her to abandon the phone kiosk and follow him.

"Why not the bench?" she asked the back of his bowling

ball–shaped head. "I'm just not comfortable wandering off with you."

He kept walking silently, heading for a ramp leading down to the docks.

She gave up, deciding to at least go as far as his boat, if only to see what the setup might be.

In single file, they reached water level, chose a dock that projected out at ninety degrees, and traveled its length to the very end, where a forty-eight-foot boat with a fully enclosed wheelhouse lay gently bobbing.

Without hesitating or looking back, Beale lightly hopped into the stern and entered the wheelhouse, leaving Lyn standing uncertainly on the dock.

He stuck his head back out briefly. "You coming? I'm gonna get a beer. You want anything?"

He was already gone as she answered, "No, thanks."

Looking through the wheelhouse windows, she saw him cross to the cabin bulkhead near the bow, descend the ladder, and vanish from sight.

She waited a moment, unsure, and then gingerly placed one sneakered foot on the boat's rail, feeling its familiar give and take as the hull rode the gentle water. She glanced around, taking in the Moosabec Reach Bridge again, now looming overhead and looking much bigger than before. Just beyond it, the largest of the Coast Guard boats was slipping free of its moorings, heading out to sea, its trim and uniformed crew bustling about.

She wished they were coming over here.

Reluctantly, she stepped onto the stern and looked around. All the familiar trappings were in place, minus the usual stacks of lobster pots. But the bait barrel, the ropes and gaffs, and the snatch block were all familiar, comforting sights. It was cleaner than she was used to— not really like a working boat—but there was nothing wrong about it, either.

She poked her head into the wheelhouse. This was pretty fancy—benches, fine cabinetry, a fridge and microwave, all the latest electronics. It made *The Silva Lining* look like a rowboat. She could hear her lackadaisical host banging around in the cabin, whistling to himself—a sound she found at odds with her first impression of him, and therefore a little soothing.

She stepped fully into the wheelhouse. "Mr. Beale?"

The whistling continued, as if he hadn't heard her, which she found believable, depending on what he was doing down there.

She approached the top of the ladder and squatted down to see into the dimly lit cabin.

"Mr. Beale?"

He came out at her like a shark leaping out of the sea, exploding from the darkness behind him, his large hand open and his powerful fingers grasping like teeth. He seized the front of her T-shirt and dragged her like a duffel bag straight down the ladder, twisting her around so that her heels bounced on the steps, her bag went flying, and her shoulder blades scraped the decking. She stared up at his empty eyes as he hauled her to the front of the cabin, using her shirt and brassiere like a suitcase handle and lifting them up around her neck.

He dropped her in a pile and stepped away as she scrambled to flatten her back against a bunk base, pulling her clothes down in a panic and tucking in her knees. There was a gun in his other hand.

The thin smile had returned. "Don't be so full of yourself. I've seen better tits before."

"What do you want?" she asked, hating the tremor she heard in her voice.

"What do *I* want? You're the one snooping around. Not that it matters. We'll talk later. Stretch out on the floor and roll over."

"What're you going to do?"

He laughed. "I'm gonna pull your clothes off and butt-fuck you. Is that what you want?"

She tightened up into an even smaller ball.

But he shook his head. "Fuckin' broads. Always thinking we want to jump your bones. Just roll over, girlie. I'm gonna tie you up and gag you till we get out of port. You're too fuckin' skinny for me, anyhow."

He reached out to a shelf near his head and retrieved a roll of duct tape.

"I won't make any noise or try to escape," she told him, eyeing the tape.

"You bet your ass, you won't," he agreed. "Now roll over like I said, or I'll do it myself and maybe forget that I don't like 'em skinny."

"Where're we going? Your island?"

He paused and studied her. "You know about that, huh? I figured as much. Nah. We're going for a little trip up north. You ever been to Lubec?"

"No."

"Right on the border. Easternmost point of the United States—the only thing they got to brag about. Lubec's where the country runs out of gas; looks it, too. Now roll over before I get mad."

Unwillingly, she straightened out and did as requested. Wincing as he knelt down, Beale straddled her hips and taped her hands together.

"The floor hurt?" he asked after he'd finished.

She nodded.

Keeping her face down, he slipped one hand through her legs and around to the front of her crotch and the other between her breasts, and lifted her effortlessly, despite her squirming, onto one of the berths lining the hull.

"There," he said. "Stay put and mind your manners. I hear a peep out of you while I'm at the wheel, and I'll hurt you like you never dreamed." He put his face inches from hers. "You believe I can do that?"

She nodded once more.

He straightened. "Fuckin' A—wouldn't be the first time."

He looked around, noticed the bag on the bottom step, and picked it up. He weighed it in his hand thoughtfully, reached inside, and extracted her nine-millimeter. "Cute," he said before finally heading up the ladder and locking the bulkhead behind him.

In a matter of minutes, the powerful engine came alive in a roar, and they headed out to sea.

All Lyn could think of was Joe. And what an idiot she'd been.

CHAPTER 22

"Where you been, boss?" Sammie asked. "We were expecting you hours ago."

With his free hand, Joe scratched his aching head in frustration, staring at the pay phone Lyn must have used to call him earlier. It was dark now, and there was no sign of her anywhere.

"I got held up. What've you got?"

There was a pause from the other end as Sam weighed this uncharacteristic terseness.

"Sorry," he added. "Bad day."

"Anything I can do?"

"No. I'm okay. Just distracted."

"More family stuff?"

His irritation flared. "What've you got, Sam?"

He had her attention. In all their years together, he'd probably snapped twice at her like that. At most.

"Got it, boss. Sorry. I'll start with the headline grabber, in case someone ambushes you with it. Les was interviewing Todd Putnam outside the P and P office on Putney Road when Todd took off, presumably to kill his wife because of Les's inference that something was going on between Karen and Wayne Castine. Long story short, Les gave chase and they were almost hit by a train."

Joe rolled his eyes toward the starlit sky. "*What?* You are shitting me. Is Les okay?"

"He's fine. They're both fine. Todd ran across the road and up the railroad embankment, with Les in hot pursuit. Neither one of them heard or saw the northbound train until it basically wiped Todd's nose for him. But it missed and we put him in custody."

"Jesus," Joe muttered, both in reaction to the story, and because he was so distant from them—and under less than legitimate circumstances. Rationally, he knew he couldn't have done anything had he been standing beside Lester at the time. But these people were like family to him, as close to his heart as Lyn, if in a totally different way, and he was feeling guilty and angry that he'd been AWOL when he shouldn't have been.

"You're sure he's okay?" he repeated. "No after-effect aches or pains? He did get whacked by that jerk on Manor Court, remember."

"He's fine, boss," Sam reassured him. "I promise."

"All right, all right." Joe let it go.

"It will get on the news, though," she continued. "It was rush hour, and a bunch of commuters saw it from the road. I called the paper and gave them our version, to head off any nosiness. I hope it'll hold them."

"Okay," he accepted. He began walking the length of the parking lot, looking for anything that might tell him of Lyn's whereabouts. "What else?"

"We did interview Todd afterward. He's pissed enough to kill Wayne now, but he swears he didn't know about the affair until Les spilled the beans."

"Lester actually *told* him about that?" Joe asked incredulously.

"No, no. I wondered the same thing. Les only mentioned that Wayne had been to the trailer. Todd just jumped to the right conclusion, probably because he and Karen have been there before. I mean, we already know about her habits—any port in a storm. If you ask me, Todd probably plays by the same rules. Anyhow, he has an alibi for the night Wayne was killed. Plus, we got something else."

"What?"

"Remember that blood sample the crime lab collected off Wayne's body? The one that wasn't his?"

"Right," Joe said. "They sent it out to be expanded, or whatever. The one with the six loci—belongs to a male."

"Right. Well, to figure out either who that is or who he's related to, we've been collecting DNA from everyone we can who lives in that trailer, which so far includes Todd, his wife, and Dan Kravitz. Willy also got a sample from Sally, Dan's daughter. The punch line is that whoever that blood belongs to, he's related to Karen—that much they can already tell, even before the expansion. So, we're now looking at one of the three sons."

Joe stopped dead in his tracks, his eyes straight ahead.

In the ensuing silence, Sam asked, "Boss? You there?"

"Yeah," he answered dully.

"You okay? You sound weird."

"Fine." He was staring at Lyn's empty car.

Sam wasn't sure. "Okay," she said slowly. "Well, we think that gives us enough for a court order, right? I mean that's the way we'd like to go, so we can round up the rest of the family's DNA and maybe nail down a solid suspect."

Joe was circling the car slowly, studying it for anything unusual. "Sounds good. Go for it."

"I don't see little Richard playing a part," Sam continued. "Which leaves Nicky or Ryan."

Joe reached out and tugged at the driver's door. It was locked. "Damn."

"What?"

"Nothing," he told her. "Include a cut in the warrant."

"A cut?"

Joe scowled, the distraction with Lyn's car making him want to simply throw the cell phone into the harbor. "A cut, a wound," he said testily. "Something to explain why the blood was on the corpse in the first place."

He could tell he'd brought her up short.

"Right. Got it."

"It's not a great blood sample," he explained. "And it may not improve with the mini-STR expansion, which means we'll need more than just DNA to make a case stick."

"Like a cut," she said. "No problem."

"Keep in mind," he added, virtually thinking on autopilot, "*that* won't be enough, either. When did the bloodstain get there? Before the killing? Afterward? It doesn't necessarily point to the killer. We know it belongs to a male, but that may not be relevant, and there may be others that the lab missed. Plus, what I'm calling a cut could've been a nose bleed, meaning you won't be able to find it now."

"I understand."

"And last as well as least, probably, have we absolutely ruled out all the other males related to Karen? Does she have a brother in town we don't know about yet? Or a father or uncle? We've still a long way to go with just the standard case-building here."

She was clearly taking notes by now. "Right, right."

"You know all this shit," he concluded. "Call me back when you get more."

She hesitated before asking, "You're not coming in anytime soon?"

He thought about lying, bringing her into his turmoil. She deserved more than he was giving her. They all did.

"No," he said. "Keep in touch."

He closed the phone, pocketed it, and pressed both his hands against his throbbing temples. God damn it, Lyn. Where *are* you?

Lyn was looking at Wellman Beale staring down at her, after an engine-thrumming, two-hour voyage across smooth seas. Ever since childhood, she'd preferred any and all of the discomforts of an open deck to the diesel-tainted warmth of a fishing boat's cabin. Age had done nothing to change that.

"What now?" she asked querulously, her nausea as yet unresponsive to the engine's silence. She'd managed to reposition herself, so that she was no longer supine. She was now sitting up, with her back against the paneling.

His eyes hardened. "Watch it. I could stop being Mr. Nice Guy."

She laughed sharply. "Right. Pardon the hell out of me. Wouldn't want you to kidnap me or anything."

In the few seconds that they glared at each other, she began wondering how far she could push the man, and even why, aside from pure rage.

For the moment, he merely shook his head and muttered, "Fucking broads—what monster even invented you bitches?"

"Problems with Mommy?" she shot back without thinking.

He leaned into her fast as she mentally kicked herself, placing his hand flat against her chest, and pressing her hard against the hull.

"Don't think for a goddamn minute that if I threw you overboard right now, anybody would know or care."

She knew she should now keep quiet, but his words proved too provocative.

"That's right," she said, trying to breathe. " 'Cause you've had practice with that, haven't you?"

He straightened, looking baffled. "What the fuck is your problem?"

"You're the one with the problem," she countered. "I just wanted to talk, but . . ."

"Oh, bullshit," he interrupted her. "I know exactly what you want. You walk into a biker bar, say your name is Silva and that you want a meet, and you think I can't put that together? I have been harassed by the cops about this crap, they sicced the prosecutor onto me, and when that didn't stick, they even spilled it to some fucking reporter, who went creeping around asking all kinds of questions. I have just about had it with the name Silva."

"You killed my father and my brother," she said, fixing him with her eyes.

He returned the look. "You are full of shit."

He briefly made fists of his hands, his whole body a study of frustration, and she thought he might beat her. He fished into his back pocket instead, extracted a switchblade, and sprang it open with an ominous snap.

Lyn felt her stomach turn over.

"Turn around," he ordered. "We're going ashore."

Relieved, she cooperated, allowing him to cut the tape from her wrists.

"Stand up and keep your yap shut," he continued, pushing her toward the ladder. "And I mean it, not one word."

They climbed up into the darkened wheelhouse, and from there to the stern, where Lyn discovered that they were tied up on the edge of a small, almost empty town. She looked around, trying to distinguish its features by a line of streetlights stretching out beyond the end of the landing. To the left of them were several more docks, the mysteriously dark and tranquil oil-black water of the bay, and in the distance—at a ninety-degree angle—a large humpbacked bridge, arcing to the opposite shore. This had to be Lubec, complete with its span to Canada. In fact, she now remembered from planning those vacation trips with her father, the bridge was actually connected to Campobello Island, made famous as the summer retreat of Franklin Roosevelt. Back in those days, however, Abílo Silva had only talked about Lubec. They'd never been here as a family.

"Come on, come on." Beale pushed her again, getting her to climb the rail, latch on to a ladder, and pull herself up.

She strolled to where the dock met the road, and read on a sign that the street straight ahead was predictably named Water Street. There was a restaurant nearby, barely populated, a few cars parked by the curb, and only one pedestrian, halfway down the block and walking away.

"Go right," Beale ordered in a low voice, prodding her with a discreetly held gun.

A second sign told her they were actually on Commercial Street, which she now made an effort to memorize. Out in the gloom of the inner bay, to her right, she could barely make out some distant fish pens—gigantic, round cages—used to raise domestic salmon. Lubec was at the base of the Bay of Fundy, with one of the world's greatest tidal exchanges—crucial for flushing the wire pens free of the waste of thousands of penned-up fish.

This town, she recalled, steadying herself mentally, had once thrived on the fishing business, then the lobster trade, then the sea urchin harvest, and now domestic salmon, all with ever-diminishing returns for the general population. No wonder Lubec felt like a ghost town—it was far from any of its former glories.

It was also quickly slipping from her sight. As Beale kept prodding her down the street, the lights of the main drag dropped back, as did the distant view of the bridge, until they were walking completely alone, in the virtual darkness, their path illuminated only by the moon above.

They were heading for a derelict collection of abandoned buildings—either an old fish-packing factory or some other kind of plant.

"What are you doing?" she asked nervously.

"Shut up."

A hundred feet farther on, he guided her off the street, down a dirt embankment, and up against the wall of one of the low buildings.

"Stay." Beale pulled a key from his pocket and fitted it to a padlock hanging from a rough plywood door cut into the wall. He removed the lock, slid back the hasp, and kicked the door open with his foot.

"Go."

She went cautiously, completely blind in the total darkness.

A sudden narrow shaft of light shot forth from a small flashlight in his hand. "Down that way."

She could make out a series of rooms ahead, all interconnected via a string of aligned doorways. There was rusted and broken equipment everywhere, and a thick carpet of debris and trash underfoot.

"What're you going to do?" she asked again.

He grabbed her hair from behind and pulled her head back, speaking directly into her ear. "I told you to shut the fuck up. Walk."

Still holding her hair, he propelled her through the first door, making her stumble. Two rooms later, they stopped. In the middle of the floor was a square hole, the top of a ladder protruding from its depths.

"Down we go," he said.

The satisfied tone of his voice made her fear what he truly meant.

A trim young woman in uniform slid out of the green Maine Marine Patrol pickup, crossed the parking lot, and entered the café as Joe rose from the counter stool to greet her. It was getting late and he was the only customer left.

They shook hands just inside the door.

"Joe Gunther?" she asked. "Randy Coffin. Cathy Lawless said you needed help."

"I'm up the proverbial creek," he admitted. "I really appreciate your coming."

"She told me a friend of yours may have met someone at the pier and then vanished?"

"I know it's a little lame, and maybe a total waste of your time."

She shook her head. "Not if the guy was Wellman Beale. That's right, isn't it?"

"That's what she told me on the phone," he admitted, and in concise detail, told her how Beale, the Silvas, and he had become intertwined—all while leading her to a stool and buying her a cup of coffee.

"But," he concluded ten minutes later, "I don't know what happened to Lyn. It's got me really worried. That's why I called Cathy. I still didn't expect you to come out in the middle of the night."

Coffin raised her eyebrows at him. "You'd do the same for me in Vermont, wouldn't you?"

"Absolutely."

She smiled and touched his cup with her own. "Well, what's good for Vermont law enforcement works for us, too."

She drained the mug, placed it on the counter, and stood up, adjusting her service belt. "So, let's go disturb a few people."

"You got some ideas?" Joe asked, dropping a bill beside the empty mugs.

"This is my patch," she explained, talking over her

shoulder as she headed for the door. "That's why Cathy called me. I spend more time working snitches on shore than I do on patrol nowadays, and believe me, you have no clue what snoops are till you've seen a fishing community."

CHAPTER 23

Sam answered the phone out of a deep sleep on the second ring, noticing as she did so that Willy's eyes were already open. She rarely actually saw him asleep.

"Martens," she answered softly as Willy, on the far side of her, rolled over onto his back and sighed.

"Hey, Sammie," the voice on the other end said cheerfully, "it's Ron. Sorry to wake you guys up again, but I thought you'd be interested—Becky Kerr was just taken to the ER."

Sam hit the speakerphone button so Willy could hear. "Why?" she asked.

"Something about a laceration. That part's not real clear. My guy wondered about it maybe being a suicide attempt."

Both of them were already out of bed and putting on their clothes.

"Who called 911?" Willy asked.

"Hey, Willy," Ron greeted him. "Sorry to wake you up."

"Answer the fucking question."

Ron laughed. "Her mom. She was a basket case, screaming her head off on the 911 tape. Dispatch told me the paramedics on the way to the ER were definitely laid-back, though, so I don't think anybody's hanging on for life."

"Who else is at the hospital?" Sam asked, tying the quick-lace boots she favored. "I'm hoping we can pick and choose who we talk to."

"The mom, for sure. Don't know about anyone else."

"Do me a favor, Ron?" Sam asked, about to hit the Off button.

"Shoot."

"Call HCRS and get somebody over there to hook up with us. I want to have a crack at this little girl."

"You got it."

"Jesus," Willy complained as they headed outside for the car. "Did you have to drag them into it?"

"Spare me," was her only response. HCRS stood for Health Care and Rehabilitation Services—a crucial mental health agency when it came to interactions between cops and people on the emotional edge, but a pain in the neck to people like Willy, whose instincts were always to fly solo.

At the hospital, ten minutes later, they found an unusually quiet ER, its hallways empty, one of its two glassed-in staff stations abandoned, and the other one held down by the ever-present Elizabeth Pace—who, Sammie was now convinced, had been there when they'd constructed the building around her.

"Hey, Elizabeth," she called out as she passed through the sliding-door entrance.

"Hey yourself," Elizabeth greeted them. "How're you two doing? Here to see our young lady?"

"Eventually," Sam answered her as Willy continued to wander the hallway, looking around idly. "Gotta wait for HCRS. Who did she come in with?"

Elizabeth indicated the waiting-room wall behind her. "You got one mother and two brothers."

"The girl okay?"

"Oh, sure. Mom's the most worked up. Daughter's just pissed off."

Sam glanced over at Willy. "Want to join me?"

"Sure."

They circled around to the waiting room's inner door and entered to find Karen Putnam sitting on a couch beside a pale-faced Richard Vial, while his brother Nicky paced the room like a restless animal, his eyes downcast and his fists in his pockets.

Sam's face broke into a smile at the sight of Richard. "Hey there," she addressed them both, sitting down quickly to be on their level. "How're you guys holding up?"

Richard smiled wanly as his mother broke out, "How do you think? Crazy kid. What the hell was she doing?"

Willy, intrigued to finally set eyes on Nicky after both the blood drop finding and what Dan Kravitz had described, approached the boy at an angle that should have forced him to stop and exchange some form of greeting.

"Hi," Willy began, but Nicky brushed between him and the wall, eyes still averted, as if Willy were part of the furniture.

Rebuffed, Willy sat down beside Sam without saying another word. The latter waved a hand in his direction, explaining, "This is my colleague, Willy Kunkle."

Karen nodded and wiped her eyes. She looked terrible, her mascara smeared, her face haggard.

"What *was* she doing, Karen?" Willy asked with the surprising gentleness he always kept in reserve.

"She had a *razor blade* in her hand. She was slicing herself. There was blood . . ."

Willy leaned forward and rested his hand on her knee, very briefly—barely a brushstroke. "Hang on, hang on. I think I understand. Was there music?"

Karen stopped and stared at him. "What?"

"The music," Willy resumed. "And the lighting. Did it look different than usual? Kind of theatrical, like she was trying to set a mood?"

"Yes," she admitted, surprised.

"And the blood. Was it a thin line, with something to absorb it underneath, like a towel or some Kleenex?"

"Yes."

"So there wasn't a lot of it?"

"No."

"Sam told me that Becky's been in the dumps lately. Is that right?"

Karen flared a little at that. "Not enough to make her kill herself."

"I don't think she was trying to," Willy reassured her.

Karen's voice rose. "She cut her wrist, for Christ's sake."

"Her wrist or her arm?"

Her eyes widened. Her mouth opened to respond and then closed.

"Her arm," Richard said in a small voice.

"That's key," Willy quickly added. "That's not suicide." He leaned forward and repeated the hand gesture, leaving it longer on her knee this time. "Your daughter was cutting herself, Karen. Huge difference."

"What do you mean?" Karen's voice had settled back down.

"It's what a lot of girls are doing to make themselves feel more in control," Sam contributed.

"That's crazy."

"It's kind of an anger thing," Willy told her. "We see it all the time. Most girls in middle and high school will try it at least once."

"Cutting themselves with a razor?" Karen asked incredulously.

"It takes their minds off their troubles," Sam explained. "Some say it's like pulling the plug on their anxieties."

"Like booze is for adults," Willy added. "We do it to numb the pain; they do what they do to make the pain something they can see."

Karen was shaking her head. "It doesn't make sense."

"Not to us," Sammie agreed. "But it works for them."

"You were totally unaware she was into this?" Willy asked.

"She's not 'into it,'" Karen protested.

"What do you think?" Sam suddenly asked Richard.

"She's been sad."

"Sadder than usual?"

"Yeah. We used to play more, and now we don't."

"Under the trailer?" Sam asked.

"Yeah."

"What did you two used to do?"

"Stuff—you know. Legos and cards and some computer games."

"But not lately?"

"She stopped coming down."

"Richard," Willy asked, "do you know if she ever cut herself before?"

He shook his head. "I never saw it."

"She wear short sleeves when you played together?"

"Yeah, sure," Richard answered, perplexed.

"What happened?" Karen asked her son.

Richard's thin shoulders shrugged. "I don't know. A few weeks ago, she just stopped, and after that, I saw she was really sad."

"But she never told you why?"

"Nope."

Willy twisted in his seat and addressed Nicky, who hadn't stopped his circular tours of the room.

"Nick," he said. "How 'bout you? You notice anything different about your sister lately?"

Nick ignored him.

"Nicky," Karen ordered. "Answer the man."

Still nothing.

"So," Sam asked Karen as they turned away from Nicky. "Let's go over this from the start—what happened tonight?"

"It was getting late," she explained, "and it's a school night, so I wanted to tell her to go to bed. I could see her light on under the door. I normally knock, 'cause she's so big on her privacy, you know? But I hardly see her anymore, so I just walked in this time."

Karen's eyes were widening as she spoke. Richard held on to her arm to calm her down. She absentmindedly reached out and stroked his hair as she spoke.

"She was sitting cross-legged on her bed, like you said, with the weird music and funny lighting, just doing . . . it. She looked so angry when she saw me."

Karen began weeping.

Sam murmured to Richard, "Did you see it, too?"

He nodded, hugging his mother.

This time, Sam reached out and rubbed his back once. "I'm sorry."

She and Willy rose, and moved toward the door. "We'll go talk with Becky now, along with someone from HC . . ."

"*She's fine*," Nick interrupted angrily, stopping at last, mere inches from Willy, his eyes riveted to the latter's mid-chest.

"What makes you say that?" Willy asked, feeling crowded but not stepping back. "Do you know what's been going on?"

Nicky shook his head, repeated, "She's fine," more calmly, and broke away to resume his circling.

Sam and Willy left the waiting room the way they'd entered, to find a woman waiting for them in the ER's hallway.

She extended a hand to both of them and introduced herself, "Carolyn Taylor-Olson—HCRS."

Sam shook hands, Willy merely said, "Hey," still distracted by his nonconversation with Nicky.

"I understand we have a situation?"

Sam indicated the waiting-room door. "Mom said she walked in on daughter cutting herself. From what we gathered, it's early onset, maybe the first time. The girl's been walking around with short sleeves up till now."

Taylor-Olson opened a file she'd been holding. "Becky Kerr?"

"Yeah. Mom's Karen Putnam."

"Oh, sure," Taylor-Olson agreed. "We've dealt with them before. Nothing too outrageous, but they've made it onto the radar."

She slapped the folder closed and smiled. "So, how do you want to proceed?"

That stopped Willy. He stared at her. "No 'stand-aside-and-let-us-do-our-work'?"

She laughed. "Gotcha. Give me a break, Kunkle. If you don't think we haven't heard about you, you really are living in outer space." She tapped him on the chest with her finger, grinning at him devilishly. "We're not here to screw you over, despite your fantasies. It ain't about you."

He stared at her, openmouthed, while Sammie, off to the side, prepared to control the damage.

But he broke into a broad smile as he glanced at his partner and told her, "They're still a pain in the ass, but I like this one."

Taylor-Olson rolled her eyes. "Spare me."

Willy patted her shoulder—a rare gesture for him. "Carolyn, right? You can play this one with Sam, here. It's not my thing. But nice job. I hope we meet again."

This time, he did shake hands, muttered to Sam, "I'll see you outside," and left the ER.

The women waited until the glass doors had eased shut before Sam asked the HCRS worker, "Did you set that up?"

Taylor-Olson tilted her head equivocally. "I didn't even know who'd be here."

"Well, you're a rare bird, to still be alive after that."

The other woman looked at her. "You seem to stand your own ground, and I hear you two are an item."

Sam laughed. "Right—a regular science experiment. It wasn't always so cozy. You want to meet the young lady in question?"

Taylor-Olson nodded. "Yeah, good idea. If all goes well, I might still be able to get a few hours' sleep."

They found Becky in the treatment room farthest from the front doors, sitting in a chair in the corner, her knees up and her arms wrapping her shins. Her left forearm was bandaged with gauze.

Sam studied her carefully, given the connection she suspected the girl had to Wayne Castine. Becky was big for her age, more overweight than developed, and remarkably plain. But she was dressed in the teasing, pubescent style that was all the fad at the moment—permed hair, makeup, tight, spaghetti-strapped crop top, short shorts. Over the tops of her knees, enough of her shirt was visible to reveal the word "Gorgeous" stenciled across the front. Her fingernails were lavishly painted and decorated, complete with fake diamonds, although now peeling and in need of a remake. She struck Sam as a girl caught out in the open—the only guest at a costume ball to have dressed the wrong way. Sam put her chronologically and psychologically between childhood and adolescence, with a firm foothold in neither.

Taylor-Olson started out, her voice supportive and upbeat, without a tinge of the cynical savvy she'd shown Willy. "Hi, Becky. I'm Carolyn and this is Sam. Not that you care, but I'm from HCRS and Sam's a police officer, and we're just here to find out if you're all right."

"I'm fine." The voice was flat and sullen.

"Your mom says you were cutting yourself, is that right?"

There was no response. Becky merely watched them over the tops of her knees.

Taylor-Olson perched on the edge of the nearby bed. "Things been a little rough lately?" she asked quietly.

No answer.

"I'd never pretend to know what it's like to be you, Becky," she continued, "but I can tell you that you're not alone—I and people like me are ready and available to help, at the drop of a hat. It's nice to know that sometimes, when you're feeling like you're all alone."

Becky continued watching them.

Sam began mentally reviewing what she knew of the family's dynamics.

"How have things been going at home?" Taylor-Olson continued.

Sam was caught by Becky's fingernails. She'd never had her own done—no surprise—but she knew it wasn't cheap. And these were top of the line—positively ornate. Way more than this kid could afford.

"I love your nails," she said suddenly.

Her companion glanced at her unhappily. Becky looked surprised.

Sam dropped to one knee, to not appear threatening. "Could I see?"

Becky's first response was to make fists of her hands.

"I hate my nails," Sam said, holding them out. "I'm always trying new stuff, but they always end up the same way, and everybody just laughs at me anyhow, so I don't know why I bother. But yours are really cool. I get mine made up that way, it might work." She wiggled her fingers at the girl. "What d'you think?"

"Maybe," she said.

Sam was wracking her brain, trying to remember what she knew of this teenage world, feeling hopelessly old.

"The shiny chips make all the difference—that and extensions, of course."

That did the trick. Becky's fingers shot out straight. "They're diamonds," she said forcefully. "Not chips—that's why they cost so much."

Sam didn't hesitate. In one smooth movement, she brought the open cell phone she'd secreted in her other hand and took a picture of the flashy nails, before Becky could react.

Sam gave her a huge smile, just as quickly pocketing the phone. "Cool. I'll show those to my nail person and see if she can do the same thing. I really appreciate it. Where did you have yours done?"

But the girl was suspicious. The nails disappeared into fists again, and she tucked her chin in defensively.

"I don't remember."

Sam backed away. "That's okay. It won't matter. Even if they don't look exactly right, I'll be better off than I was. How much did they cost, just so I can be prepared?"

Becky shrugged.

"That's all right, Becky," Taylor-Olson said softly, giving Sam a sharp look. "And they are very pretty."

Unrepentant, Sam stepped outside the examination room. Becky's problems were her own, in the long run. For her part, Sammie had a job to do, and right now that didn't include counseling and comfort.

Willy was back walking the corridor. He showed his surprise as she closed the door behind her. "That was fast."

"That was useless," she said. "The kid's a clam and I don't have the time. HCRS can have her." She pulled out the phone and opened it up to check her photographic skills. "I got this, though."

He sidled up next to her and peered at the small screen. "What the hell?"

"Her fingernails," Sam explained. "Very over-the-top. A little ratty now, but primo when they were new."

He stepped back to study her. "And your point is?"

Sam looked at him pityingly. "They cost a fortune, Sherlock. So who paid for them? I'll guarantee it wasn't her or Karen."

His face cleared. "No shit. Nice work."

CHAPTER 24

Randy Coffin led the way up the gangplank to the deck of an older, sturdy ocean trawler, rigged with enough lights to make it look like a Broadway stage, albeit one where each bare bulb fairly hummed with a swarm of nocturnal bugs. Once aboard, however, she and Joe didn't encounter either thespians or sailors, but a massive confusion of piled-up netting, with a single rough-hewn man sitting in its midst. To Gunther's untrained eye, he seemed to be repairing the net, although how on earth he knew where to find what needed attention was beyond Joe's comprehension.

"Neil," Randy called out upon clearing the rail.

The man looked up and smiled broadly. "It's Ranger Randy. How're you doin'?"

"Old joke," Randy murmured over her shoulder to Joe as she picked her way across the deck to where their host was perched on an upended milk crate.

There was no shaking of hands or introductions, apparently stemming from an understanding that such gestures were frivolous and unnecessary.

"How's life been keeping you?" Randy asked him.

"Can't complain," Neil admitted, his hands smoothly at work, weaving in and out of the net's meshing.

"Finding fish out there?"

"Enough to keep me fed."

"Seen anything I'd like to hear about?"

Neil didn't miss a beat, nor did he take his eyes off his task. "Funny you should ask. You might want to check what George Mullins maybe could be keeping in that shed out back of his equipment barn."

"Oh?" Randy smiled at Joe over the top of Neil's bowed head. "Any idea what that could be?"

"Damned if I know for sure, but there's a possibility that gear you were asking about last month found its way out of the weather."

"No kidding?"

This time, he glanced up quickly, fast enough to flash her a grin. "No kidding."

"That's good to know," she told him. "How 'bout Wellman Beale? You seen him around lately?"

That stopped him. His hands suddenly froze in midmotion and he straightened, taking in Joe carefully for the first time.

"Beale?"

"Yup."

He considered the question, as if how best to approach a dangerous animal.

"I guess so," he finally conceded.

"Tonight?"

Neil cocked his head and shifted his gaze to her. "Maybe."

"So you did."

"Don't guess I actually said that."

Randy nodded deliberately. "No. You didn't. That's true."

"Someone else might've, though."

"Assuming Beale had been around to be seen, you mean?" she asked.

"Right—assuming."

Joe joined in. "Along those same lines," he suggested, "might someone have seen a young woman with him— slim, good-looking, light brown hair?"

Neil studied him again and smiled. "You catch on fast. Yeah—I'd say that was right. Somebody might've said she didn't look real happy about it, too."

"Where did they go, Neil?" Randy asked directly.

But the old fisherman shook his head. "Can't tell you. Got on his boat and went out."

"Anyone else with them?"

"Pretty sure it was just the two of them."

"How long ago?" Joe asked.

"Maybe four hours," Neil suggested.

Randy patted him on the shoulder. "Thanks, Neil. You done good."

Neil had returned to his handiwork. "You take care, Ranger Randy, and don't forget about George's stash."

"Allard called," Lester told Willy as the latter entered the office late the next morning. "Looking for Joe again."

"You didn't throw him under the bus, did you?" Willy asked.

Les didn't rise to the bait. "Just so we're all on the same page, I told him the boss had been up half the night and was still out working an angle."

Willy laughed. "That's good—wish we knew what the hell that was." He paused before adding, "Sam probably does, but she's not talking."

He then updated Les on their midnight activities. "We met with Karen, Nick, Richard, and Becky at the ER last night. Becky was caught cutting herself and Mom wigged out."

"You get anything out of it?" he asked.

"Sam got a nifty picture," Willy said dismissively, just as she entered the room. "And I got to see Nick acting crazier than a rat in a box."

Sam showed her cell-phone image to Lester, explaining, "Becky's fingernails."

Lester pegged the significance immediately. "Whoa. Expensive. How'd she swing that?"

Willy turned from dumping a file on his desk. "What the hell do you know about painting fingernails?"

Lester laughed. "You don't have a daughter."

Sam snapped the phone shut. "Wayne paid for it."

"You don't say so?" Willy asked.

"That's where I've been," she explained. "There're only a couple of places in town to get this done. I got lucky first time. Flashed the photo, talked to the Asian guy who did it, and he ID'd both Becky and Wayne—didn't blink an eye."

"Pretty convenient," Willy cautioned.

"Pretty memorable," she countered. "Wayne grossed the guy out. He was all but sticking his tongue in her ear. The manicurist said it made him sick. He also said she was eating it up."

"That would fit," Lester commented. "Immature girl on the outs with her friends and family, falls for an older guy who flatters the hell out of her. I wouldn't doubt he told her she was ten times the woman her mother is."

"Gross," Willy growled. "True, but gross."

"That also explains her being shut down last night," Sam ventured.

"It's one explanation," Willy said.

"What's another?" Sam asked.

"She killed him," he suggested. "He dissed her and she carved him up."

"What about the drop of blood?" Lester asked. "It's from a male related to Karen."

Willy shrugged. "Maybe she had help."

"Like Nick?" Les proposed. "You said he was crazy."

Willy was dismissive. "Yeah, but crazy-loony; not homicidal. He walks in circles like a kicked dog."

He crossed to his desk, suddenly reminded of something. "Hang on, hang on. Did I get a call or anything from Waterbury? A woman named Alice Plouff?"

"You're kidding," Sam said.

He wasn't. "Damn. I knew she'd screw it up."

He dialed a number on his phone and began speaking in a jarringly upbeat voice. "Alice, hey. How're you doin'? . . . No, no, that's okay. I know we all get busy, and it was a favor, right? Anything you could do would be a hell of a lot faster than going through channels. That's why I called you first. I just forgot that I hadn't followed up . . . So, you did it? It matched? No joke? I mean, you're sure? Damn, girl. Dinner's on me next time I'm up."

He hung up, smiling, before raising an eyebrow at Sam. "She's three hundred pounds. You're safe."

"Like I care. What was that?"

Willy was feeling good. "Since none of you has collected a DNA sample from Ryan Hatch yet, that was confirmation that Karen's firstborn has a sample on file in Waterbury that hasn't gotten into the system yet. Also"—he held up his index finger—"my new best buddy Alice just compared it to the six-loci sample collected off of Wayne's body, and it's a perfect match."

"Given only six loci," Lester cautioned.

Willy frowned at him. "Six is still a one-in-a-million match, especially since none of those boys has a father in common. I always liked Ryan for this."

"How'd you think of checking?" Sam asked.

"Ryan's rap sheet," he explained. "He got nailed on a felony assault charge last month—some bar brawl involving a bunch of guys and a few pool cues—but in order to duck any inside time, the judge had him agree to a DNA sample." Willy flipped his hand in the air. "Just took a little digging."

"I guess we better have a talk with him," Sammie said, letting him bask in his glory. She also remembered her impression of Ryan when she met him at the trailer. "He is the eldest," she played along, "he's hot tempered, and I bet he's pissed about Todd coming back home from prison. If a guy like that found out his little sister was being boinged by a scuzzy bastard like Wayne, I'd lay odds he'd have an up-close-and-personal with him."

Willy laughed. "I'd say what we got qualifies. I'm up for squeezing Ryan."

Sam glanced at Lester, who lifted a shoulder, not so much agreeing as not offering any opposition. "He's right about Karen being the only shared parent among them," he said. "That pretty much guarantees a six-loci match being good enough, at least for our purposes—be different if two or more of them shared a father."

"I'll run it by Joe," she said, opening her phone. "Grabbing Ryan might be a little premature, since he's probably not going anywhere and we still haven't done our homework yet."

She punched in the number, held the phone to her ear, and then almost immediately snapped it shut, visibly disappointed. "Out of cell range," she announced.

Willy scowled. "Fuck him, then. Let's do it."

Joe closed his phone slowly, hanging on to the pole supporting the *Zodiac*'s small roof above the steering console Randy Coffin was manning.

"No service," he announced in a loud voice, over the roar of the twin outboards.

"Maybe later," she shouted back, keeping to her task and increasing speed. The boat could reach over forty knots—a rate that demanded she avoid even the smallest obstacle.

Joe kept watching the small island they'd just left, recalling when he'd first seen it, at night, weeks ago, when he'd had his one and only encounter with Wellman Beale.

Beale hadn't been there this time, though. All they'd found was Dougie O'Hearn, his grizzled sternman, who'd allowed them to tour the place, and had obligingly told them—while he couldn't swear to it—that he thought his boss might be in Lubec, where he owned some property.

Joe could still see the old man far behind them, a stick figure standing on the dock, studying them as they blended into the northern horizon. If Wellman Beale is in Lubec, Joe thought, then I'm the proverbial monkey's uncle.

Lyn startled awake at the sound of a scrape overhead. She was sitting curled up against one wall of the cellar Beale had placed her in hours earlier, extracting the ladder as he left.

"Hello?" she called out toward the pale gray opening of the overhead trapdoor, barely visible in the thin daylight from the windows above.

A bulky shadow appeared in the frame. "That the best you can do?" Wellman Beale asked. "Not, 'Hello, asshole,' or something?"

"Would that get me out of here?" she asked, fighting to keep her voice strong and direct, hoping her fear couldn't be heard.

"Nah. Probably not."

A pinprick of bright red light suddenly leaped from the shadow's midst—a laser beam, as from a gun sight—it began dancing cheerfully across her body, a Tinker Bell with lethal intent.

"What're you going to do?" she asked, trying to ignore it, while transfixed by its erratic wanderings. "If you're worried about a kidnap charge or anything, I'm happy to keep my mouth shut. Nobody needs to know about this."

He laughed. "Right." He sat on the edge of the square hole, dangling his feet into her cell, better to steady his aim. "We'll just let bygones be bygones—until some fucking SWAT cops come kicking down my door."

"Then what do you *want*?" she blurted out, instantly regretting the despair she heard echoing back off the enveloping concrete.

"I don't know yet," he said lightly, as if he'd just been asked what kind of sandwich he wanted at a picnic. The tiny red dot settled down between her legs. "Maybe I'm getting interested in seeing the color of your panties."

She stared up at his shadow in muted terror, half expecting him to simply drop down on top of her. Please, Joe, she thought, wrestling with her panic, *find* me.

CHAPTER 25

The Harmony parking lot is located in the heart of Brattleboro. It is as hemmed in by downtown's shoulder-to-shoulder nineteenth-century buildings as a large castle courtyard, complete with only three entrances—a narrow, arched, one-way tunnel from High Street, a two-way gap about a quarter block wide, leading out to Elliot Street, and a driveway next to it by the bank. Over the years, the lot had been planted with small trees, to soften its appearance, and targeted by town leaders and police against making it a magnet for teens and euphemistically labeled "young adults"—both considered troublemakers. The trees were coming along; the population control efforts remained iffier.

Sam, Lester, and Willy arrived there in two cars from the Putnam trailer in West Bratt, where small Richard had told his friend Sam where he thought his oldest brother might be. Lester entered the lot from the north—High Street—while Sam and Willy came in from the south, parking illegally by the lot's outlet. In that way, they were positioned like cowboys, hoping to head off any skittish horses that might choose to bolt from the corral.

They were connected by radio, discreetly accessed by sleeve mikes and earbuds.

"You all set?" Sam asked Lester after they'd exited their car.

"Yup. Looking around as we speak," came the answer.

"Willy—you want to split up or work this together?" Sam asked over her shoulder. Hearing no response, she checked, and found him already gone.

"Gotcha," she muttered to herself. "Glad we talked."

The lot wasn't overly crowded—a couple of small groups in odd corners, unsurprisingly near the few stores facing inward that either catered to the kids or simply ignored them. But visibility was still a challenge, what with the trees and the hundred or so parked cars.

This explained another reason for the location's popularity among the less-than-desirable—while automobiles had limited access to it, pedestrians could pass through like water through a colander. A dozen stores facing out had rear entrances servicing the parking lot. Intended to address fire codes or simple convenience, this porosity afforded drug dealers and others seeking discretion multiple ways of transecting the block without drawing attention.

That alone made Sammie nervous—that they hadn't done enough preparation only worsened it. With Willy's DNA match, Ryan was no longer a mere interview subject; he was a murder suspect. That meant that you delved into his background thoroughly, scrutinized his personal habits, found out the best place to isolate and grab him, and only then took action. It didn't mean you wandered around a parking lot, hoping to get lucky.

But Willy was Willy, and Joe wasn't around—again. That put Sam in the position of dancing with the devil she knew all too well, versus holding off until Joe surfaced, knowing that Willy would be in motion on his own in the meantime.

At least this way, she might be able to run interference.

"I got Maura Scully," Lester said quietly over Sam's earpiece.

"Where?"

"She just left the bakery, east side."

Sam walked in that direction, soon spotting the young girl's hank of long blond hair.

"You want to tag her first?" Les asked.

"Yeah," she answered. "I want this nice and quiet."

Sam saw Lester idly leaning against his car, beyond where Scully was chatting with two other girls. He was pretending to be having a cell-phone conversation.

Sam approached the trio casually. "Hi," she said, addressing them all before looking directly at Scully. "Are you Maura?"

"Who's asking?" Scully wanted to know.

Sam smiled and stuck her hand out. "Oh, right—duh. I'm Sam. I work with HCRS. I just wondered if I could ask you a couple of questions."

Predictably, and as Sam had hoped, Maura rolled her eyes. "God, what is it with you people?"

"I know, I know. This is just so I can fill out some paperwork and not get fired. I am sorry. I know what a hassle we can be."

Maura put on a show of being peeved, mostly for her companions, but conceded in the end. "Whatever."

Sam hesitated. "It's kind of confidential."

"I can't leave," Maura told her. "I'm waiting for somebody."

"No, no. We can just move across the way a little." Sam glanced at the other two. "That's okay, isn't it? Just two minutes of privacy? I'll be as fast as I can."

The other girls looked uncomfortable being asked permission. "Sure," one of them barely murmured.

But it was enough. Scully followed Sam across the

parking lot's traffic lane, until they were standing out of earshot.

"Where's Ryan?" Sam asked, out of the blue but for the sake of the microphone. "I thought he'd be with you."

"In the bakery," Maura told her without thought. "What do you want?"

From the corner of her eye, Sam saw Lester leave his post and stroll toward the bakery's far entrance, so that Ryan would be boxed in.

"I guess you heard that Becky had a meltdown last night," Sam said, watching over the girl's shoulder to check on any activity at the store.

"So? What's that got to do with me?"

"Well, you live at the same address, right?"

"Yeah."

"So, I was wondering what you could tell me about life in general there, specifically relating to Becky's state of mind."

Maura's forehead wrinkled. "What?"

"How's Becky been acting?"

"She's a stuck-up bitch. I don't have nothing to do with her."

"Still, you must have some impressions."

Sam saw Les enter the store. Almost immediately, she heard his surprised voice mutter, "Shit. Willy's making his move."

Sam stiffened, not listening to Maura anymore. So that's where he went.

As if on cue, she heard Willy say, "Hey, shitbird. Drop the goods and show your hands."

That was instantly followed by a loud bang and a crash, Willy letting out a grunt and Lester yelling, "Go, go, go. He's a runner."

The door behind Scully banged open to reveal Ryan

Hatch, his eyes wide, stopping for a split second, looking around, and then preparing to sprint for the Elliot Street exit.

Sam shoved Maura out of the way, pulled her gun from her holster, and yelled, "*Do not move. Police.*"

Ryan didn't hesitate. He pulled his own gun from under his T-shirt just as Maura regained her balance and threw herself against Sam.

Ryan's gun cracked sharply once before he took off. Sam, grabbed by a bullet low in her right leg, spun around and fell as Maura began screaming.

Lester appeared outside first, and ran over to Sam. Willy flew out behind him, instinctively took in his partner's grimace and the nature of her wound, and went after the fleeing Ryan.

The latter's speed served him well, allowing him to cross the lot, straddle the motorcycle none of them had noticed, fire it up, and begin rolling, just as Willy came within two feet of laying his hand on the young man's shirt.

Willy didn't hesitate, even as the bike squealed away in a plume of burning rubber. He threw himself behind the wheel of his car, and—covert siren and lights ignited—followed the motorcycle out of the lot, turning right and heading west up Elliot, toward the fire department's central station.

It was a short chase, even with the bike's speed and agility. Willy, not radioing for help or pursuing Ryan from a safe distance, crushed the accelerator instead and sent the car off like a rocket. Pedestrians and traffic scattered before him, he bounced off the side of a car parked beside the dry cleaner's, and just as Ryan had to slow down for a vehicle entering from the side, Willy simply ran him down at top speed, smashing him between his front bumper and the side of the obstructing car.

Ryan flew over the roof as if shot from a catapult and landed in a heap in the middle of the street, a pool of blood slowly spreading from under his head.

Willy swung out of his wrecked car, ignored the other driver, who was shaking his head in a daze, and walked around to where Ryan lay motionless.

He stared at the body for a moment, noticing the slightly moving chest, and said softly, "You're it, asshole."

CHAPTER 26

Joe hopped from the bow of the *Zodiac* and quickly looped the line around the nearest cleat. Randy Coffin spun the wheel, snugged the rest of the boat up fast against the piling, killed the engines, and did the same with the stern line.

They were one dock down from where Beale's boat was quietly bobbing on the water.

"See anyone?" she whispered.

It was midmorning in Lubec, and yet the view down Water Street wasn't much more crowded than in the middle of the night.

Gunther studied the distant lobster boat for half a minute. "Nope."

They left their mooring spot and circled around to the other dock—watchful, hands on holstered weapons, sensitive to any movement either on board or in the immediate surroundings.

But all remained serene.

"*Ahoy,*" Randy finally called out. "Maine Marine Patrol. Anyone aboard?"

Hearing nothing, she cautiously stepped on deck, with Joe close behind, and approached the open cabin door.

"Nothing," she announced.

They went below and saw the cut loops of duct tape lying on the floor.

"No blood," she commented hopefully.

Joe was already headed back up. "Where the hell's Cathy?"

They had finally reached Cathy Lawless via radio from the *Zodiac* and got her to agree to meet with them here.

Randy followed him back out and scanned the two streets visible from the dock.

"There." She pointed to a car approaching from the distant corner, where Water Street met the bridge over to Campobello Island.

The two of them walked to the edge of Commercial Street and waited for the dark sedan Randy had spotted. Inside were Cathy Lawless and her monosyllabic partner, Dave Beaubien.

"Hey, guys," Cathy greeted them. "You made good time." She glanced beyond them. "That the boat?"

"Yeah," Randy told her. "Empty. Found this." She dangled one of the loops of duct tape.

"Ouch," Cathy said. "Sorry, Joe." She reached over the back of her seat to move a bag out of the way. "Climb in. Let's figure out what's what."

Joe and Randy complied, transforming the car into a miniature office.

"Hey, Dave," Joe greeted Beaubien glumly.

Dave merely nodded his response.

"Did you get the town clerk to find out what property Beale owns?" Joe asked, following up on the second half of the conversation they'd shared on the radio.

"Two she could identify," Cathy told them. "A residence on Mowry and an abandoned warehouse somewhere ahead of us." She pointed down Commercial Street. "As far as I could tell, the Mowry address is our best bet—the clerk said she was amazed the warehouse was still standing. Plus, the address on that one was a little vague."

Randy looked at Joe. "We're just along to watch your back. What's your preference?"

He paused. "The house seems more likely, and I'm worried about losing more time."

"Want to leave half of us here, while the rest go to the house?"

"Where's 'here'?" Joe asked. "I thought you weren't sure of the warehouse's location."

Cathy nodded. "Cool. What about the boat?"

In answer, Randy dangled the ignition keys from her hand.

Cathy pulled away from the side of the road. "Done."

Mowry Street may have been on the far side of town, but that only translated to a three-minute drive across five blocks. Lubec was sparsely populated, hosting only a handful of lobster boats; its school was facing extinction, its locals were selling their homes to wealthy vacationers, and employment often consisted of a round robin of blueberry picking, Christmas wreath making, and the odd carpentry job. Although appreciative of many a spruced-up and handsome home—and of a neat and picturesque village, overall—the four cops weren't startled to see a rundown, tiny house surrounded by rusting metal lobster traps and three abandoned cars by the time they reached Beale's property.

"La Maison Beale," Cathy announced, killing the engine. She twisted in her seat before asking, "Just so we all stay on the same page, what're we looking at?"

Joe understood the question and, despite his anxiety, tried to answer it professionally. "Possible kidnapping, maybe worse, but the evidence is thin. Lyn somehow arranged to meet Beale. Randy and I interviewed a guy who saw them step onto Beale's boat, but no signs of coercion aside from the informant saying that Lyn didn't look happy."

Cathy pulled a face. "That could mean she didn't like getting seasick, too."

Joe swallowed most of his protests. "Before she vanished, she did tell me she would stay put till I got there."

She smiled at him. "Good enough for me. Let's kick some ass."

They got out and slowly approached the decrepit house in a spread-out straight line, covering all entrances. Joe and Cathy then met at the front door, on which she hammered unceremoniously with the heel of her hand.

"Wellman Beale? Open up. Police."

To their shared amazement, the door opened within seconds, revealing the same heavyset, scowling man Joe had met weeks earlier, and whom he'd interviewed in vain about the disappearance of Lyn's father and brother.

Adding to the surprise, Beale immediately recognized Joe and gave him a sarcastic smile. "Couldn't find Vermont?"

Joe nodded to him. "Came back for you."

"Wellman Beale?" Cathy asked formally.

"Trick question, right?"

"Where were you last night?"

"Taking a shit."

"Were you or were you not in Jonesport?"

"Like you don't know."

"Answer the question."

"I were. Do I win something?"

"Nothing you'll like," Cathy said. "You were seen with a woman, getting onto your boat and leaving harbor. Do you admit that?"

Beale glanced at Joe and raised an eyebrow. "A lot of

women have gotten onto that boat, and not one of them's ever complained."

"Answer the question."

"Yeah, I gave a quick tour of the harbor to some skinny broad. She wanted to see the sights."

"That include taking her to Lubec?"

A quick shift of his eyes from one to the other of them preceded his answer. "Bullshit."

Cathy leaned forward slightly. "You really think after all the crap you've pulled that you can walk around without our knowing? We've been putting your tax dollars to work, Wellman."

He shifted his weight. "Well, you wasted your money. I dropped her off, like I said."

"Then you'll invite us in to look around."

His readiness gave him away. He stepped back and waved a hand. "I'm real embarrassed. The maid's a cow. The place is a mess."

"We'll survive," Cathy said, brushing by with Joe, as Randy and Dave stayed at the door to watch Beale.

Of course, it led to nothing. He was right about the mess and, unfortunately, about there being nobody else on the premises.

Joe and Cathy paused alone in what passed for a living room.

"No surprise," she said softly. "What do you want to do?"

Joe pulled on his ear, fighting to keep focused. "We can't roust him for anything."

"Nothing that'll stick."

"She's got to be in the warehouse—it belongs to him and it's near the boat."

"Don't have a warrant," she reminded him, "not that we couldn't use exigent circumstances."

He pointed to the front of the house, where they could

hear Beale talking to the other two. "We have the man with the key. Why don't we let him use it?"

"You mean tail him?" Cathy asked. "He's going to know we're watching."

Joe smiled. "Unless he thinks it's his lucky day. Call Dave on his cell phone and try this out . . ."

Moments later, Dave Beaubien stepped back a couple of paces from Beale's front door to answer his cell. He nodded a couple of times, snapped it shut, and spoke to Randy. "Get them out of there. We've got a cluster fuck just north of Machias—a tractor-trailer into a school bus."

"Oh, my God," Randy said as Dave shoved Beale aside.

"Move it," Dave said. "*Cathy*," he called out. "We gotta go. Big-time ten-fifty outside Machias—multiple casualties. They need everybody."

Cathy and Joe appeared from the house's dark interior. "What happened?" she asked.

"Truck versus bus. We'll have to do this later."

Joe protested. "Wait. We got the son of a bitch right here."

Cathy turned to him as the other two headed for the car. "Sorry. Maybe the sheriff can spare a babysitter to keep you company. We'll drop you off at his office on the way." She pointed a finger at Beale, who could barely contain a smile. "You stay put, jackass. I hear you've moved one foot off this property, I will bury you. You understand? We'll be right back, so you better be here."

"Yes, ma'am," Beale answered her. "Absolutely will not move a muscle."

Joe hesitated. "I'll stay with him."

Cathy looked peeved. "You don't have a car, you have no jurisdiction, and we'll be right back. Get in the car, for Chrissake."

Defeated, Joe avoided eye contact with Beale and angrily joined the rest of them in the car. Cathy took off with tires spinning.

"Think he bought it?" she asked as she turned off Mowry onto Pleasant and began heading back to the boats.

"Bought what?" Randy asked.

"Our bullshit. We wanted to leave the coast clear for him."

"We hope he'll beat feet for the warehouse," Joe explained. "Sorry."

She laughed. "No problem. Better that than a bunch of mangled kids. What's the plan?"

Cathy stopped at the corner of Washington Street, which paralleled Mowry one block away. "Only two ways for him to leave—this corner and where Mowry does a forty-five to hook up with this road one street up. One of us gets out here and tucks into the pucker brush to watch; another does the same at the other corner; and Joe and I stake out the warehouse. Whoever sees him first gets on a cell to update the others about what's up. If we're right, we'll be back together on Commercial Street in a few minutes."

Randy had already opened her door. "Got it. Talk to you soon."

Cathy swung left, dropped off Dave, and then took Church Street and Eureka to return to Commercial and the harbor. As Joe sat in the passenger seat, watching the gently hilly neighborhoods speed by, he couldn't focus on the quaint wooden buildings, the church, or even the town's most prominent feature—a bright blue, towering, silolike structure, presumably a water tower, stamped with the town's name. Instead, he thought only of Lyn, and hoped they were still in time.

As it turned out, the warehouse's vague address explained itself instantly—it was the only such structure standing, if barely. Cathy hid the car out of sight behind a pile of weed-choked dirt, and she and Joe chose their hiding places far to either side of the place's entrance.

Then they waited.

As hoped, it didn't take long. Joe's cell buzzed on his belt fifteen minutes later.

"It's me," Cathy told him from her spot. "Dave called. Beale just drove by, slow and careful and looking all over the place. If we're right, he should be here right about now."

"Got it," Joe told her, adding, despite his instincts, "Let's see what he does."

"What do you think that'll be?" she asked skeptically.

"What I'd do," he told her. "Put Lyn back on the boat and head out to sea. That's his comfort zone."

"He won't just kill her?"

Joe appreciated her directness, while hating the thought. "If he comes here, it means she's either still alive or he needs to dump her body. Either way, he'll want to get back on that boat."

After a moment's pause, Cathy responded, "Well, you're right about the first part. I can see his car now."

The phone went dead. A few seconds later, Joe saw what Cathy had, and Beale's car slid into view onto the hardscrabble parking area adjoining the warehouse entrance.

Keeping out of sight, Joe saw his nemesis stay at the wheel for half a minute, watching for any movements, before finally easing out of the car. Then, again, he surveyed everything around him, wary and tense, until, finally, he walked quickly to the warehouse door, unlocked it, and vanished inside.

Joe's phone vibrated again. Irritated, he held it to his ear and growled, "What?"

Willy Kunkle's voice filled his ear. "'Bout time you plugged that fucking thing back in. I don't know where the hell you are or what the hell you're doing, but while you been screwing around, Sammie's been shot. See you at the hospital, dipwad."

Stunned, Joe stared at the dead phone, his chest hammering. Fumbling, he dialed a Brattleboro number.

"Emergency Room. How may I help you?"

"This is Joe Gunther of the Vermont Bureau of Investigation," he said softly, struggling to control the quaver in his voice, his eyes glued to the door ahead of him. "An officer of mine was brought in with a gunshot wound. What's her condition?"

"Joe?" the woman's voice said. "It's Elizabeth."

"Willy just called me," he said. "I'm stuck out of state. What the hell happened?"

"It's Sammie, Joe," Elizabeth Pace told him. "And she's fine. She got winged in the lower leg. The bullet fractured her fibula, but it's not bad. Very clean. You want me to put someone on? There're a lot of them here right now—it's like a cop convention."

"No, not now. I'll be there as soon as I can. They get the shooter?"

Her voice dropped. "What's left of him. He's being operated on right now."

Joe saw Cathy's head appear from behind her hiding place. She looked at him quizzically and gestured as if she were also holding a phone, asking him what on God's earth he was doing.

"I gotta go, Elizabeth. I can't thank you enough."

He pocketed the phone and gave a thumbs-up. Willy's histrionics aside, everything important back home seemed to be under control for the moment. One disaster at a time.

Joe slipped away from his spot, approached the building from a blind angle, and sidled up to the door that Beale had used earlier.

Cathy did the same from the other side, until she was

positioned across from him, her back against the wall, waiting for either a legal justification to enter, or simply for Beale to reappear.

The latter occurred first. Startling them both, the door suddenly squealed open, followed by a familiar voice ordering someone, "Wait there. I gotta look around."

Beale stepped into view, allowing Joe to place the muzzle of his gun against the man's temple.

"You move, you die," he said quietly.

CHAPTER 27

Late at night, Joe entered Sam's hospital room gingerly, half expecting to find Willy there, mad as hell and gun in hand.

He didn't blame the man. He was naturally high-strung, had just seen his lover shot, and had then almost killed the perpetrator in return. Not to mention that it had all occurred on Joe's watch and in his absence—a double sin in the eyes of each of them. Joe's leadership had been wanting here from the beginning, and now—as a direct result—a member of his team had almost paid the highest price.

But Willy wasn't there. Joe crossed the room to stand beside the bed, and looked down at Sam's pale, sleeping face—perfectly smooth and trouble-free. He'd paused at the nurses' station outside, and had spent hours making calls on the drive back from Maine. He now knew it was a clean break, just above the ankle, and that Ryan Hatch's bullet had passed through the meat of her leg, barely glancing the fibula. A plate had been screwed into place and a cast applied. The doctor had told Joe that Sam should be as good as new in six weeks, aside from some PT.

Impulsively, Joe leaned forward and kissed her on the

cheek, touching her hair with his fingertips. She always gave everything she had to him and the job, and he felt terrible now, seeing her laid out so.

He settled into the chair adjacent to the bed, still studying her face, and began reviewing the last several hours.

At least, the worst of his distractions were now officially settled. Beale was under arrest for a felony he'd be hard placed to beat, and Lyn was back in Gloucester with her mother and brother—shaken but intact. It had been she who'd insisted he return straight to Brattleboro, rather than accompany her home. She'd assured him that Beale had done no more than scare the hell out of her.

Of course, many questions remained—why had he grabbed her? What role, if any, did Dick Brandhorst play in it all? What had Abílo and José been up to in the first place, and what exactly had befallen them in the end? And, lastly, what of all this was still obviously in motion, stimulating the vandalism of *The Silva Lining*?

But Lyn was at least safe, and Joe could now concentrate on the metaphorical oil slick that was spreading around the still unsolved murder of Wayne Castine.

He laid his head back against the cushion of the visitor's chair, feeling the weight of no sleep bearing down on him.

And more good news? Willy hadn't killed Ryan Hatch. The boy had undergone hours of brain, rib, and hip surgery, and remained on the critical list at Dartmouth-Hitchcock Medical Center, where he'd been airlifted, but the doctors there had assured Joe they anticipated only improvement.

As for Willy's fate legally, the Windham County state's attorney had been cagier, at first. That phone call had begun with Jack Derby reciting Kunkle's trespasses, foremost being his reckless disregard for public safety. But added was a total failure to coordinate his actions with local law enforcement or, for that matter, his own team. According to Derby—since Joe hadn't yet asked Willy for his version—Willy had undermined the planned low-key approach to Ryan Hatch in the bakery, instead marching up to him, grabbing him by the collar, and throwing him against the wall, thereby causing the boy to drop and scatter the drugs he'd been selling to another kid at his table.

Joe had successfully argued the obvious—that Ryan was a suspect in a homicide, that he'd run when apprehended, shot an identified police officer, and sought to elude capture. What better example did the state's attorney need of an ongoing, active threat, which had been so rapidly and completely dealt with?

An old and practiced pragmatist, Derby had only grumpily conceded, suggesting that this could come back to haunt them—including possible civil suits—once the shock wore off and the facts were aired. In his words, in a town as politically sensitive as Brattleboro—and as left-leaning—"such a demonstration of police exuberance is unlikely to be left to drift away like a bad odor."

With a sigh, Joe had then called Bill Allard, perversely grateful that all this chatter was keeping him from falling asleep at the wheel. Nevertheless, Allard's tone had only joined the chorus of disapproving voices. What had Joe been thinking? Was Bill going to have to start reviewing basic tenets of VBI's organization? Was Willy Kunkle still so indispensable an asset, and Joe still so eager to pin his own future to his?

Joe had barely heard it. The smooth black pavement had drawn him in like a soothing melody, and he'd abandoned himself to simply staying between the white lines, only just noticing any oncoming headlights . . .

Joe opened his eyes, unaware they'd fallen shut. Standing beside Sammie in the dark hospital room was a thin, small boy. He was staring fixedly at her, his hands slack by his sides and his mouth slightly open.

Joe spoke in a near whisper, thinking he knew who this might be. "Hey there."

The boy gave a twitch, as if he'd been caught daydreaming in class. His wide, guileless eyes took in Joe.

"You okay?" Joe asked him.

"Yeah." He pointed his chin at Sam. "Is she?"

Joe lifted his head off the seat cushion behind him. "She's fine. Just a broken leg. They probably gave her something so she could sleep. You're Richard, right?"

The boy nodded.

"She really likes you."

Richard considered that for a moment. "She's cool."

"I think so, too. I was sorry to hear about your brother."

Richard returned to watching Sam. "Yeah."

"He hanging in there?"

"Yeah."

"You seen him yet?"

"Nah. My mom's up there."

"The whole family must be pretty upset."

"I guess."

That answer told him a fair deal. "I don't suppose you've been home much."

"Nope."

Sammie stirred at their voices. She reached out gently and touched Richard's chest with her fingertips. He stared at the IV attached to the back of her hand.

"Hey, Richard," she said softly, as if she, too, were being careful not to wake anyone up. "You come to check up on me?"

"Yeah."

"I'm fine. Honest. Just a broken bone."

"I'm real sorry Ryan shot you," he said.

"I'm sorry he got so messed up," she countered. "I think we scared him."

"Wasn't your fault," Richard said firmly. "He was wrong."

"How's your sister taking all this?" Sam asked.

Richard glanced at Joe. "That's what I was telling him. I don't know. I been pretty much hanging out alone."

Sam turned her head to see Joe for the first time. She smiled tiredly. "Hey, boss."

"Hey, kiddo." Joe reached out and squeezed her other hand briefly.

"He's your boss?" Richard asked.

"Yeah. This is Joe. Joe—meet Richard Vial."

"We've been chatting," Joe admitted.

Sam's smile broadened. "I like doing that with Richard, too. He's one of the good guys—a real trooper."

Joe sensed the boy's hesitation, and rose to his feet. "I think I'll go get some coffee. You two all set?"

Sammie nodded. "Yeah, Joe. Go for it. I'll see you in a bit."

He left them alone and walked down the empty hallway. Hospitals have an eerie stillness at night, like an anxious person wrestling to sleep, knowing the next morning will be filled with chaos.

He reached the nurses' station, where a lone woman glanced up from the magazine before her and inquired, "She okay?"

He wondered if Richard had managed, by pure habit, to slip in here unnoticed.

"Fine," he said. "I'm just going for coffee."

"There's a machine one floor down. To the right off the elevator, at the end of the hall. It's not too bad."

"Thanks. You want any?"

She shook her head. "Thanks. All set."

He rode the elevator down, and stepped through the doors to come face-to-face with Willy.

"Look what the cat dragged in," he said sourly. "Been making your apologies?"

Joe ignored that. "Met Richard Vial. They're talking right now. I thought I'd give them a little privacy." He pointed down the corridor. "Buy you a coffee?"

Willy studied him a moment before allowing a half shrug. "Okay."

They fell into step beside each other. Willy, to his credit, dropped his outrage long enough to comment, "You look terrible."

"Been a long few days. You don't look much the worse for wear. How're you doing after the shootout?"

Willy said instead, "I hear you been working the phones."

"Oh?"

"Allard, Jack Derby."

"What did they tell you?" Joe asked, genuinely curious.

"That you're the only reason I haven't been fired." He suddenly stopped in his tracks and stared at Joe. "What is it with that anyway? Why're you always saving my butt? Why do you give a good goddamn? Am I the son you never had or some bullshit?"

Joe smiled. "Jesus, I hope not."

"Then what?" Willy was almost shouting, his face red and his body tense. Joe knew not to tell him to settle down.

"We've had this out before, Willy," he said quietly instead. "Maybe we're salt and pepper, or yin and yang, or polar opposites that make for a good whole." He reached out and laid his hand on Willy's shoulder—a gesture he was surprised the other man accepted. "But I benefit from having you around. You're a good cop, an honest man, and you speak your mind. The fact that you're a pain in the ass takes second place."

He resumed walking down the hall, adding, "Maybe you should turn the question around—why do you stick around, when you seem so hell-bent on getting fired all the time?"

Willy joined him, but didn't respond, staring in silence at the floor as they went.

Now it was Joe's turn to stop and face his colleague. "And I do apologize," he said. "For what it's worth. I screwed up. I should've been there."

Willy wouldn't play. Joe saw him consider several responses, but his final choice was vintage Kunkle. "We didn't need you."

"'Cause you got the bad guy?"

"He shot Sam."

"Did he kill Castine?"

Willy broke away and resumed their quest. "Doesn't matter."

Joe didn't disagree. "For your sake, you're right."

"What's that mean?"

"That, for the record, you ran him down because he shot Sam, and that I saved your bacon based on the same reason—a nice, clean whitewash, covering up the fact that none of you should've been there in the first place."

"Fuck you. You don't get to quarterback after the game."

Joe shook his head. "I do this time. All those phone calls I made tonight? One of them was to David Hawke. I called him at home. He told me they got the mini-STR results a few hours ago and will fax them over this morning. They were able to stretch out the DNA to nine loci. Bad news is that the reason you went in all fired up to grab Ryan Hatch fell apart—his DNA no longer matches the sample."

Willy didn't answer. They'd reached the coffee machine, but neither of them turned to it. Instead, Willy stared out the window overlooking the darkened parking lot, studying his own translucent reflection.

"Where the fuck *were* you, boss?" he asked tiredly.

Joe looked at him, startled by the question's plaintiveness. For all of Willy's rudeness and rage, he was an honest man. But he was also a lost soul.

Joe knew why Willy stayed around, at once wrestling with self-destruction and clinging to the likes of Joe and Sammie. Despite his fury, he yearned for salvation, and perhaps saw the two of them as the only way to achieve it.

Not that he'd ever admit it.

Joe stepped up beside him and commingled their reflections in the window. "I was doing the same thing in Maine that you were when you ran down Ryan," he explained.

Willy turned to look at him. "What?"

"Lyn got kidnapped by some guy who had a hand in her father's and brother's deaths. I was getting her back."

Willy scowled at him. "You are such an asshole, you know that?"

Joe shrugged. "We all have our moments."

"One word, and we would've been there. Is this a New England thing? This I-am-an-island, screw-my-friends, do-it-alone-and-get-fucked attitude? Jesus, Joe, what happened to all your no-'I'-in-TEAM shit?"

Joe was laughing by now, his exhaustion combining with the irony of this speech coming from this source.

Willy let him settle down before asking, "Wild guess—she's okay?"

Joe wiped his eyes with the back of his hand and finally addressed the coffee machine, feeding it change from his pocket.

"Yeah," he said. "Thanks for asking."

Willy nodded, his universe back to as close to normal as ever.

"What else did Hawke say?"

Joe extracted one cardboard cup from the machine and handed it over. "The nine loci match Ryan's brother,

Nicky. Turns out they're full brothers, with the same father. Nick took on the last name King because he hates his old man."

Willy turned that over in his head. "Crazy Nicky whacked Castine?"

Joe fed the machine more money, amazed by how he constantly had to rein the man in. "Maybe. The science is just saying that a drop of his blood was on Castine's body. Right now, that's all we've got."

Lyn was no longer sure what she had. Having all but pushed Joe into his car to get him headed back toward Brattleboro, she'd spent hours with a succession of Maine police officers, repeating her story, onerously working her way through the ritual until she could finally reclaim her car in Jonesport and return to Gloucester, where Steve and their mother were still hiding out in a motel.

All that, she'd taken in stride, even using it to isolate herself from what she'd experienced at the hands of Wellman Beale.

But it turned to naught when the three of them at last reached home. As Lyn pushed open the door to her mother's apartment, she had to reach out to steady herself against the jamb.

"You okay?" Steve asked from behind, his hands full of belongings.

He shoved by her to find the apartment as ransacked as his boat.

"Jesus Christ," he said disgustedly.

Lyn was suddenly struck by fear and pulled him back onto the landing. "They might still be here," she cautioned.

But Steve was having none of it. He stormed in as Maria Silva tentatively sidled up beside her daughter and peered over the threshold.

"Come on out, you sons of bitches," Steve yelled, as it turned out, to no one.

The two women waited until he'd checked every room, swearing and waving his arms in frustration, until he finally sat heavily on the living-room couch, his hands between his knees, moaning, "What the hell's going on?"

Lyn entered then, still nervous, with their mother trailing behind, uncomprehending. She made a more analytical tour of the place, trying to assess both the damage and the intent of the break-in, her own anger displacing the cold fear that had initially gripped her.

She stood before Steve and asked him, "Any ideas?"

He looked up at her, his eyes wide. "Me? How should I know? I don't know who did this."

"I think I do," she told him. "What I don't know is why."

"And I'm supposed to know that?"

"You're being pretty defensive about it."

He stood up abruptly, forcing her to step back. "You're full of crap." Their mother approached them and began muttering nervously, touching them both, her hands fluttering like hummingbirds.

Lyn reached out and draped her arm around the older woman's shoulders. "It's okay, Momma. We're just a little upset. Let's get you settled in."

She glanced at her brother. "Sorry, Steve. Let me start over."

She could see from his face that he was ready for more, finally tired of being tarred for misdeeds he considered far behind him. But he swallowed his protest and responded quietly, "All right. Go for it."

She spoke as she steered her mother over to a chair, which she righted and placed before the TV set. "This look like the boat to you?"

"What do you think?" he asked.

"No, no. I don't mean the mess. I mean the nature of

it." Lyn turned on the set, searching for a channel she knew Maria would enjoy. "Does it look like vandalism, or theft, or what?"

He glanced around instinctively, at first nonplussed. "How the hell do I know? A search, maybe."

She faced him directly. "Exactly. They tossed the boat, looking for something, and now they've done the same here. That tells me—just maybe—that whatever they're after was either moved from one place to the other, or is small enough to be easily missed."

He spread his hands out wide. "What's that mean, sis?"

She steered him into the kitchen where they wouldn't disturb Maria, who was already transfixed by the program Lyn had chosen. "Steve, let's face it. Dad and José were into something—smuggling, running drugs, something that probably got them killed. What I'm saying is that whatever it was looks like it's still hanging around. Did you take anything off the boat and bring it here after we got it back?"

He scratched his head, trying to remember. "There wasn't all that much. Beale had pretty much cleaned it out. There were some old charts; some equipment, like rope that I didn't trust. I threw all that out."

"Electronics?" she asked. "Any radios you replaced?"

He smiled at the thought. "Not with our money. I took Grandpa's old barometer off the wheelhouse wall. It didn't work and the glass was cracked. I figured it would be better off here."

"Show me."

He led her to the bathroom. Behind the door was the ancient, oblong, meteorological indicator of yore, now stained and beaten and quaint. He removed it from its nail and handed it to her.

"Don't know what you can make out of that."

She stared at it, wondering the same thing. "That's it?" she asked.

"All I can think of."

She turned it over in her hand, squinted slightly, and then moved it under the overhead light. "Look," she said, pointing at something on the back.

"The screw?" he asked.

"Yeah—it's shiny. Well, shinier, like it's been fooled with. They all are. You got your knife?"

He handed her his pocketknife. She opened the screwdriver blade and inserted it into each of the four screws holding the instrument's back in place. Crouching down in the middle of the bathroom floor, so as not to lose anything that might fall out, she gingerly worked the wooden back free.

"What do you see?" he asked, crowding next to her.

Instead of answering, she placed the back on the floor and tipped the barometer into the palm of her outstretched hand. A small, shiny, plastic object dropped into view.

"What is it?"

She took the plastic case between her fingers and pried it open, revealing an even smaller, tablike structure, smaller than a stamp.

"Looks like it belongs in a computer," she said.

CHAPTER 28

"Good to have you back, boss," Lester said, looking up as Joe entered the office, holding the door open for Sammie, who was on crutches right behind him.

Willy was already there, barricaded behind his own desk, which, as usual, looked like a recycling center for gun magazines and periodicals.

"Give the man a break, for Chrissake," he growled, making Lester stare at him as if he'd just sprouted a third eye.

Keeping his counsel, however, Les got up, pulled Sam's chair around so that she could more easily collapse into it, and commented, "How's it feel this morning?"

She propped her casted leg up onto the desk and readjusted the ice pack swathing it, grimacing as she did so. "Like a pain in the ass."

"Meaning you refused the Vicodin?" he surmised.

She smiled ruefully. "Yeah, yeah, yeah. I hate that stuff. It's not bad if I keep it elevated and cold."

He left it at that, knowing where a suggestion that she take a few days off would land.

Joe took up his place, sitting on the edge of his desk, and addressed them all. "I apologize for my behavior recently. As I told Willy last night, Lyn got into a jam in Maine—to be more accurate, she ended up being kidnapped—and I felt I had to do something about it."

Lester burst out laughing. "Nope—sorry, boss—but that was way out of line. Next time, tell her to either suck it up or pull that kind of stunt when it's more convenient, okay?" He then suddenly froze in mid-smile and asked, his face reddening, "She all right? Sorry—should've asked."

Willy shook his head. "No, jackass, she's on life support."

Les's eyes widened with horror.

"She's fine, Les," Joe said quickly. "Thanks for asking. It's still an ongoing case, but the locals got it, and it looks like the worst is over. Have you three critiqued what happened yesterday with Ryan Hatch?"

"We talked it out at the hospital, right after Sam got out of surgery."

"She was still dopey enough not to tear my head off," Willy said.

"We fucked up," Sam added. "We know that."

"It'll probably stay where it is," Joe reassured them. "I've spoken several times with the SA and the investigators from the VSP—up to just a half hour ago—and they're all hoping to keep things simple. You were there to interview Hatch, he wigged out, and you did what you had to do. No one's going to open the can of worms about why you were there in the first place—or your lack of homework and preparation, the absence of any tactical coordination, your Keystone Kops approach, or your not having a backup plan for when all hell broke loose."

"Cool," Willy commented. "Thanks for not bringing it up."

"No problem," Joe told him. "Keep in mind that somebody might file a civil suit—the guy whose car you used as an anvil, for example, or even Ryan Hatch, assuming he survives, which is looking good, by the way."

"Swell," Willy muttered, unrepentant. "Maybe someone will knife him when he gets to prison."

"Hatch doesn't strike me as the type to come after us," Joe continued. "As for the driver you hit, who knows? Maybe he votes Republican."

Joe rose and moved to the open window, where the morning breeze was beginning to pick up the first of the sun's warmth.

"I assume you all know by now that the mini-STR came back, proving the blood we thought was Ryan's isn't, and instead fits his full-fledged brother, Nicky."

Sam's hand fluttered up like an embarrassed schoolgirl's. "That was my bad."

Joe stared at her.

"Richard told me Nick had changed his name," she explained. "I should have asked him then to spell it out for me."

Joe waved it away. "Doesn't matter. But it does mean we need to locate Nicky and find out how and why he got that close to Castine. And we need to do it using a slightly different approach than what was used on Ryan."

"You're a riot, Joe," Willy cracked. "Sure they don't want you back in Maine?"

Joe smiled. "You're stuck with me now, pal."

"How do you want to do it?" Sam asked, still clearly self-conscious.

The phone rang and Lester picked it up. He listened for a few seconds, made a couple of comments, ending with, "We'll be right there," and hung up.

He leaned back in his chair and gave a lopsided grin. "Don't know what it is, Joe, but this is never going to go the way you want. That was Ron, downstairs. His people just called in from Karen Putnam's trailer park. A unit was sent there for a domestic in progress—now it's a hostage situation."

Willy rolled his eyes and started to laugh.

"Who's involved?" Joe asked.

"The man himself. Nicky's barricaded inside with Becky, supposedly holding a knife to her throat. Karen made the phone call. Sounds like the family's been having a knock-down-drag-out all night long."

Joe rose from the windowsill. "Okay, so much for the organized approach. Guess we're onto Plan B."

Cathy Lawless walked down the dark, crowded hallway of the Gloucester police department, sidestepping several stacks of boxed files, and smiling about how certain items, like storage, plague every department she knew. At the end, near the bathroom, she found the tiny office of Detective Brian Wilkinson.

She stuck her head around the corner and waved. "Hey there. Cathy Lawless—MDEA. You Brian?"

Wilkinson struggled to stand without dumping the folder he was balancing on his lap. The computer was on before him, and he had obviously been trying to compare one source of information with another—another common challenge in the business.

She quickly entered and waved him down before he reached his full height. "No, no. That's fine. Sit, sit. Been there, done that. No formalities needed."

He settled back with a grunt, mashing the folder in place with a large, meaty hand. "Thanks. I hate this stuff."

"Still," she said, sitting on the edge of a worn-out office chair. "I'll let you get back to it if you want to tell me what you got."

He was wearing half-glasses, and looked at her wearily over the top of them. "Forget that." He smiled. "I called you, after all. Guess I've lost whatever manners I ever had. You want coffee or anything?"

"Nope. Thanks. All set."

Wilkinson carefully laid the open file across his keyboard, and slowly backed away from the desk before rising again. "Okay. Why don't you come with me, then, and I'll show you what we found."

He led the way back down the hallway, out into the parking lot, and over to an unmarked car, unlocking the doors remotely with a key fob as they approached.

"Like I told you on the phone," he said, "we got a call for a vandalized boat a while back—Steve Silva's *The Silva Lining*. Looked pretty standard. It happens now and then—they cut lines or trash each other's equipment in some stupid spitting contest." He started the engine after Cathy had slammed her door shut, and headed for Gloucester's main drag.

"Anyhow, this one was different. A lot of us think Silva is running drugs from offshore—he just got out of the can where he did time for dealing. So, I was thinking about that when I got there. His sister was with him— she's a bit of a hothead; used to tend bar in town before she took off for somewhere—and she gave me a little shit. She's got a cop boyfriend in Vermont. Decent enough guy. I met him on another case a few years back."

Cathy looked around as they drove down toward the harbor. She resisted the urge to come clean with her knowledge of all this.

"Yeah," she said instead. "I met some of the players."

He glanced at her quickly. "Oh, yeah. Well, okay. Then I'll cut to the chase. I checked out the boat after I got rid of them, and it was pretty clear it hadn't really been trashed, but tossed, like by people looking for something."

"Right," she said evenly. "So I gathered." She was

beginning to wonder if the long drive down here hadn't been a total waste of time.

He laughed. "Shit. 'Course you do. Well, I'm not too sure what you know and what you don't, right? So, better too much info than not enough."

He pulled up to the curb, killed the engine, and—for a man of his bulk—swung easily out of the car.

"I gave it the once-over at the time," he continued, heading toward the docks. "But, to be honest, I wasn't too confident. Still, I took pictures, did sketches, all the rest. You know—the routine. And then I hit pay dirt."

"Right," she said absentmindedly, admiring the traffic in mid-harbor—boats large and small churning through the water, bent on the commerce of the sea. Unlike what she knew of farmers in their fields, which had always struck her as a fundamental and straightforward relationship, fishermen and the sea remained elusive and slightly menacing. Her own experience with the water, whenever she went out swimming, was to wonder about what might be lurking in the deep, weighing her value as a meal. To think of people in flimsy boats, atop a vast and restless ocean, dropping lines into that same water in the hopes of catching the very same creatures, made her happy she worked on dry land.

They reached *The Silva Lining*, aboard which Wilkinson hopped with an easy familiarity, paying no attention to Cathy's more cautious approach.

He stood in mid-deck and waved a hand about. "I asked Steve Silva to leave things as they were, so this is pretty much how I found it. It's not like I had to preserve a chain of custody or anything, but I figured you'd like to see it for yourself."

Cathy was still wondering why she was here, much less in need of an all-but-preserved, unsecured crime scene. She nodded vaguely, looking around and observing the mess. It did look like a toss job.

Wilkinson crossed to the wheelhouse and pointed at a couple of gouged holes in its wooden casing. "After you guys picked up Beale, grabbed his gun, and circulated its IBIS data, I compared that with what I dug out of the wood here a couple of days ago. They matched."

Cathy scowled and joined him to study the two large cavities, her interest suddenly sharpened. IBIS was the Integrated Ballistics Identification System—a federal database shared by hundreds of departments nationwide. "You found a bullet matching Beale's gun?"

"Two of them. It was dumb luck, to be honest. A few waves rocked the boat while I was poking around; I reached out to steady myself, and put my hand right on a thin patch of wood that was screwed in place and painted over, but it made no sense where it was. It was weird—at least I thought it was—so I took it off, and voilà."

He grinned. "The place was a mess anyhow; I figured there couldn't be any harm adding a little damage with a penknife, right? But here's the real punch line: The lab told me they got blood on them. Wanna bet that goes back to one of the Silvas?"

Cathy smiled, utterly forgiving him for not telling her any of this on the phone. "I do," she answered him.

He then reached into his pocket and extracted an envelope. "That's not all," he continued. "The Silvas' apartment was dumped here in town, just like this. Lyn got curious, grilled her baby brother, and did a little digging on her own. She found an old barometer Steve removed after they got the boat back from Beale." He tapped the wheelhouse wall closer to the instrument panel. "Used to be attached here, screwed in place, but it was busted and didn't work anymore—purely sentimental now—but a great place to hide something small, which is what she thinks her dad did, maybe as insurance, maybe to hold back for more money."

He opened the envelope and showed her an evidence baggy, containing the small and shiny object Lyn had found. "Don't know what it is yet, but it fits a computer, and I'm thinking it's what got the Silvas knocked off. Between it and the bullets, maybe you or whoever runs all the way with this case can crack Beale wide open."

Cathy looked at Wilkinson with newfound respect. From the near bumpkin she'd thought she was meeting fifteen minutes earlier, she now saw one of the rare, true team players—who'd bothered to do his homework, and then think of any other agencies who might be interested in what he'd found.

She slapped him on his burly shoulder. "Damn, Brian. You've done some nice work here." She considered for a moment his concluding words, and added, "But I'm hoping we won't have to stop with Beale. Let me tell you about a guy named Dick Brandhorst. You ever hear of him?"

CHAPTER 29

The four of them shared a car, parking in the staging area, out of sight from the trailer. From there, they walked up a side street—Sam on crutches—to where Ron Klesczewski had positioned his converted ambulance command post.

Ron was inside, keeping in the air-conditioning and keeping out all the people milling around, who were either waiting to be assigned or just sharing the excitement. Cops, like firefighters, are as prone to gawking as they are to being useful.

"Hey, Joe," Ron said as Gunther alone entered the already cramped space.

"Hey yourself," Joe answered him, nodding to the other man there, a young patrolman he knew only by sight, who was sporting a pair of headphones and manning a laptop computer. "What's the situation?"

"From what we know, the trailer's empty except for Nick and his sister." He pointed to the other man. "Bill's about to set up a phone link to the inside, so I can start talking with Nick, assuming he picks up. Then we'll move to a throw phone, as usual, so we can better control communications—again, assuming he plays along. Basically, we're just getting started."

Joe sat on the edge of a bench seat. "Where's Mom?"

"She was the only other one inside when we got here. From what I could get out of her, the three of them were fighting all night about everything that's been happening, and it finally came to a head when Nick took a swipe at Karen with a knife. That's what got her to call 911, and why she's now at the hospital."

"She badly hurt?"

Ron shook his head. "He didn't actually make contact, but I think it pushed her over the edge. She's pretty hysterical. When our first units got here, she came running out, and Nick was seen at the door with the knife at Becky's throat. At that point, we pulled back."

"Any sign of Dan Kravitz or his daughter? She's Nicky's girlfriend, sort of."

"We're trying to locate them. Neighbors told us they might have moved out, what with all hell breaking loose, but so far, that's just a rumor."

Joe wondered if Sally Kravitz's departure might have played a small role in triggering Nicky. He'd been to so many family blowups, he knew what fragile ties sometimes kept everything in check. And Nicky was obviously a special case, anyhow.

He got back up and put his hand on the door handle. "I'll get out of your hair while you set things up, unless you need me for anything. I better find a spot for Sammie, too—she insisted on tagging along, crutches and all."

Ron laughed. "Surprise, surprise. Send her in here. Can't beat the temperature, and since she's the only one who's been inside the place, maybe she can help me out."

"Will do," Joe told him, and opened the door to leave.

Outside, of course, Sammie was nowhere to be found. Willy was leaning against a trailer, in the shade.

He didn't wait for Joe's question. He merely jerked his thumb down the way and said, "She couldn't help herself."

The command post was located on a parallel street to the Putnams' address, nearby but out of sight, shielded by a row of neighboring trailers. Joe followed Willy's direction and soon found Sammie crouching awkwardly behind some bushes, directly across the dirt lane from where she'd first met young Richard.

"Jesus, Sam," he muttered, crawling up beside her. "What the hell do you think you're doing? This isn't our scene, and you just got out of the hospital."

But she wasn't listening. She pointed at the trailer instead. "Look, behind the latticework around the foundation. Just as I thought."

"What?" Joe asked, squinting to see what she was showing him.

"It's Richard. He's still in his hideout." She waved discreetly, barely sticking her hand through the leaves before her.

Joe watched carefully and saw a slight pale movement behind the crisscrossed slats.

"Shit. I better tell Ron."

But Sam laid her hand on his arm. "Hang on. Someone should be with him."

He squeezed her hand to draw her attention. "Sam," he said, his face inches from hers, "you are not to act on this. You have a broken leg. You shouldn't even be here. You get impulsive, you screw it up for everyone, including your little pal over there. Do you hear me?"

Unlike with Willy, he knew such an approach would work with her.

"Yes," she said simply, adding, "but you should know that I already communicated with him—as much as I could—and he's refusing to come out."

He pulled out his radio and switched it over to the

tactical frequency he knew Ron was using. "Ron? It's Joe."

"Go ahead," Ron's voice said seconds later.

"You get a report yet from your people on movement under the trailer?"

"Affirmative."

"That's Richard—the youngest member of the clan. Sam's behind the bushes across the street, making eye contact with him. The kid's refusing to leave."

"Okay." The word was drawn out, Ron waiting for more.

"Sam won't be attempting to get under there with him, but it might be a good idea if somebody does."

"You volunteering?"

"If you recommend it. Otherwise, no."

"What's the access point?"

Sam took the radio from Joe's hand and answered, "Straight shot—the slats open like a door facing the street."

After a brief pause, Ron responded, "Okay. Get back to the CP, Joe, and get fitted with a vest, helmet, and the rest, and let me know when you're ready to go. Meantime, I'll put together a diversion."

Fifteen minutes later, Joe was back beside Sammie. In the meantime, Nick had picked up the phone inside the trailer, and had agreed to a throw phone being deposited at the front door.

That was Joe's promised diversion. As Nick was presumably being distracted by this delivery—and therefore facing south—Joe slipped free of the bushes, scurried across the dusty street, eased the latticework open, and crawled under the trailer to where young Richard was waiting.

Joe held his finger to his lips and whispered, "Hey, Richard, how're you doin'?"

Richard whispered back, "Are my brother and sister going to be okay?"

"I hope so," he answered him. "But you can help that happen."

"How?"

"You can get out of here with me, to someplace safer."

Richard shook his head emphatically.

Joe switched gears. "Then you've got to tell me what you know about them and the layout above us. The point here is to make sure everybody comes out of this safe and sound. You understand?"

The boy studied him carefully, especially after Joe took off his Kevlar helmet and laid it aside.

"Are you the man from last night, in the hospital?"

"Yes. Joe. Did you and Sam have a good talk after I left?"

"Yeah."

"You know why I couldn't let her come over here, don't you?"

"The leg?"

"You got it. She's supposed to be resting at home right now, except that none of us wanted you guys to be left hanging. What happened, anyhow?"

Richard stared at the ground. "Big fight. Mostly about Wayne."

"What about him?"

"I think Nicky did something bad to him."

Joe settled down cross-legged opposite him. "What did he say, Richard?"

Richard was still looking at the ground, and now began to poke his finger at the old rug they were sharing, exploring the holes into the dirt beneath. He didn't look up as he spoke. "Maybe he hurt him a lot, 'cause of something Wayne did to Becky. I couldn't really figure it out, 'cause I think he did something to Mom, too, but Mom said he didn't."

"What did Becky say?" Joe asked, still whispering.

"She couldn't make up her mind—it was like one way and then the other. That got Nicky really mad. I couldn't tell if she liked Wayne or hated him. But I do know Nicky surprised them together."

Joe nodded. "Okay, let's not talk about it anymore. Time we did something to help, instead. First off, how many people are up there?" He pointed above.

Richard looked surprised. "Nicky and Becky."

"Anybody else expected back in the next hour or so, that you know?"

The boy shook his head.

"How 'bout guns? Any of those around?"

"Mom's got one under her bed."

"Loaded?"

"I guess so. She says it is when she tells us not to mess with it."

Great, thought Joe—that sounded like an accident waiting to happen. "Does Nick know about it?"

"Sure."

"Do you think he might use it?"

"I don't know. Maybe."

Upstairs, they both heard the distinctive sound of the throw phone's ringing, interrupted by someone picking it up.

"How do Nick and your sister get along?" Joe asked suddenly.

"Fine, I guess. They're both a little weird."

"But do you think he might actually hurt her?"

The answer was equivocal. "I don't think so."

Joe rolled onto his back a moment and studied what he could see of the flooring overhead, finally reaching for his flashlight to better study its details.

"What're you looking at?" Richard wanted to know, his voice still very low.

"Just wondering how I can take a peek up there, see what's going on."

"You could use my door," he suggested simply.

Joe straightened and stared at him, feeling foolish. He'd just assumed Richard used the front entrance and then ducked under. "I sure could," he conceded. "Where is it?"

The boy pointed farther down the length of the trailer. "It's a trapdoor, over there."

"You push it down, or up?"

"It opens up, into the hallway near the bathroom."

"So, it's on hinges," Joe half mused aloud. "Which way do you see when your head's sticking through it?"

Richard pointed toward the street.

"Meaning I could see Nicky talking on the special phone right now, if I did that?"

"Right."

Overhead, Nick was speaking, his voice too muffled to be understood. Joe knew Ron was running through the standard hostage negotiator's protocol, establishing rapport—a sometimes long and subtle process.

"Wait here," Joe told his companion, and awkwardly but silently crawled back into the gloom, searching for the trapdoor.

He found it easily enough, positioned himself on his knees, and—with his forehead just touching the surface of the door—placed both palms flat against it and pushed very gently, hoping it wouldn't stick and thus pop open under pressure.

It didn't. No doubt due to Richard using it so regularly, it rose almost immediately, without a sound, and allowed Joe the thinnest of cracks, through which he could see the same quasi-living-room area where Sam had interviewed Karen Putnam.

This time, however, Nicky King was sitting on the edge of the coffee table, the throw phone in one hand and a large knife in the other. Next to him, sulking on the couch, Becky sat with her arms hugging her legs.

Joe dropped back down, pulled out his radio, screwed its earpiece into place, and keyed the mike.

"Ron?"

Sammie answered, "He's on the phone, boss, talking with Nick. What've you got?"

"Access to the central hallway from below. Richard showed me the trapdoor he uses to get in and out. I just took a peek and saw Nick on the phone."

"Becky okay?"

"She's fine. She may not even be in real danger, except that Nicky is holding a knife. We need a diversion of some kind—somehow to either get him walking in my direction or looking so hard out the window that I can climb in and sneak up behind him."

Sammie sounded doubtful. "How big is that trapdoor?"

Joe smiled. "I'll forget you asked that, but it ain't huge. I'd prefer the first option."

"Roger that," she said. "I'll call you right back."

Joe returned to where Richard was staring through the latticework. In every direction, cops could be seen, tucked behind shelters of all types, dressed in black BDUs and helmets. It was like being on the wrong end of a war movie.

Joe slipped his hand over the boy's shoulder. "I talked to Sam just now. We're putting a plan together to end this peacefully."

Richard pointed outside. "They don't look like they heard it."

"They only do what they're told," Joe tried reassuring him. "Right now, they're supposed to sit tight and look scary. They doing a good job?"

Richard nodded silently. Above them, Nicky's muffled

voice continued as Ron kept him occupied. So far, it had been a near textbook recipe of time-tested procedure mixed with serendipitous opportunities, like the discovery of the trapdoor.

Ten minutes later, Sam's voice came over Joe's earpiece. "Joe?"

He keyed the mike and spoke softly. "Right here."

"You better get in position. We're about to head him down your way."

"Give me one full minute and then go," he told her. "Don't bother trying to get me on the radio. I'll have my hands full."

"Got it."

He told Richard to stay put again, and resumed his post under the trapdoor. Unbeknownst to him, one of the Special Response Team stepped out into the street and, in full view of the trailer's living-room window, gestured to two others to run down to the unit's far end, presumably to attempt an entry from the back.

At the same time, Joe eased the door up, just in time to see Nick straighten suddenly—phone still in hand—stare out the window, and begin looking around in a near panic.

"*You lied to me,*" he shouted on the phone, before throwing it away and running down the hall, straight toward Joe, his eyes glued to the far end.

Joe waited until the last possible moment, the young man's hurtling body growing to absurd dimensions, before he threw the trapdoor back on its hinges and stood up to his full height—a super-sized gopher abruptly leaping from its hole.

Nicky's eyes popped wide just as Joe seized him around both knees and brought him down like a tree stump—hard and with a single resounding crash. The boy hit the floor with enough force to stun him momentarily, making Joe fear that he might have fallen on his knife.

But it wasn't quite over—in the sudden, startling silence, Joe heard a motion over his shoulder, in time to turn and see Becky running toward him, brandishing the very same knife.

She never closed the gap. Through the trailer's front door to her left, a member of Ron's team appeared like a charging Ninja and simply catapulted her into the opposite wall like a human-sized rag doll.

In all, it took under ten seconds, leaving everyone—as Joe had promised Richard—alive.

CHAPTER 30

"She came at you with a knife?" Lyn asked him, her eyebrows high. "I thought she was the victim."

"She was," Joe told her. "But in more ways than one." They were in a car, driving toward Bangor, where they were to meet with Cathy Lawless and members of ICE, or Immigration and Customs Enforcement, the federal cops whose jurisdiction included most crimes involving the nation's borders.

Joe took his hand off the steering wheel to count off on his fingers. "First, by her own family dynamics, including two brothers acting as knee-jerk fathers; an all-but-invisible jailbird stepfather; a real father no one seems to remember; and a nearly totally dysfunctional mother. Second, by Wayne Castine, who was either sleeping with her mother to get to her, or just discovered her in the same house and decided on a two-for-one conquest. And third, by the head game Nicky played with her after he caught her with Wayne in that apartment, and forced her to watch him butcher the guy."

"What *was* that all about?" Lyn asked.

"This comes from the HCRS shrinks, the SA's office, and our own interviews, but it looks like Nicky figured out

about Wayne and Becky, which not only offended his sense
of order, but further diminished his place in the family
pecking order by adding another male, as if there weren't
enough already. So, one night, he followed her to Babbitt's
apartment, waited until they got comfortable, and then
pounded on the door, calling out Wayne's name. That
must've surprised the hell out of *him,* even if it didn't catch
the ear of a single one of the neighbors—at least supposedly. Of course, as soon as Wayne opened up, that was
it—and the beginning of Nick and Becky's strange trip."

"What did he do to her?"

"Nick?" Joe asked. "As I see it, where Wayne won her
over with flattery and painted nails, Nicky brainwashed
her with how she was the one really responsible for
Wayne's death. Nicky had her believing that she'd se-
duced Wayne, and had forced Nicky to act as a result."

"No wonder she was self-mutilating," Lyn said quietly.

"In the end," Joe continued, "she flew at me because I
was threatening the last defender she had left—the only
one of the whole bunch who'd sacrificed everything to
protect her."

"So, the hostage thing in the trailer was bogus?"

"On that level, yes," he answered her. "Although, given
Nicky's thinking, who knows what he might've done if
we hadn't found that trapdoor. He could've rationalized
killing her to guarantee protecting her virtue. Funny," he
added a moment later, "that we figured most of it out
from a single drop of blood. Wayne hit Nicky in the nose
as he was going down—barely, but just enough."

Lyn stared out the window at the passing landscape.
They'd been on I-95 for hours, and were nearing Bangor's
outskirts.

"How do people get so messed up?"

He glanced at her. "Are we talking about the Putnam
clan, or yours?"

She gave him a faint smile. "Good point."

"For what it's worth, Lyn," he told her, "and I know we haven't gotten the whole story yet, I think your father was a straight arrow. I'm not saying he didn't screw up. But I'll almost guarantee you he was doing the best he could for his kids, right up to the end. People can be stupid, and it can cost them their lives. But I'm not a big believer that they change personalities just because the situation demands it. Keep your good memories of him alive. He deserves that."

He returned to negotiating the thickening traffic as she went back to watching the scenery.

"Thanks, Joe," she said after a couple of minutes.

They parked by the side of a large modern office building, overlooking the Kenduskeag Stream, which Lyn immediately recognized as being close to Dick Brandhorst's place.

"What exactly's going to happen here? They going to arrest him?" she asked, climbing stiffly out of the car.

"They already have," Joe told her. He pointed to the building looming alongside. "He's in an ICE holding cell in there. ICE and the MDEA are cooperating on this, since it involves both drugs and the border. They're allowing us to watch as a courtesy."

She considered that a moment before stating, "They're allowing *you*."

He circled the car and slid his arm across her shoulders, kissing her cheek. "There are too few of us north of Boston to not be friendly, Lyn. Everybody knows what this cost you, and what you mean to me. I may be dead wrong, and if I am, I'll apologize later, but I'm hoping that seeing this interview might help you out—and maybe answer a few of your questions."

Joe escorted her inside, rode the elevator up, and was

met by a thin, somewhat dour woman whom he introduced as Dede Miller, the ICE agent assigned to neighboring Washington County. She had been part of the same task force of weeks earlier.

Miller led them down a hallway, talking as she went. "We only picked him up a half hour ago. He waived his rights, of course, cocky bastard. Probably thinks we got nothing on him. Cathy and I were thinking of playing good-cop-bad-cop on him, hoping two women in the same room will mess him up."

She opened an unlabeled door, using her security pass to get them deeper into the building, and waved them in without uttering another word.

The room was dark, lighted solely from a large glass window overlooking a similar space next door. It was a standard, if high-end, interrogation setup. Already there were two men, standing before the one-way window, who turned upon their entrance.

The older of the two stepped forward, hand outstretched. "Joe and Lyn, right? I'm John Ferraro—the SAC for this area." He waved a hand at the other man. "And you've already met Dave Beaubien, Cathy's partner."

Silent Dave merely nodded his greeting. Beyond the glass, trying to look bored but with his eyes moving nonstop, sat Dick Brandhorst.

"He say anything yet?" Joe asked, joining the first two in a single line—like spectators at an execution.

"Just the usual innocent one-liners: Who me? This is an outrage, etcetera," Ferraro said.

They heard, over the speaker mounted on the wall, the opposite door's lock suddenly snap, and both Cathy Lawless and Dede Miller stepped in, the latter carrying a slim file, which she placed before her as she sat across from Brandhorst. Cathy remained standing, leaning against the wall beside the viewing window.

Brandhorst smiled affably. "How many others are hiding behind the mirror?" he asked. "They should come out and join the party."

Miller merely opened the file and said, "Not sure I'd look at it that way, Dick. You're in deep trouble. You know a man named Wellman Beale?"

"Am I supposed to?"

"Not good, Dick. When you avoid a direct answer, we call that a lie."

His eyes flicked between the two of them, although Cathy hadn't moved. The smile stayed in place. "I meet a lot of people. I don't always catch their names."

"Mr. Beale says he knows you."

Brandhorst nodded agreeably. "I don't doubt he does."

"You don't know the people who work for you?"

His eyes widened slightly. "I don't know the people at the phone company or the people who pack my groceries. You could say they work for me, too. Tough question to answer."

Dede Miller remained unperturbed. She slid a piece of paper across the table at him. "Speaking of the phone company, these are your office records, showing that you call Mr. Beale on a regular basis, and have for years."

Brandhorst didn't look at the record. "You sure he uses that name when he deals with me?"

Miller slid a photograph over, covering the phone bill. "That's a picture of you and Beale. We've got others."

This time, he glanced at it, if only briefly. "Oh, yeah. Okay. Maybe I do know him—as John Clark."

Behind the mirror, Joe nodded approvingly. Dede Miller was starting well.

"Why did you say you didn't?" she asked.

He considered his response before smiling and spreading his hands wide. "I guess he was protecting his identity for some reason. Wellman, you say? Weird. Yeah,

I've known him forever. Bit of an asshole but a good fisherman—knows where to find the big ones."

"You're saying for the record that you only know him as a fishing guide?"

A tiny but telling hesitation was followed by, "Yeah."

Without comment, Cathy Lawless left her position and moved to the opposite wall, just enough out of Brandhorst's line of vision that he had to glance over his shoulder to see her.

"Remember," she said softly, speaking for the first time, "we only need confirmation for what we already know, and that's for your sake. The prosecutor will be looking at this video later, to see how straight you've been. Could be a jury'll do the same thing, down the line."

"I haven't done anything wrong," he told her.

Miller acted as if Cathy's small exchange had never occurred. "When did you last see Mr. Beale?"

Brandhorst faced her. "I don't know. When was the last time you saw your dentist?"

"Would you say it was a week ago, a month, or a year?"

He licked his lips. "It might've been a few weeks."

She made a pointed effort to write a note to herself on a pad beside the open file.

"How 'bout when you last saw Abílo Silva and his son José. Was that in the company of Mr. Beale?"

No hesitation this time. The response was almost too fast. "Never heard of them."

Dede Miller sat back to study him. "You know, for a man who's trying to be careful, you sure have some sloppy habits. Do you really think if we got your office phone records, we didn't get everything else—including a long talk with Lyn Silva?"

"What's the difference if I met some lobsterman and his kid?" Brandhorst challenged her.

"The difference is they died in your company." She

leaned toward him again before concluding, "Because you killed them."

Joe felt Lyn stiffen. "I thought he was just the money-man," she whispered.

Brandhorst's face reddened. "I had nothing to do with that."

"Interesting answer," Cathy said from behind him, making him whirl around.

"It's the truth," he insisted.

She smiled. "No, it's not," she said quietly.

Joe took hold of Lyn's hand. "You okay?" he asked her.

She nodded once, not taking her eyes off the scene before them.

"There were three of you that night," Miller intoned next door. "You, Beale, and Beale's sternman, Dougie O'Hearn. We already have Beale in custody."

"You need to be straight with us, Dick," Cathy said, almost into his ear. "This is not the time to screw up."

"Beale's lying to save his own ass," Brandhorst said, all pretense abandoned. "He had an ax to grind with Silva I knew nothing about. One minute we're talking—the next, he opens up. *He's* the one who killed them."

"The evidence could support that," Cathy commented.

Brandhorst half rose in his chair, until Cathy laid a hand on his shoulder. "You know I didn't shoot those two."

"Then tell us what happened, Dick," Cathy urged him. " 'Cause right now, you're an accessory."

He hunched forward to stare directly at Dede. "It was a simple dope deal. No big shakes. A few pills for a few bucks. I was along for the ride. I barely knew Silva. His kid owed me for gambling debts and the old man figured he'd square the books. I was the bank, Beale was the dealer, and Silva was the mule. I introduced them a while back, after Silva asked me how to raise extra cash. Turns out they'd met a few years ago in Jonesport, on vacation or something. Anyhow, that's all I knew till Beale invited me out for a boat ride—that's what he called it. And then, there we were, meeting up with Silva. I was bummed—I try to keep a low profile, you know? I was angry at Beale, but what could I do? So, I hung back, trying to be inconspicuous, but then, all of a sudden, all hell breaks loose—they start yellin' at each other, and before I can move, Beale shoots them both. I have no clue what triggered it."

"Where did this happen?" Dede asked.

This time, Brandhorst was direct. "At sea. Like I said—boat-to-boat, off Grand Manan. We were standing on Silva's stern. O'Hearn was on Beale's boat, manning the wheel."

Dede cupped her cheek in her hand and looked at him pityingly. "Yeah—O'Hearn. He is the fly in the ointment, isn't he? The guy who really messes up a nice and tidy story." Her face became serious when she added, "Because we got him, too, and he says things went down a lot differently."

Brandhorst scowled. "Well, *duh*. O'Hearn *works* for Beale. What the fuck do you expect him to say?"

"We *got* Beale, Dick," Miller countered. "We got the gun, we got the bullets—one of them even has Silva's DNA on it. And O'Hearn fingered Beale as pulling the trigger."

Brandhorst straightened, spreading his hands wide. "Well, there you have it."

"Not quite. You said you didn't know why it happened—that it was just a dope deal gone south."

"So?"

This time, Cathy produced the evidence, dangling a small plastic envelope before his eyes. Even from the observation room, they could see the same small computer component that Lyn and Steve had discovered in the old barometer.

"So," Cathy said. "We were wondering why this doesn't look like dope."

Brandhorst froze at the sight of it, inches from his face. Then his shoulders slumped, his eyes dropped to the tabletop, and he muttered, "Shit."

"Talk to me, Dick."

He shook his head. "If that greedy bastard hadn't held that back for more money, we would've been fine. But he wanted the whole debt wiped clean—his kid off the hook."

"So you ordered them killed," Cathy stated, "like O'Hearn and Beale claim you did."

Brandhorst almost sounded sad. "It was the principle of the thing. The deal was for the dope. That"—he indicated the contents of the envelope—"was a favor—something Silva was supposed to bring over for free. But we couldn't find it afterward, when we went through their pockets. I didn't make a big deal about it then, 'cause I'd kept Beale outside the loop. I figured I'd search the boat later. But the stupid jerk told me it sank in a storm. He sacrificed a fortune for the value of a goddamn boat. Whole thing was a fucking disaster."

"Until Silva's daughter walked into your office."

"Yeah," he mourned. "I couldn't believe it—looked like the break of a lifetime."

Lyn broke away from the line at the window and walked unsteadily toward the door. "I feel sick," she whispered.

Joe grabbed her by the waist, dance-stepped her into the hallway, and down two doors into a unisex bathroom they'd passed earlier. There, she hovered before the sink, her hands resting on its edge, her breathing coming fast and deep.

Joe rubbed her back with one hand and held her hair back with the other. "Feel free if you need to," he urged her.

"It's not like I didn't know," she gasped. "It was just listening to that son of a bitch. I'm just a little dizzy. I'll be okay."

She reached out and ran the cold water, cupped some in her hand and splashed it on her face. She looked up and caught his eye in the mirror. "He will go away for this, won't he?"

Joe nodded, handing her some paper towels from the nearby dispenser. "'Cause of the border involvement, it's a federal rap; O'Hearn says Brandhorst ordered Beale to shoot; and both Beale's and O'Hearn's stories are perfect matches. Pinning the computer piece to Brandhorst was the final nail. Whatever it is, it's clearly worth a lot, and once they analyze it and find out where it came from, that should guarantee his going away for a long, long time—he and Beale, both."

She straightened and vaguely mopped her face dry.

"Would you like to leave?" he asked. "It's a beautiful day."

She looked surprised. "That's okay?"

"Of course," he told her, and led the way.

Outside, he steered a course across the parking lot toward the nearby Kenduskeag Stream, which in this section of town was mostly a concrete canal. The sun felt good on their shoulders after the air-conditioning behind them, and the water's noisy rush to meet the broader embrace of the nearby Penobscot River added to Lyn's recovery.

She stood by the bank, lost in the gentle tumult before them, as Joe slipped his arm around her waist.

"I read something once," she commented at last, "probably an article in a doctor's office—I don't remember. It was about distant fathers. How they become larger than life because we never get to know them. They grow to be godlike, guaranteeing that, sooner or later, their kids will pay the price."

Joe thought of the remnants of the tattered Putnam family, and considered Lyn's words in the light of his never having seen or met a single one of the many fathers responsible for Karen Putnam's various children.

"Godlike to some kids," he said, "maybe just absent to others."

He turned to her then and asked, "Are you angry at your dad?"

She pursed her lips, not looking at him. "I was. It looked like he chose José over Steve and me, and threw us all away as a result." She sighed. "But now . . ."

The image of two driven, desperate kids in a trailer, armed with a knife but otherwise clueless, floated up in Joe's mind.

"Maybe we do the best we can with what we've got available—fitting it into the big picture later is what drives us crazy."

She finally took her eyes off the water and looked at him. "It's that shallow? That random?"

He kissed her cheek. "Damned if I know. I just do what I can to pick up the pieces."

Read on for an excerpt from

RED HERRING

Archer Mayor's new novel, available in hardcover from Minotaur Books!

CHAPTER 1

Doreen Ferenc slipped her nightgown over her head and let it fall the length of her body and gently settle onto her shoulders. This was the reward of every day, this threshold moment, when, as though dropping a heavy burden, she exchanged her regular clothing, complete with belts, buttons, zippers, and elastic, for the sensual, almost weightless comfort of a simple shift of light cotton.

Not that the day had been more onerous than usual. Her mom had been in good spirits, minimally judgmental of the nursing home staff. They'd served Indian pudding for lunch, a perennial favorite. Her mother had once been an expert at the dessert, and it had led them both down a path of happy memories while they'd worked on the quilt for Doreen's new nephew. Doreen's brother, Mark, had recently married a much younger woman in Nevada, where they lived, and she'd just delivered their first child.

Doreen and Mark weren't particularly close, as siblings went, but they got along, and their mom loved them both. She preferred Mark, as Doreen well knew, but only because he was in a position to present her with a grandchild. Doreen had never found marriage appealing, and by and large didn't like kids, which, thank God, she was now safely beyond having anyway. The quilt had become a salutary talisman of good tidings to which Doreen could contribute guilt-free.

She left the bedroom in her bare feet and dropped her clothes into the laundry hamper in the darkened bathroom, pausing a moment to admire the unexpected snow falling from the night sky onto the enormous skylight she'd spent too much money having installed. The house was an almost tacky prefab ranch—virtually a trailer with pretensions—but she knew in her heart that it was also the house she'd most likely die in, so why not splurge a little, like on the skylight and the heat she poured on to make the whole house as toasty as in mid-July? She loved winters in Vermont, including flukily premature ones like this year's. She'd known them her whole life, and had, at various times, enjoyed skiing, snowball fights, and even shoveling the driveway. But no longer. Now she just wanted to watch the weather from the comfort of an evenly heated, boring modern house that was fussed over by a handyman man complete with a snowplow—assuming he'd attached the plow to his pickup yet. She had started working full-time at seventeen, decades earlier, and now she was going to enjoy all the fruits of a slightly early retirement.

Entertaining such thoughts, she pursued the next step in her nightly routine, and entered the small kitchen. There, she dished out a single scoop of vanilla ice cream, splashed an appreciable quantity of brandy over its rounded top, and retired to the living room couch, which was strategically angled so she could watch TV from a reclining position.

It was snowing—heavily, too—and only October. People hadn't switched to snow tires, sand deliveries were still being made to town road crews, and cars were going to be decorating ditches all over the state by morning. But

Doreen didn't have to care about any of it. She was as snug as the proverbial bug.

Settled at last, she hit the remote, dialed in her favorite channel, and heard the doorbell ring.

"Damn," she murmured, glancing at the digital clock on the set. It was just before ten pm. "Who on earth?"

She placed her bowl on the coffee table, struggled up from her place of comfort, and sighed heavily as she crossed the room to the tiny mudroom and the front door beyond it.

Enclosing herself in the mudroom to preserve the heat, she slipped on an overcoat from the row of nearby pegs, hit the outside light and called out, "Who is it?" She could see the outline of a man standing before the frosted glass of the door.

A weak voice answered, "You don't know me, ma'am. My name's Lyle Robinson. I've just wrecked my car about a half mile up. I was wondering if I could use your phone."

So much for keeping immune from the woes of poor weather. She then heard him cough and bend over as he clutched his chest.

"Are you all right?"

"I think so, ma'am. I wasn't wearing my seatbelt, like a damn fool . . . Sorry. Don't mean to offend. I think I just bruised my chest, is all."

She hesitated.

"Ma'am?" he said next. "Not that it'll matter, but I'm a cousin of Jim and Clara Robinson. They used to live just outside Saxtons River. I don't know if you know them."

"I do," she blurted out. "So, you're related to Sherry?"

"Yes, ma'am, although what she's doing way out west is beyond any of us."

Doreen threw open the door.

She was only aware of two things after that: the bare blade of an enormous knife, held just two inches before her eyes, and, behind it, a man disguised by a hooded sweatshirt worn backwards, two holes cut in the fabric for his eyes. She now understood why his voice had sounded weak.

"Okay, Dory," he said. "Drop the coat and step back inside. You and I are gonna get acquainted."

CHAPTER 2

He wasn't sure how it happened—he hadn't been paying attention—but Joe Gunther was now all alone in the room. Aside from the body, of course—one Doreen Ferenc, according to her driver's license, her neighbors, a computer check, and her mail. She herself was silent on the matter, not that he didn't think she had a few things left to tell him.

Joe sat gingerly on a wooden chair to take advantage of the sudden stillness, dressed in a white Tyvek suit that made him look more like a nuclear plant worker than a cop.

Crime scenes, especially homicides, were busy places—all bustle and talk, sketching and taking photographs, lifting prints and logging evidence. Along with a platoon of people—from cops to medics to funeral home employees to state's attorneys and unwelcome official gawkers.

It left little room for quiet contemplation.

Gunther didn't worry about where everyone had gone. They'd be back too soon anyway. Instead, he sat motionless, studying both room and victim for what they might tell him.

It wasn't much. There was a single glistening drop of

blood on her forehead, presumably from a scalp laceration above the hairline, and no obvious signs of disruption
around her—a slightly displaced coffee table and a wrinkled doormat that could have been mere casual
housekeeping. By all appearances, the entire house
looked like what it had actually been: the home of a spin-
ster of fifty-four who'd had a habit of lying on the couch
every night to watch TV, accompanied by a plate of
slightly spiked ice cream.

That was her expression of the wild life, from what
they'd been told by a nurse at her mother's nursing home,
who'd also said that Dory came to visit every day for four
hours, without fail, morning and afternoon, equally di-
vided into two-hour increments—the best and most consistent relative or visitor the place had ever known.

Prior to Joe's arrival, another cop had spoken to the
nurse on the phone—not the usual place to discuss a
death. Joe preferred to break such news face to face. But a
call had been made to the retirement home to make sure
they'd have someone to speak with, and the nurse—
Brenda Small by name—had immediately blurted out, "I
knew it. She's dead. That's the only way she'd miss visiting her mom." The cop had been too stunned to disagree.
Joe didn't think it mattered. Small had vowed that she'd
keep the death to herself, and volunteered what little they
had on Doreen, including the brandy garnish on the ice
cream. She claimed that she and "Dory" had become virtual sisters over the years—unsurprising given that Doreen did little aside stay at home and tend to her ailing
and needy mother.

Joe had his doubts. He suspected Doreen got out more
than Brenda imagined. In his experience, of which he had
decades, people were quick to pigeon-hole each other,
reducing them to caricatures. As in using the word, "spin-
ster."

He imagined she had been that only literally. There was no evidence in the house stating otherwise—pictures or documents attesting to husbands or children, alive, dead, or estranged. But there were travel books and brochures, signs of a love of cooking, and a dozen albums and several cameras speaking to both an enthusiasm for, and an ability in photography. This was a woman who, for whatever reasons, had chosen to hand over the majority of her time to accommodating her mother's needs, but who'd also managed to work in the basics of what appeared to be an enviable, if solitary life.

Except for its last moments. Those had, by all appearances, been a waking nightmare.

Up to now, Joe had employed a favorite time-tested technique at death scenes—while acknowledging the body, he didn't start by focusing on it, choosing instead to work from the fringes inward. But he'd done that by this point. He'd wandered through the small, neat, house, asked many of the preliminary questions, and gathered an overall sense of Doreen's daily rhythm.

Now he gazed at her, supine on the couch, her mouth agape, the blood shining on her forehead, her clouded eyes fixed on the ceiling as if she'd died wishing herself someplace else.

Joe didn't fault her there. The most compelling aspect of this entire scene, and which had transfixed every other investigator here, he feared, was the story suggested by her position. Her legs were apart, her nightgown pulled up to her waist and torn at the bodice, and her underwear dangling from one foot.

By all appearances, Doreen Ferenc had been raped and murdered.

"Are you the head guy?"

Joe glanced over to the door leading to the kitchen. A bearded man in his mid-thirties with longish hair was leaning over the threshold, hesitant to enter. Like everyone else, he was dressed all in protective white, but his self-consciousness about it was transparent.

Joe rose from his seat. This was no cop. "Yeah. Joe Gunther. VBI."

VBI stood for Vermont Bureau of Investigation, the state's major case squad. Joe was in fact its field force commander—a title that in more populated states would have guaranteed him a spot behind a desk. But not in Vermont.

Joe crossed the room, careful to stay on the floor's butcher paper travel lane—a crime scene detail designed to curtail contamination.

He stuck out his gloved hand. "And you?"

The younger man flushed. "Oh, damn. I'm sorry. Jack Judge. I like John, to be honest, but everybody calls me Jack. Holdover from when I was a kid. I'm the new assistant medical examiner. Sorry I'm late. The snowstorm caught me by surprise."

Gunther smiled, amused by his self-deprecation. It was a nice break from all the other overachievers.

"Welcome, John. You want to see the main attraction?"

Judge smiled back. "I guess that's why I'm here."

Joe led the way. The rule was that no one touched a body before the ME. This wasn't always observed, but it had been this time, Joe being in charge. Back in the day, AMEs, as they were now called, used to be volunteer local doctors, but as the world had become more litigious, violent, and complicated—even in this rural corner—they'd been replaced by trained investigators. Though not full timers, they were often nurses or paramedics, used to responding to chaos in the middle of the night, working alongside cops, interpreting medication labels, and filing prompt paperwork.

"You just start?" Joe asked.

"Yes and no," Judge answered him. "I was a medic in the service."

Gunther looked at him more closely. "See any action?"

Judge nodded. "Iraq."

Joe, ex-army himself, nodded and circled the couch to introduce the AME to the reason he'd been called. "Tough," was all he said, before stating, "Doreen Ferenc; DOB 5/24/56, making her fifty-four."

Jack Judge squatted down, his forearms on his knees, and studied the body's face.

Joe kept speaking, knowing the drill. "Some of this is sketchy—it's still early—but we think she lived alone, led an orderly life centering mostly around her mother, who's in a nursing home. She had a regular doctor, whom she saw yearly, but had no medical problems and was only on an acid reflux med. I don't remember the name. One of the other guys has that."

Joe pointed at the small bowl of melted ice cream. "She supposedly had a little vanilla laced with brandy every night in front of the tube, so this looks like it happened last night."

Judge cast a glance at the darkened TV.

"We turned it off," Joe filled in, adding for no reason except to slightly humanize the victim, "It was on the Nature Channel. She had an iron-clad routine, going to the nursing home every morning and afternoon to spend time with mom, so when she didn't show up today, someone over there began calling. A neighbor finally saw this through the window and called 911."

"Who saw her alive last?" Judge asked.

"You're kidding, right?" came a voice from the doorway. "What the hell do you think we're all doing here?"

They looked up to see a scowling man with a withered left arm, the hand of which had been shoved into a pocket of his Tyvek suit to keep it from swinging around. This fellow, the arm notwithstanding, had cop stamped all over him.

Gunther said with a frown, "Willy Kunkle—John Judge, from the ME's office. Willy works for me, although nobody knows why."

Judge nodded, but Kunkle smirked. "They call you Jack, right? Jack Judge. Cute. Sounds like a cartoon."

Joe didn't say anything, recognizing the futility of educating Willy, but Judge, to his credit, simply answered, "Jack or John—doesn't matter. I heard of you, too."

Kunkle laughed. "I bet. You do her yet?"

"We were about to," Joe said.

Willy drew near, but had the courtesy to stay quiet. Joe didn't doubt that he'd give Judge more grief later. Hazing fit him like a glove, showcasing the least flattering of his many, often conflicting personality traits.

Jack Judge went back to studying Dory, finally rising enough to hover over her like a parent delivering a goodnight kiss.

He spoke softly. "Nothing jumps out at first glance. I see no signs of strangulation, or bruising around the face or shoulders." He reached out and deftly checked under the remnants of the torn nightgown before pressing against her sternum and along her collarbones and ribs, one by one, lifting each exposed breast gently to do so. Joe had seen several such exams, and even conducted a couple, but admired the man's sensitive touch, as if the patient were still alive.

"She's cold and in full rigor," Judge continued. "I'll check lividity in a bit, but I suspect that's fixed, too. That would fit your idea that this happened last night, right here."

He pulled a penlight from his outer pocket and moved to the scalp, where he parted her hair and began scanning the skin beneath. After a while, he straightened, frowning. "Can't find the source of that blood right off, but there's not much of it." He quickly shined the light into each nostril and raised her stiffened lips off her teeth, also peering into the mouth. "It's not castoff from there, so it may have come from whoever did this."

"You can call the guy an asshole, John," Willy chided him, emphasizing the name. "Nobody'll mind."

Judge had shifted to her hands, which he handled like porcelain, bending his body rather than manipulating them, so as to preserve their positioning, not to mention any trace evidence that might still be clinging there. Watching him, Joe suspected he'd done well as a medic, both highly competent and impervious to the likes of Willy.

"Nothing obvious here, either," the AME muttered. "Her nails are long enough to have done at least some damage, if she'd used them, but I don't see anything."

He took a step to the left, directly above her midriff. Again, from his pocket, he extracted something Joe couldn't at first identify, which turned out to be a small, powerful magnifying lens. Using both light and lens, Judge bent even closer to the body's exposed pubic hair.

Willy took a half pace backward. "You are shitting me."

Despite the circumstances, Joe smiled to himself. As unlikely as it seemed, cops were often squeamish around the dead, even tough guys like Kunkle. Joe wondered if Judge wasn't subtly wreaking a little vengeance with this show of interest; Doreen would be going upstate for an autopsy in any case, encased and sealed in a body bag. That's where prints would be lifted, fingernails scraped, hair combed through, tissue samples collected. Not that Joe minded Judge's thoroughness here and now—it gave them all a better snapshot—but he sensed with satisfaction a little psychological warfare taking place.

Judge continued his close visual examination from her groin to her knees, paying close attention to the inner thighs, but looked disappointed when he finally straightened.

"Nothing," he stated. "No deposits, no stains, no signs of violence."

Willy scoffed. "Right. The expert. No offense, but I'll wait for the doc's vote on that."

"You've done this before," Joe suggested, both to clarify and, he hoped, to set Willy right.

Jack Judge nodded. "I was asked to investigate a few rape/homicides in Iraq."

Willy, also a combat vet, although carrying more baggage than most, looked away, pretending to be taking in the plate of melted ice cream, admonished but not willing to show it. "So, what do you think happened?" he asked as a peace offering.

Judge shrugged. "Maybe less than it seems? Why, I don't know." He looked at Joe. "You ready for me to roll her over?"

"Gently," Joe agreed. "Yeah."

She wasn't a large woman, and her stiffened state made it easy for Judge to simply lift an arm and a leg pivot her onto her right side, just enough for the other two to bend down and examine the body's underside.

"Whoa," Willy exclaimed.

The cushions beneath were soaked with blood, which also covered the entirety of Ferenc's back.

Judge's position put him at a disadvantage. "Can you see what caused it?"

"Negative," Willy commented, reaching out toward a hole in the nightgown, at about mid-lumbar level.

"Hold it," Joe said, touching Judge on the shoulder to get him to set her back into position. "We'll let the ME give us that. I don't want to disturb any more than we have. Knife, gun or ice pick, we know something was used, and we know for sure we have a murder. Let's just bag her hands carefully, wrap her up safe and sound, and do what we do best."

For once, Willy didn't argue, straightening up. He turned to Judge and asked with a tired, collegial half-smile, "All right if we call the perp an asshole now?"

"Fine by me," Judge told him.